A Mystery of
Grace

S. Lee Fisher

NEWMAN SPRINGS PUBLISHING
320 Broad Street
Red Bank, NJ 07701

First originally published by Newman Springs Publishing 2019

ISBN 978-1-64096-907-0 (Paperback)
ISBN 978-1-64096-908-7 (Digital)

Printed in the United States of America

To my parents with love.

SPECIAL THANKS TO BOB AND Jean Fisher, who lived every day in love and faith.

To my husband Ralph; my 'Best Shirt', my 'Hoke', my friend. He tirelessly listened to every write and rewrite.

To Mac and Ralph, for their expertise on the U.S. military system.

To Dar and Greg, for their encouragement and support.

To Bridgie, for her endearing friendship.

And to Megan, for her gentle nudges.

Overture

Chapter 1

1951—Southern Alps

THE SCREECHING OF TIRES AND a screaming voice pierced the frosty night air. Unexpected scattered snowflakes, a starless sky, and a bora wind teased of a cold night and morning to follow.

"Eddy. Come on! Let's go. We need to be back on base in twenty minutes."

Standing in only his standard issue boxers and T-shirt, broad shoulders and muscular arms exposed; Eddy looked around the modest two-room cottage at the straw-covered dirt floor. The entire contents of his footlocker were stuffed into his army duffel and thrown onto the single bed, whose tattered quilt was sprouting stuffing shoots. The small table was covered with a red check tablecloth, with two chairs that were painted white. A warm crackling fire served as both stove and heat source. Nothing adorned the walls except a small crucifix and a single shelf. Flour sacks provided minimal privacy for the windows. In summertime, the view of the Alpine foothills was breathtaking. Majestic mountain peaks still covered with snow served as a backdrop to sweeping meadows and wildflowers. A small bouquet always occupied an empty wine bottle on the window. However, soon, winter wind and snow would mean a long, sometimes bitter, wait for spring.

His eyes met those of the petite teen clearing the table of their meager meal of polenta and dried pork. Her dress was clean but tattered; a remnant of prosperity past. The garment served during the last months of her pregnancy. Tonight, it was cinched around her waist with a shawl. Her long locks piled loosely on top of her head.

A wisp of jet black hair curled across her face. She tried to hold back her tears as she quietly began to sob.

"Eddy, please go. I don't want trouble for you." She turned away from the young corporal to hide her now flowing tears.

"Wally, go. Go now, before I chicken out! *Go!*" was his answer to his buddy driving the jeep.

Eddy wrapped his muscular arms around the weeping girl. He drew her near and kissed her tenderly. "Shh. *Amore mio.* I'm staying." He picked up the boy wrapped in a thin blanket and caressed his head. *We'll need some warmer clothes for him,* he thought. The baby cooed at his father's touch. "Rosa, you and little Joey are my family. I love you," he whispered softly in her ear. To himself, he admitted his willingness to abandon all creature comforts, family, and country for this beautiful young girl and infant.

As Rosa melted into his embrace, the canvas-covered jeep sped away.

Twenty-one-year old Eddy Kepler was now AWOL.

Chapter 2

Current day—Campbellsville, Pennsylvania

"Daddy. I think we have covered everything." She really meant "I have covered everything. Per the funeral director's text, I just need to pick out a dress and some jewelry to drop off at the funeral home tomorrow morning before nine o'clock. I was thinking that pink boucle suit. It looks so cute on and she wore it frequently for special occasions." She continued to put neighbor-donated food, consisting of the standard mix of casseroles and cold cuts, into the refrigerator.

"How about the sweet little string of pearls you brought back from the army? The pearl earrings I gave her when I graduated from college will complete the look. I can't forget her pink pumps. The woman was a shoe horse. Yes, she would have liked this outfit. If it wasn't so tacky, I'd throw in her fox stole. The woman loved that awful thing and wore it long after it was out of style!"

"The Daughters of the American Revolution service will be at 10:00 a.m., before the funeral service. I think members from Jacob Ferree, Fort McIntosh, Massey-Harbison, and maybe even General Richard Butler chapters will be attending. I ordered the DAR marker for her gravestone. I never understood Mom's lack of excitement concerning DAR membership. Her lineage is something of which to be proud. I'm proud of both of your lineages!"

"Luncheon will be at your country club," she continued to ramble. "We are serving a buffet luncheon with three choices of entrees—beef tips, chicken marsala, and vegetable lasagna. There are four different side dishes. I thought you would like a salad, with green beans almandine, rice pilaf, glazed carrots, and potatoes au gratin. Of course, for Mom, lots of desserts and cookies. Oh, and there will be appetizers first, in case any guests beat us back from the cemetery. Cousin Jenny will be going straight to the food line." She smiled at the thought of her cousin eating four plates of cheese and then complaining of lactose intolerance.

She poked her head into the office. "Are you listening? You haven't said a word since we got home. Please take something for your nerves! The doctor gave you a sedative prescription which I filled this morning. It's late—you must be tired. Please think about going to bed, and for goodness sake, try to sleep. Stop worrying. I am here. You know I always take care of you."

"She really is in a better place. Her world was so empty and dark. I don't know how she stayed sane all those years. For that matter, I don't know how you managed to tolerate her smothering you. She gave you no room to even breathe and was always underfoot. Remember the time you both fell because she hovered too close and got her leg twisted in your cane. You were both sore for a week, not to mention the cuts and bruises that you tried to hide from me!"

"Now she is with God. All she talked about was how at peace she was with people once her memory totally left her. Good thing too, because she carried around a ton of baggage! She was ready to leave us and meet her Savior. And anxious to catch up with Grampa too, even if she couldn't remember him. It's what she wanted. God gave her happiness, something that she often fell short of during her life!"

Most of this was spoken to try to comfort herself. Even if her father wasn't drained, Shelby Patrick was mentally and physically exhausted. Her mother's decline began slowly. Her memory slipped into oblivion slowly over the past several decades. At first, it was just a person or two. Then her personality changed, becoming agitated and rigid. Her temper quickened, keeping everyone on edge. She finally lost memory of most life events. Her obsession was to love her husband. It painfully took a toll on both caregivers, daughter and father, as they watched the once vibrant, spirited, intelligent woman slip into a shadowy existence.

The old man sat rigid in his chair. He stared straight ahead, his red eyes glazed but dry. Memories washed over him with the rage of a wild waterfall. He did not hear a word his daughter spoke. He was lightyears away, lost in his thoughts.

Chapter 3

Early 1900s—West-central Pennsylvania

OLIVE WESTCHESTER BAILEY WAS A proud, pretentious woman with a quickly ignited blazing-hot temper. Her hard exterior penetrated to her very soul. The local children were terrified of her. Heaven forbid your ball roll into her yard. It was gone forever.

She exemplified the female version of Ebenezer Scrooge on a bad day. No one dared knock on her door for a donation. She never attended or tithed a church. She was the town miser. Yet, when a local veteran died, she was the one to canvass the neighborhood, asking for money to buy a funeral wreath.

Partially orphaned at age three when her mother died of influenza, she was raised by her older sisters. Youngest of eight children, Olive frequently went unnoticed. Easily underfoot of her four brothers working the farm and the brunt of frustration for her sisters; contrary to her personality, it was better for Olive to remain invisible. Her father, Henderson Westchester, was absent of parenting. He worked fifteen-hour days to manage his prosperous farm and to feed his growing family and thus had little time for his youngest little girl. Disappointed by her gender at birth, Henderson made no effort to endear the child.

As a young man, Henderson was pressured by his father and uncle to study law. Both his uncle and cousin were members of congress. Uncle James was a civil war hero who lost his leg fighting at Gettysburg. Being a war amputee contributed to his political success. James' son, cousin Jethro, rode to fame and fortune on his father's coattails. The plan was for Henderson to follow them to Washington

DC. Rather than choose public service, Henderson chose to take over his grandfather's estate and run the four-hundred-acre farm—land given to his great-great grandfather as compensation at the end of the Revolutionary war.

The Westchesters owned a thriving farm which employed a dozen farm hands. Henderson grew corn and wheat. He also grazed many head of livestock. Uncle James helped ensure the farm's success with a small government contract that began during the Spanish-American war. Like most pork belly agreements, the contract automatically renewed itself without further negotiation.

Henderson was a pillar of respect in the neighboring communities. However, for this long-established family, the same could not be said of his children. Most were spoiled and rebellious.

Money was not an issue; morality was. Despite attending church every Sunday, the Bible's teachings were lost on Henderson's brood. Without female supervision, his teenage daughters were considered "wildlings." Edwardian times did not tolerate non-chaperoned courtships. The Westchester girls did. Already the two oldest girls found themselves unmarried and pregnant by their sixteenth birthdays. Henderson required they continue with their farm chores of milking cows, tending chickens, slopping pigs, and grooming horses. Their household chores included all manners of running a prosperous farm, including all social requirements for entertaining. With the addition of their own infants, they did not want to be bothered raising their little sister.

Olive was bullied and tormented by her brothers and sisters. It was often best to make herself invisible, even though she preferred being the center of attention. She developed a deep sense of self-preservation. Known as the "feisty" Westchester child, she often acted out in public to fulfill her craving for attention. She was a drama queen whenever she found an audience. It was no wonder that, given little nurturing as a child, as an adult Olive possessed no knowledge of how to nurture her own children.

***

In January of 1930, Olive's oldest daughter was already eleven. The first birth was followed by two other girls and a boy. After missing two monthly cycles, it was obvious that a fifth pregnancy was afoot.

"Look what you've done! I'm pregnant!" she hissed at her husband through pursed lips and clenched teeth.

Tobias Bailey, a.k.a. "Tabs," was a diminutive, soft-spoken man. Olive considered him beneath her, socially. His family owned neither wealth nor property. Tabs, his father, and brothers were all laborers in the local factory owned by her Uncle James. Olive's opinion of Tobias differed when he and his fellow doughboys returned from World War I. In the family tradition, Olive celebrated more than one soldiers' return home. Suffering her sisters' destiny, impregnated, Tobias Bailey was a noble gentleman and married Olive despite their twelve-year age difference.

"Olive, dear, you are my wife. Am I not entitled to husbandly pleasure? Please calm yourself. Your excitement can't be good for the baby. We'll work through this. This summer, we shall add another blessing to our family," was all Tabs could mutter before Olive started flinging jelly glasses at his head.

Across town, Abigail Kepler hummed a lullaby and nursed her baby boy.

Part One

Chapter 4

1700s—Colonial Pennsylvania

GREGOR CAMPBELL'S FAMILY IMMIGRATED TO the colonies from Edinburgh, Scotland, in the early eighteenth century. His parents sailed to New York harbor but decided to settle in the Philadelphia area. The Campbell family were always town dwellers. Gregor's father was a shop- and innkeeper. Campbell's "Tartan Inn" was popular with the Scott and Irish population of the colonial city. Being born in Pennsylvania, Gregor, a native colonial, was privileged to an education and the life of colonial gentry. As a young man, Gregor dabbled in local politics. At the time of the Revolution, he was a respected magistrate.

The Campbell family lived in a large, two-story brick home on two acres of land. The grounds consisted of formal gardens outlined with boxwood hedges, a rose garden, a cutting garden, and a vegetable garden. The Campbells were not slave owners; however, they were quick to employ indentured servants.

Colin Westchester also immigrated from Scotland, although he was British. Colin's father was stationed in Inverness, Scotland, in 1727. Unlike most officers who left their families in London, Col. Westchester thought it would be an interesting adventure for his young wife to follow him to Scotland. Lady Westchester lived in luxury at Inverness castle. Her husband was always close at hand. It was no surprise that she found herself with child before the end of the decade. Master Colin was born and raised in the Highlands by native Highlanders. He loved the beauty of the land. Colin knew no other life; in his mind, he was part Scot.

By age sixteen, with the help of his father, Colin was presented a commission in His Majesty's army. Colin and father proudly represented the Crown, even if it meant a skirmish or two with their Scottish friends and neighbors. They were, after all, the ruling country. That is, until the battle of Culloden.

Father and son were so disgusted and appalled by the quickness and ferocity of the outright slaughter of the Highlanders that they both resigned their commissions and sailed for the colonies. Upon arrival, they declared themselves Scots, despite their contradictory last name.

Living peacefully on a farm in Berks County, Pennsylvania, Colin was the first in line to sign up for the patriot forces when the colonies began revolting against the Crown. Due to his knowledge and skill in warfare, he was immediately given a commission and the rank of colonel.

Gregor Campbell was also quick to side with the colonists for independence. Despite being a man of learning, he worked his way up through the ranks. He finished the war as Lt. Gregor Campbell, serving under his fellow Scotsman, Col. Colin Westchester.

At the end of the Revolutionary war, Gregor, was given land, same as Olive's ancestor, Col. Colin Westchester—in west-central Pennsylvania.

West-central Pennsylvania was already populated by settlers following the Forbes Road and the army to Fort Duquesne during the French and Indian war.

Colin received six hundred acres; Gregor, two hundred acres. The men were friends; therefore, they found it easy to, together, cultivate a new community of villagers and farmers.

The acreage was about eighty miles east of Fort Pitt, twenty-five miles north of the former Fort Ligonier and ten miles west of the former Fort Palmer. Westchester took to farming, dreaming of the Scottish Highlands while Campbell designed a town.

Campbell's town was laid out in a large grid fashion featuring generous lots. Gregor set himself up as magistrate, built a large house, and hoped to entice eastern colleagues in joining him on the frontier. The Conemaugh River flowed directly through the center of the grid. The town offered beautiful vistas of the surrounding Allegheny Mountains and ample river access for industry.

***

Campbell and Westchester both retained contacts in eastern Pennsylvania. They convinced friends to journey across Pennsylvania to their new land. For those patriots who were looking for space either in a town or on a farm, west-central Pennsylvania was a popular destination, although Indian raids were not uncommon. The construction of the National Highway made it accessible.

Irish and Scotts migrated to its scenic picturesque hills and ridges. Campbellsville soon attracted many Germans living in the eastern cities. It reminded them of the Mosel river valley of the fatherland.

Gregor sold one-acre village lots while Colin sold twenty-five-acre farms plots.

Per Gregor's design, large houses were soon built in the corners of each grid segment. Gregor opened an inn for travelers and troops on their way to Fort Pitt and beyond. The Germans opened a store and a lumber mill. The Irish opened eateries, farmed, and prospected for coal. The Scotts farmed and opened a woolen mill. The river provided easy access for light industry to the newly born town. The families intermarried. Thus, the town and country grew along with the American heritage.

Chapter 5

1937—Campbellsville, Pennsylvania

IN THREE WEEKS, HARRIETT JANE Bailey would celebrate her seventh birthday. She just completed first grade and she loved school. Harriett was an instant scholar. Even at an early age, she showed a natural acumen for learning. Her teachers applauded her curiosity and enthusiasm. By the end of the school year, Harriett was already reading her brother's third-grade primer.

She was so excited to turn seven. In her mind, being seven signaled being a "big girl." Not that Harriett would ever really be big; she was the same small stature of her father. She secretly confided in Tabs, "Papa, I hope that, somehow, mother will find a way to bake me a birthday cake." She remembered tasting cake two years ago at Christmas when her mother's great aunt hosted a rare party. "Cake is really delicious."

"Janie," Tabs answered with the pet name for his little girl. "If you wish really, really hard, maybe your wish will come true."

Harriett Jane wished all week, with all her energy and devotion.

Harriett's birthday also signaled seven years of economic depression for the country. Months earlier, financial indicators gave false hope for a long-awaited recovery; however, unemployment remained high and in 1937 the country slipped into a recession within a depression.

Tabs Bailey lost his job three years ago. Congressman Westchester kept Tabs on as long as possible, being his great niece's husband. But the business just wasn't there. Simple example of supply and demand. The factory received no orders and employed a skeleton crew, of which Tobias did not make the cut. Tabs picked up odd jobs here and there.

To feed his family, he hunted squirrel, deer, and rabbit. Poached was a more accurate description, since his hunting was done out of season. Tobias did not care; he had personal family responsibilities, one of which was a very unpleasant wife. Luckily the local forest was full of small game. Many of the town's men hunted out of season. Tabs was one of the more skilled hunters. He could shoot and trap, ensuring frequent meat for the table. The Baileys were blessed with a catch at least once a week.

Harriett usually accompanied her father on his trips to the woods. She climbed trees and swung on grapevine swings, often falling, knees and elbows always scraped. Tabs taught her the names of birds, plants, and animals. She even knew most of the local insects. Harriett didn't mind not having pretty dresses. She was happy as a "tomboy" because she was with her beloved papa. Harriett and Tabs were inseparable.

Tabs harvested and sold ginseng and sold the furs of his prey for some extra cash to help pay the mortgage. Harriett helped Tabs pick berries, wild cherries, and mushrooms. The family planted both an apple and plum tree and a large grapevine that not only provided shade for lounging, but wonderful grapes for jelly, when they could find sugar to buy. A chicken coop and a small vegetable garden, spread across the top of their property next to an alleyway, supplied the family with eggs, potatoes, onions, tomatoes, and various squash.

Survival was a family effort. Olive's part was saving every extra available penny, even during good times. By sewing money into a mattress and avoiding the banks, Olive also managed to avoid the cash crash and lost minimal in 1929. Considering the state of the average American, the Bailey family managed to survive, even without regular employment. Janie worked hand in hand with her papa every step of the way.

***

Henderson Westchester, in failing health and his seventy-seventh year, turned the farm management over to his sons' years earlier. Blame it on the depression, or blame it on the sons' lack of ability—the farm was also failing. The boys lost their government contract with the implementation of the New Deal. People were hungry, but no one could afford to buy wheat or corn. Some of the wheat was ground into flour and used by the family, but the family didn't buy. The town bakeries closed a few years earlier. The granary also closed. The Westchester's kept several milk cows left from the once thriving herd, the milk consumed by the family. Unfortunately for Olive, she rarely benefited from the flour and milk, being disliked by all her siblings.

During the prosperous twenties, the boys financed acreage to purchase updated equipment and an irrigation system. The irrigation overwatered the first year and ruined crops. The second year was more profitable but not enough to make up for one year's loss. Now deep into a depression, they could no longer afford to repay their banknotes. Acreage and livestock was sold off, reducing the farm to about a hundred acres with the herds depleted. If the economy didn't improve soon, they would lose the entire beautiful farm given to their ancestors so long ago by the First Continental Congress.

***

The day before Harriett's birthday Olive hiked the three miles out of town to the farm. She hated to approach her family for supplies; however, Tobias pleaded with her to bake a birthday cake for his little Janie. *It is not my nature to coddle the child*, thought Olive, *but cake would be a wonderful treat. I'm tired of doing without. I want cake!* she decided, and off she went.

"Please, Ben. I only need four cups of flour and one cup of milk," she begged her oldest brother. "It is Harriett's birthday. I want to bake her a cake. She is turning seven tomorrow." Olive held money to pay for the food; however, she was testing her brother's generosity.

Ben shook his head. "No," thinking his sister never cared about her child's birthday. Too angry with Ben's quick dismissal, she refused to ask again and refused to mention payment.

Ben tried to soften the denied request. "Olive, we barely have enough to feed ourselves." Olive spun on her heel and stormed out, muttering some profanity under her breath.

"We are going to lose the farm if we don't come up with one thousand dollars by the end of the month. Care to help with that?"

Capable of providing the needed funds, Olive found satisfaction in her brothers' misfortune. She knew she could always manage to pay her mortgage. She saved enough cash to last at least another seven years, and Tabs brought in extra money. Her home was not yet in jeopardy, and with any luck, never would be.

The two-story, corner lot, three-bedroom brick structure was Olive's pride and joy. It once belonged to the town doctor before Olive and Tabs bought it. It was one of the bigger houses in town, with both front and back porches.

All the corner houses in Campbellsville were large, being built by the prosperous first inhabitants. Smaller houses built for factory workers filled in the street blocks as local industry grew.

The second floor of Olive's palace consisted of three bedrooms and an inside bath, complete with running water, water closet, and claw-foot tub. Olive naturally claimed the biggest bedroom in the front of the house. It was large enough for Olive's full bed and Tabs' cot. Tabs lost all bedroom privileges due to Olive's last pregnancy. She was determined that it would be her last. In the summertime, when windows were open, she could hear the train whistles blowing softly at the end of town. In this economy, the train depot was usually deserted.

The three older girls, Ester, June, and Alice, shared one bedroom and Janie shared the smallest bedroom with her nine-year old brother, Albert. Olive would need to split the two youngest children soon. *Perhaps Tabs could scavenge some wood scraps and build a partition in the attic for Ester, their oldest? Or maybe the girl will find a husband and get out of my hair. She's eighteen. Time to leave the nest. That's the solution of choice.* thought Olive. She didn't have to wait long. Like mother, like daughter, Ester was pregnant, married, and vacated by the end of summer.

The enclosed staircase opened into the dining room. Olive polished her mahogany dining table to a mirror finish. She purchased a set of blue and white floral bone china back in the twenties, which was kept on display in the matching mahogany breakfront. It was the closest pattern in her price range that Olive could find to the English flow blue that was so popular. The family only ate in this room for special occasions. No such events occurred over the past seven years, not for even the birth of a child.

Olive's front parlor was decorated to modern times. A floral green and white magnolia print upholstered the settee and two stuffed arm chairs. A leaf pattern woven into a woolen rug covered the shining buffed wood floor. Silver and wood framed pictures of family adorned the side tables. Freshly cut flowers from the gardens occupied a niche in the wall. This was Olive's special place. To the rest of the family, it was "off limits." They were sequestered to the large kitchen.

The kitchen had a coal burning cook stove/oven. An oversized corner farm house sink accommodated the largest of jelly pots and roasting pans. A Hoosier was the baking center, when supplies were available. Its flour and sugar bins remained empty for the most part. Two huge pantry rooms stored a wringer washer and usually an array of preserves, jellies, and dried meat. Olive's stock was dwindling but still in existence.

A painted white cabinet contained mix and unmatched dishes which were used for everyday dining and an extensive collection of salt and pepper shakers. Olive obsessed over her menagerie of cactus, alligators, skunks, rabbits, and miscellaneous animals, windmills, palm trees, circus clowns, wine bottles, and even a bizarre pair of outhouses; all used to dispense the white or black condiment.

In the center of the room was a large oak pedestal round table and eight mismatched oak chairs. This was the only room in which the family was permitted to gather.

Milk or no milk! I shall never offer them a roof if they lose that farm, she thought as she began the trek home. *I have the space. Let them sleep in the woods.*

***

The morning of Harriett's birthday arrived with blazing heat and humidity. Olive was almost glad not to have to fire the coal cook stove to bake a cake, but she now craved cake, wanting it more than Harriett.

Harriett was playing in the alley by the chicken coop. Suddenly, a scruffy ragged man appeared out of nowhere. Harriett was startled.

"Come here, little girl," beckoned the tattered man. His pants were mere shreds of fabric held up by a piece of rope. His shirt was collarless and saturated in sweat.

"No. Leave me alone! You stink," she was quick to quip back.

The hobo took offense to her insult and moved closer to the chicken coop. He raised his voice, now sounding menacing.

"Fetch me some eggs. Hurry," he snarled at Harriett. Harriett was really scared, and being so small, offered no kind of threat. The hobo moved in yet closer to Harriett. Sensing trouble, she picked up a stick and went on the attack. She charged the hobo, switching his back and face with the stick, all the time yelling at the top of her lungs. Having the element of surprise, the hobo faltered long enough for Tabs to hear his daughter's cries for help. He bounded across the yard, arriving with a twenty-gauge shotgun in his hand, while Janie continued hitting the hobo with her stick.

"Mister! You better back away from my little Janie, or I'll splatter you with buckshot," growled Tabs. "Janie, get over here behind me. Now, Mister, I know you're hungry, so I'm givin' you one egg. You take this egg and you get a move on. If I see you around these parts ever again, I'll shoot you. You hear?" Tabs waited for an answer. "You hear? I'll shoot you dead on the spot."

Janie moved to the safety of her father but tripped over a root and landed in the middle of the chicken coop. She was covered with mud and chicken poop. The hobo slowly backed away while grabbing an egg from Tabs' hand. He began sauntering slowly down the alleyway. Tabs shot a round at his feet. Purpose served, the hobo ran off toward the train station.

***

"What in the name of God did you get into?" screamed Olive. "Look at you. I can't possibly bake a cake now. You require a good scrubbing." Olive made it sound as if it were the child's fault that she was not getting a birthday cake. *Why should I admit failure?* thought Olive, *when I can blame it on someone else.*

Poor Janie sobbed, looking at her filthy clothes and shoes. "But Mama, there was a hobo and I fought him off. He was trying to steal a chicken and I fell."

"Enough of your stories. I don't want to hear such nonsense. Go strip down to your panties while I run your bath. No cake for you today!" was all her calloused mother said.

Not wanting to heat the stove, Olive filled the wash basin with chilly water from the tap. Janie sobbed and shivered as her mother scrubbed her hair and skin with an unwarranted roughness. Ordeal finally complete, Janie dressed quickly in fresh clothes and sulked away to hide. Her mother would not permit her to return outside.

Tabs was not around for the exchange between mother and daughter. He followed the hobo to the end of town, making sure he was long gone. When he returned home, he found a squeaky-clean Janie sobbing in the corner of the kitchen.

"What's wrong, precious Janie?" he asked as he wrapped his daughter in his arms.

"Mother doesn't have time to bake my cake because I fell and got dirty and she had to take time to give me a bath. I wanted cake." She sobbed.

Tabs flashed his wife a look of disbelief. How can she blame this on the child, having no intention of baking a cake? Tabs look was met with a snarl.

Tabs gathered up his little girl and carried her outside. His exit was followed with Olive shouting, "Don't you let her get dirty!"

Tabs carried Janie to a big wooden Adirondack chair where they sat together under the grapevine. He reached in his pocket and pulled out a package wrapped in old newsprint.

"Here, honey. It's not much, but it's for your birthday," soothed Tabs.

Janie looked at her papa lovingly and stopped crying. She unwrapped a loosely hand sewn rag baby doll with button eyes and a mop crop of hair.

"Oh Papa, I love her. She's so beautiful. What shall I name her?" responded the innocent child.

"Let's call her May, in honor of my mother," Tabs answered. *That should be enough to get to Olive*, he thought. Janie was never allowed to meet her Grandma May. To Tabs' regret, Mother May died without ever meeting his darling daughter. Olive, of all people, considered May white trash, undeserving of the Westchester family and social status.

Tabs also pulled a wrinkled piece of foil out of his pocket. He opened it to reveal a melted cube of chocolate. "Janie, dip your finger in the chocolate and lick it," Tabs instructed. Together, father and daughter sat and ate the melted chocolate.

"Papa, this is the best birthday ever!" Janie's eyes beamed as they met her father's. Tabs' heart melted. How could this sweet child be the offspring of a woman filled with such hatred and selfishness?

Chapter 6

1940s—Campbellsville, Pennsylvania

THE VILLAGE OF CAMPBELLSVILLE, PENNSYLVANIA, braced for additional challenging times with the bombing of Pearl Harbor and the announcement of another war. The town never really recovered from the previous decade of depression; how was it going to survive another World War? Mistakenly, the last war was reported to be the war to end all wars. The reporters were wrong.

Now devoid of most men, boys, and young adults, the town's women were left to struggle on. Storefronts closed during the depression remained closed. Females taught school, ran the shops, planted victory gardens, attended to town politics, and raised their children. Many boys not yet old enough to enlist left the village and moved to larger towns to work in the factories and steel mills in support of the war effort. Houses were abandoned when many of the women joined the exodus. Although small, Campbellsville contributed many Rosie Riveters.

Absent competent teachers, Harriett Jane Bailey managed to complete her high school education by supplementing with self-study. Sadly, college was out of the question. Academic scholarships were almost nonexistent, and although Harriett was a dynamite tiny athlete, she was much too small to play on any sports team other than an intramural team. If academic scholarships were hard to procure, college athletic opportunities for women were impossible.

Most of the money saved by Olive was spent during the past two decades. Now that work was available, Tabs was too frail and too old for strenuous physical labor in the factories or mills. To Olive's dismay, Tabs worked custodial jobs. However, the Baileys survived the depression with little loss. The exception was the loss of Olive's dignity. Her "high and mighty" family lost the farm and lost their prestige. Her siblings moved to the nearby cities. She was alone with her maiden name and no one to remember it. A total assault on Olive's Westchester lineage—complete.

***

Harriett's classmate, Edgar, chose the road of least resistance and did as little studying as possible. That is, as little without jeopardizing graduation. Edgar copped an attitude. He carried a chip on his shoulder. He felt cheated that he did not have the appropriate coaches to promote him for a college sports scholarship. His athletic prowess included baseball, basketball, and he excelled in football. Edgar was six-foot tall, muscular, had blonde curly hair, and was extremely handsome. He looked older than his seventeen years and was often chastised by townsfolk for not enlisting. Four of Edgar's brothers, Earl, George, William, and Roy, were veterans of the war. Earl and Roy served in the navy, in the Pacific Theater, fighting against the Japanese. George served in the African army tank division. William, air force, served in Northern Africa also. Luckily, all returned home with minimal physical harm and proceeded to work in the steel mills.

There were four additional older siblings, two boys and two girls. Abigail essentially bore two different families. The four oldest being born shortly after her marriage at age eighteen. In their seventh year of marriage, Edgar traveled out of state for work. Abigail gratefully accepted a break from pregnancy. Four years later, upon the return of her husband, she spent the next six years pregnant. Edgar was a surprise. Four years younger than the next closest brother, Edgar ushered in Abigail's change of life.

Being the youngest sibling and spoiled by his family, Edgar hoped to change the family work trend by playing college football. He held all school records and most state records in rushing; however, the women teachers did not know how to comply with college rules for athletic scholarships. Edgar's dreams were negated by a local lack of knowledge.

Graduation came and went with the war in 1948. Neither Harriett nor Edgar attended college. Harriett worked the summer after graduation in a local food store. She possessed the same miserly skills of her mother and managed to save enough money to start secretarial school in the fall. Edgar worked as a butcher in the same store. They never spoke despite Harriett's secret crush on her coworker. She was much too shy to compete with other women.

Edgar squandered his salary on beer and the local girls, of which there was no shortage for the handsome young stud.

In September of 1948, Harriett enrolled in secretarial school in Pittsburgh. She worked as a nanny for a wealthy family for room and board and some extra cash.

Edgar bought a used, cream colored 1941 coupe and followed his brothers to work in the steel mills.

Chapter 7

1950—Campbellsville, Pennsylvania

"MOM. I'M LEAVING FOR WORK," Harriett yelled as she ran down the steps to catch her ride. It was a beautiful summer day. Her classes should have taken eighteen months to complete. Always the over-achiever, Harriett obtained her associate degree in only twelve months and found a secretarial job at a small company Dugan & Co. in a nearby city. She literally fell into the opportunity when their vice president, Thomas Roland, attended a job fair at her school.

Harriett was so tiny that she was below eyesight of the six-foot five-inch Roland, who stumbled over her. Her hair and dress were modest, verging on forgettable. However, the executive was so impressed with Harriett's composure and obvious intelligence that he offered her a job in the secretarial pool on the spot. The mousey tiny girl joined fifteen other secretaries.

Her first day of work, Harriett was given a desk from a group inside a large half-walled cubicle. She was supplied with a typewriter, steno pad, pens, pencils, staple remover, and letter opener. The sta-pler, typing paper, copy paper, and pencil sharpener were located centrally within the cubicle and to be shared by all fifteen women.

Harriett was overwhelmed with the incessant chatter. "How do these women work in this condition?" she asked herself. She learned how to tune down the noise with the help of cotton ear plugs. Although she overheard snippets of weekend conquests; the drama of love lost and found. She knew she would never share such intimate thoughts with these women; not that she was ever invited to join them.

Keeping stride with past achievements through exceptional arduous work, it took four months for her to work her way up to assistant to Mr. Thomas Roland, VP, CFO.

The move to private secretary suited Harriett. She continued to occupy a half-walled cubicle, but now, it was directly outside of Mr. Roland's office. A phone was added to her list of equipment. Shared supplies were among the three executive secretaries only. Living in more civilized surroundings, Harriett enjoyed the company of mature co-workers.

Harriett loved the freedom of earning a wage. She was very diligent, more than any of the other company employees. Her record was spotless. At times, all three of the companies' executives required her skills when other secretaries failed to produce. They admired the dedication of the little brunette and rewarded her with bonuses whenever possible.

Harriett never dated and was rarely asked to participate in after-work activities. The other secretaries were jealous, but not willing to exert equal effort. Like every good girl that maintained a spotless reputation, Harriett lived at home with her parents. She paid them monthly rent and helped to buy groceries.

Life with Olive and Tabs was almost pleasant. Her older siblings were all married and owned homes and had children of their own. Tabs moved into the girl's bedroom and enjoyed escaping his wife. Harriett remained in the room she once shared with Albert. It was small but quiet, in the back of the house. She purchased a new flowered bedspread and matching draperies to create an oasis of privacy. Her closet was meagerly furnished; however, the few items were of high quality. Harriet owned two business suits, two skirts, three blouses, two sweaters, two pairs of trousers, and three pairs of shoes; black and brown heels and beige flats. All clothing matched, extending the look of her wardrobe with some creativity and additional accessories.

Olive delighted in her newfound income, resulting in a more amicable personality.

"I'll stop at the pastry shop on my way home," she trailed as she raced off.

Mother and daughter both had a sweet tooth. Unlike during the Depression, pastries were now plentiful.

As the post war economy boomed, so did Campbellsville. Several small businesses opened plants in the town. Empty real estate was purchased. People had money. They took pride in their property. Houses were freshly painted, yards were groomed, and fences whitewashed. Victory gardens were replaced with flower gardens. Instead of tomatoes and onions, the alleys were lined with bearded iris and day lilies.

Cars became commonplace. Chicken coops were converted to car ports or garages. Bus service to and from Campbellsville carried travelers to several nearby towns and cities, offering additional work opportunities.

Industry returned, and storefronts opened. Several small groceries, two pastry shops, a five-and-dime, a department store, a shoe store, hardware store, and a stationary lined Main Street. They were joined with several restaurants, a coffee house, and multiple taverns.

Three veteran's clubs opened, where vets from both World Wars gathered and commiserated in their common experience.

Campbellsville boasted a pharmacy, a doctor's office, movie theater, bowling alley, tennis courts, baseball field, post office, and two banks. The village morphed once again into a prosperous town.

The steel mills in neighboring cities boomed. Any man returning home from the war easily found a job as the women reluctantly relinquished their positions and headed home. Edgar was making good money and spending it just as quickly. One of only a few young men in town who owned his own car. Although it was an older model, Edgar sported wheels. With his good looks and private transportation, the bachelor enjoyed having his choice of any girl from all the neighboring towns.

"Hey, Ed!" yelled his older brother, Earl. "Turn on the radio."

Edgar hurried to the family Zenith and dialed in the local news station. The reporter was finishing a report stating that the Communists of North Korea crossed the 38th parallel. President Truman was ready to join UN troops in retaliation.

The thought of yet another war was a topic at most dinner tables that night, including Edgar's. His mother, father, and brother shared their concern with the youngest family member.

The oldest four Kepler children moved to Detroit to find work during the Depression. The four World War II vets stayed in Pennsylvania.

"Ed, if you want to escape the draft, you need to get married. And I mean right away," argued brother Earl over beef stew. Earl was Edgar's favorite brother and the only brother still living at home. Earl always tried to protect Edgar as a child, although Edgar towered over him as a man.

"I think Earl may have a good point," joined Abigail, not wanting her youngest son to experience the horrors of war. She listened unnoticed when her sons shared stories of their "adventures" and near-death experiences.

Edgar picked at his food. "Married," he mumbled. "Well, son-of-a bitch."

Abigail wrinkled her forehead in objection to such language at the dinner table.

"This is a real downer. I guess this cool cat gig can't go on forever. Nope! Not stopping. It's too soon? Shit! But who am I going to marry?" Edgar looked at his brother. "I have already deflowered most of the lookers in a ten-mile radius. None of them are suitable to take as a wife. Well, my brothers and Dad may approve, but you won't, Mom."

Abigail looked at her son with disdain. "Ed, you are twenty, already a man. It is time for you to finally become a responsible adult. Have you really been that much of a Tomcat? Have you no respect for women or yourself?"

The infidelity of Abigail's husband was a well-known fact. Edgar Jr. inherited his good looks and physique from father, Edgar Sr. Father never grew up, why should son? Junior also followed Senior's example of womanizing.

"Mom. I'm a legend! I have the respect of every cat in town," Edgar proudly pronounced. "But I don't want to marry any of those girls. Too loose, with a taste of the wild. When I settle down, I always thought I would look for a respectable girl, someone like you, even if I have to travel several hundred miles to find her." He laughed uncontrollably.

Edgar Sr., Earl, and Edgar Jr. were heartily laughing. Abigail joined reluctantly. She was a creative, loving, pious woman who was aware of their sins. She prayed daily for the souls of her wayward husband and sons.

"The problem remains. You need a wife or you'll be drafted." Earl brought the group back to reality. This assumption was based on pure conjecture. "Little brother, war really is hell. Don't take this lightly."

"I'm going out. This is too depressing. If I must find a wife, at least let me have one last day of fun." With that, Edgar charged out the door to his car, like a rutting bull moose. Speeding out of town, Edgar happened to pass the pastry shop just as Harriett Jane Bailey exited with her boxes of treats.

Hmm. Problem solved! thought Edgar. *I'll start working on her tomorrow. Tonight, I party!*

Chapter 8

THE KNOCK AT THE FRONT formal door surprised both Olive and Harriett. The Bailey's were visited infrequently, and never through the front door at nine-thirty in the evening. Tabs rose from a kitchen chair where he was rolling cigarettes and walked to the inner sanctum of the drawing room. Olive watched hawk-like to make sure he did not litter loose tobacco on the woolen rug.

"Janie, sweetie, you have a visitor," he called as he opened the door to a strapping muscular young man. "Please come in, sir."

Even at twenty years of age, Harriett looked at her mother for permission to enter the parlor.

"Go. What are you waiting for? Git rid of whoever it is. I don't want strangers lurking 'round wantin' to steal from me," was her mother's response for granting passage.

Harriett approached the door cautiously, wondering who would be calling. She had no close friends. If the knock was a surprise, the vision of Edgar was an outright shock. She worked in the same store as he for an entire summer and never exchanged a word. What was he doing at her front door asking for her this late at night?

"Hi, Harriett," began Edgar carefully. The ever-confident boy was in uncharted waters. He did not know how to behave around respectable girls. Harriett was the shy, wholesome, resourceful, modest girl that every mother wanted for her son but that no son wanted for himself.

"Edgar?" was all Harriett managed.

Sensing that she was more uncertain then he, Edgar gained some confidence.

She always carried a crush on you. Don't be such a chump. You'll have her charmed in a week, he thought with rising bravado.

"Harriett, who's Janie?" he asked. "Never mind, it doesn't matter. I was wondering if you would like to see a movie with me. How about tonight? The late show?"

"What? I couldn't possibly go out tonight. I'm up early for work. My day usually starts around 5:30 a.m. Oh, Jane is my middle name. Papa calls me Janie," responded Harriett. She immediately regretted sounding so juvenile by saying "papa."

"No?" Surprised, Edgar was not familiar with rejection. Confidence wavering, he continued somewhat sarcastically, "I'm sorry. How thoughtless of me. I forgot you are a career woman. Perhaps we could try for another night?"

Fending off his sarcasm, Harriett answered, "I shall look forward to the movies Saturday night. Not the late show. Pick me up around seven? I want to be in before eleven."

"It's a date. See you Saturday." Edgar turned and walked indignantly down the porch steps. *This may be harder than I thought*, crossed his mind as he opened the car door.

"Oh, and please use the back door. Mother does not permit me to receive guests any place other than the kitchen. Good night," yelled Harriet before the door was closed.

Holy crap! What twenty-year old is in by eleven? No way in hell will this work! were the groans in his head as he drove away.

"Who in the name of sweet heaven was that?" pried Olive as Harriett returned to her kitchen chair.

"The craziest thing. That was Eddy Kepler."

"You mean that Tomcat offspring of Abigail and Edgar Kepler? What on earth did he want?" asked Olive.

"He asked me out on a date. We are going to the movies Saturday night," answered a blushing Harriett.

"Janie dear," Tabs gently put his arm around his daughter. "Please be careful with this boy. He is no gentleman. I hear the men talking. His reputation is worse than his adulterous father's. Eddy Kepler is not to be trifled with."

"Pious Harriett!" sneered Olive. "You think you are so much better than the rest of us with your education and fancy job! You go ahead and date this Eddy Kepler and you'll end up pregnant just like Ester!"

"You mean just like you!" Harriett flashed a look at her mother. It felt good to be on the giving end rather than receiving end with Olive.

"I shall date whomever I please and I shall *not* end up pregnant. I possess something you do not, and that is self-control. If that makes me better than you, then so be it!"

Harriett rose and walk out of the kitchen. As she climbed the stairs to her room, she smiled. "Boy, did it feel good to finally let loose on my bully mother. That was years overdue."

Tabs remained in the kitchen and hid his grin from his hissing wife. "Janie will be okay with Edgar Kepler Jr.!"

***

Harriett was all butterflies the next day at work. The smolder of a crush was ready to burst into a burning inferno of the heart. It was difficult to maintain focus, but she managed. Today was payday, and she feverishly counted her dollars. A saver like her mother, she knew this month's rent was already put aside at home, with a sizable account in the bank. She decided to indulge herself and buy a new dress for her date. She didn't own any dresses. They were too impractical. Dresses offered limited ways to mix and match in a minimalist closet.

Harriett wanted in the worst way to share her excitement with someone; however, she had no close friends. It was inappropriate for her to tell her boss, Mr. Roland, although he worried that his young associate partook in no social life either inside or outside of work. The other two executive secretaries were twice her age. Enthusiastically, but alone, she left the office.

She cashed her check, placing all but ten dollars in her wallet. Time to shop! It was Thursday; therefore, the stores in town remained open until nine in the evening. Harriett checked the bus schedule and headed toward Gimbels department store.

Once inside, she was met with a barrage of scents and cosmetics. Harriett never wore makeup. *Maybe I should buy a lipstick too?* she thought.

Decisiveness was not a shortcoming. Harriett quickly chose a navy blue sleeveless cotton dress with large white dots. The waist was cinched with a wide white belt. It looked darling on her tiny frame. Many of the styles were brighter colors and patterns; however, Harriett went with a more conservative, versatile fabric. Cost: $8.50. More than she wanted to pay but still within her ten-dollar budget; enough money remaining to buy an expensive Elizabeth Arden red lipstick.

On her way to the cosmetic counter, Harriett passed the shoe department. "White shoes would complete the look," she mused. "But white is so impractical! Can't be worn before Memorial Day or after Labor Day. Look for blue. They can be worn to work."

After adding $4.50 to her budget for "T-strap" navy pumps, Harriett gathered her shopping bags and headed to the bus stop. She felt like an heiress carrying multiple shopping bags. She would have to borrow a white cardigan sweater from one of her sisters. Fifteen dollars was all she could splurge for her first date.

At home, she eagerly engaged Tabs and Olive in a session of "show and tell."

Tabs clapped his hands in admiration. Olive was fast to criticize the purchases.

"Red lipstick! Do you want to look like a common whore?" She spit the slur at her daughter.

"Mother, red lipstick is all the rage. The woman at Gimbels showed me twenty-five different shades of red. I picked the least bright. At twenty, I am old enough to wear some lip color."

"Whores can wear red lipstick at any age. You are just asking for it!" sputtered Olive.

The elation and excitement of a wonderful day shattered, Harriet slung back at her mother. "Well, I guess you would know." The second night in a row, she made a quick exit to avoid further verbal wrath and flying objects aimed in her direction.

Harriett rose early the next morning. She wanted to miss any encounter with her mother. She felt badly about their words last night; however, she wasn't ready to apologize. Harriett admonished disrespect in others. She wasn't sure why she was so disparaging last night. But she admitted that it felt good to release pent up feelings.

Arriving thirty minutes before her clock-in time, Harriett went to the lobby to look at magazine ads. She needed to justify her red lipstick purchase. Comforted, Harriett found many ads and many popular brands promoting red lip color. Eyebrow pencil was also a popular feature. *"Perhaps that is my next purchase?"* she thought as she walked to her desk.

Despite her workload, the day seemed to drag. Her mind wondered. How should she act on a date? What would she do if he tried to hold her hand? Would he try to kiss her? She was never kissed by any man other than her papa. What if she liked him? She remembered her crush on him, when she worked at the grocery store; feeling a flutter in her stomach. What if he didn't like her? Why did he asked her out in the first place? She was not his style. Eddy went for flashy easy girls, why me? These and other questions plagued her day.

Harriett decided to inspect lip color of the secretarial pool.

"Red is the color, hands down."

Finally, she was ready to go home to face her mother with new found confidence and, admittedly, some remorse.

Tabs went hiking in the woods that day, hunting ginseng. With any luck, he would manage to bring in some extra money and avoid his wife. It had the makings of a brilliant day.

Olive decided she was not feeling well. She was not the least bit used to being challenged by her family. The loss of overall power was disconcerting. She would certainly see that it was not repeated.

Harriett returned home and made dinner sandwiches for herself and Tabs. Olive was not eating. Harriett was not much of a cook, but neither was Olive, unless she wanted something special for herself.

Tabs and Harriett listened to their favorite Friday night radio programs. The Baileys did not own a television. TV was a rarity in Campbellsville. After what seemed an eternity, bedtime arrived. Harriett washed her hair, set it in bobby pin curls, wrapped her head with a scarf, and went to bed with wet hair. Hair rollers were popular with the girls. Harriett neither owned them nor wished to sleep on them. She overheard the girls at work complaining of morning headaches caused by their use. Pin curls were fine for her budget and taste.

Sweet dreams remained elusive. Harriett was much too excited to really relax. After hours of tossing back and forth, she managed to achieve a dreamless stupor.

The smell of bacon drifted through her open bedroom window. The window, which remained open most of the summer for air circulation, was directly above the kitchen. Dressing quickly in a pair of boy leg shorts and waist tied top, Harriett raced downstairs to see why she smelled such a treat.

Tabs was at the stove, frying bacon. He smiled as his daughter, hair still in pin curls, entered the room.

"Good morning, sweetie," he said with a grin.

"Bacon?" questioned Harriett.

"I made some money on ginseng yesterday. Bacon, to celebrate my little girls first date, and to smooth things over with your mother."

"Papa, you are so thoughtful!" Harriett threw her arms around her father and kissed him on the cheek.

Their exchange was witnessed by Olive, also exploring the source of the mouthwatering aroma.

"Always her favorite! What are you two up to?"

"Oh, Mother, I'm so sorry for my rudeness last night. I didn't mean the nasty things I said." Although she was lying, just a little. "Please forgive me." Harriett tried to make amends with her dismal mother. "I don't know what ever possessed me to lash out."

As she tried to kiss her mother on the cheek, Olive pulled away. Unforgiving and indifferent, Olive muttered, "Harrumph," and sat down at the table to eat the morning treat. It never occurred to her that she also owed Harriett an apology.

Chapter 9

EDDY KNOCKED AT THE BACK door exactly at seven o'clock. He was met by a petite girl with brown curly hair brushed away from her face. She wore a soft red lipstick. Her dotted summer dress looked new. A white sweater draped over her shoulders was fastened by a pearl sweater clip. She looked like a fashion model with her matching blue shoes.

Eddy inhaled. *Wow, she really cleans up. She's a real doll*, he thought. To Harriett, his compliment was cautious.

"You look nice. Let's get going."

Harriett yelled goodbyes to her parents as she followed Eddy to his car parked out front.

Eddy jumped into the driver's seat. Harriett went around to the passenger side. She stood waiting for Eddy to open her door. Already turning over the ignition, Eddy looked out the window, thinking that Harriett probably never rode in a car and didn't know how to open the door. He motioned to the handle. Harriett stood firm.

What the hell? he thought.

Harriett just stood waiting. Finally, it dawned on Eddy that she was waiting for him to open the car door.

Good God! A 1950's suffragette. Not sure this is worth the trouble, although she is a knockout tonight.

Eddy dutifully got out of the running car and opened Harriett's door.

"Thank you," was all she said.

"What's your pleasure?" he asked.

Before he could list the movies at his favorite frequented drive-ins, Harriett responded, "the seven-thirty showing at the Crown Theater."

The Campbellsville Crown Theater was owned by Sydney Crown, businessman from a neighboring city. He owned most theaters in a twenty-mile radius. His vision was ahead of his time. The theater was open on Wednesday, Friday, Saturday nights, and Sunday afternoon for a matinee. He built two separate viewing screens within the building. One viewing area also converted to a stage that a small Pittsburgh group used for summer theater camp productions each July and August, bringing big city culture to the villagers of Campbellsville.

The theater brought in two movies per month. Because of the two viewing areas, they could offer one new movie every two weeks, keep audience interest, while minimizing costs. Crown movies were usually several months after release, which also kept down cost. The town's folk didn't mind. They were happy to have a theater other than the drive-in a.k.a. the local "make out" spot.

This month's features were both headliners. Often Crown showed both an "A" and a "B" movie. The older listing was *The Big Lift*, starring Montgomery Clift, Paul Douglass, and Cornell Borchers. It was a movie about the Soviet blockade of Berlin, post-World War II. The newest listing was an Irving Berlin musical, *Annie Get Your Gun*, starring Betty Hutton, Howard Keel, and Benay Venuta. Harriett was hoping to see *Annie Get Your Gun*.

Although the Crown was at the end of the street on which Harriett lived, Eddy took a circuitous route. Harriett wondered if he was either showing off his date or working up nerve to go through with it. Finally, Eddy parked and jumped out of the car. Expecting Harriett to follow, he bounded up to the box office and ordered two tickets. He looked back to see Harriett sitting in the car.

Now what? Good God, she's waiting for me to open her car door! he realized.

Slowly he walked back to the car. *Does she really expect this every time?*

As he opened the door, he presented Harriett his hand. She took it and exited the car.

They entered the theater and Eddy gave his tickets to the usher. They were led to a door marked *The Big Lift*. Harriett hid her disappointment. With the talk yet of another war, she did not want to see a war movie. Eddy could barely hide his excitement of seeing what he called "a shoot-em-up."

Despite being escorted by a rake and watching a war movie, Harriett still enjoyed being on the arm of Eddy Kepler. Heads turned as they entered the theater.

Eddy led her to a seat in the mezzanine. She refused. Although Harriett never sat in the mezzanine, her sisters said they were the "kissing seats." She asked to sit in the middle of the main floor, not too far forward but not in the back. Somewhat discouraged, knowing it would be a scoreless evening, Eddy led Harriett to the main floor. Finally, he found suitable seats in the sixth row on the aisle.

Harriett worked up the nerve to ask for some refreshments. She figured that if Eddy was void of sufficient manners to open her car door, he would certainly not offer her a drink. Annoyed, Eddy left Harriett to buy popcorn and Coca-Colas.

"Hey, Eddy," called a voice from across the aisle. "What are you doing in a regular theater? I thought you preferred the drive-in?" questioned one of his buddies.

"I'm here with Harriett Bailey," Eddy answered.

"You've got to be kidding! With all the babes hanging off you, why Harriett?"

"I've changed my ways," smirked Eddy. "Strictly good girls for me from now on. And Harriett is actually a looker. You'd never recognize her from high school."

"You are probably right, because I never paid any attention to her in high school, and I don't intend to now." His buddy laughed. "She'd be the last girl I'd be caught dead with."

"Your loss." Eddy mustered as much bravado as possible, trying to save face. He wasn't convinced that Harriett was worth all the trouble of marrying a "good girl" just to avoid the draft. It might actually be easier to fight a war.

Harriett heard the exchange. She wondered why his sudden switch to "good girls." The comment made no sense. She decided to let it go and enjoy her surroundings.

Art deco sconces dotted the walls. The theater smelled of popcorn and stale cigarettes. Red carpeting covered the main center aisle. The floor under the worn cushioned seats was wood for easy clean up. Cheap velvet draperies covered the screen.

Harriett watched couples file in and take their seats. She wondered if this was the first date for one couple that held hands and gazed into each other's eyes as they walked to the front row.

She looked up and back and managed to catch a glimpse of one young couple already necking in the mezzanine.

Glad I avoided that! Too awkward for a first date.

The projector started to hum, and the screen lights flickered. The curtains pulled open, allowing previews of future movies to fill the screen. A newsreel reminded moviegoers of the trouble brewing with North Korea. The audience groaned.

Harriett's excitement was mounting. She was on a real date. All her childhood notions of romance surfaced. She thought of Cinderella's lost glass slipper and Snow White's poison apple and life-saving kiss. Could she possibly find her own Prince Charming?

"Poison. That's a possibility with my mother!" she chuckled to herself.

What would it feel like to kiss a boy? The butterflies fluttered again in her stomach.

Eddy's return brought her back to reality. She looked up and smiled brightly at him.

She really isn't that bad of a looker, he thought as he grinned back. Harriet's heart melted. Direct hit; Harriett became the newest victim of Eddy Kepler's charming smile.

To his surprise, Harriett allowed Eddy to hold her hand during the movie. His touch sent tingles through her body. However, later, his advance to get closer was blocked with an arm and a whispered "No." Harriett knew that she could not let her resolve sway.

They ate the buttered popcorn, drank their colas, and watched the action on the screen. Harriett was careful not to drop any food on her clothes. Oil stains were so hard to remove. Eddy seemed to be enjoying the production. Harriett ignored the movie but enjoyed the date. She was glad that she bought herself a new dress and lipstick.

All was worth the effort and money. She knew Eddy was surprised to see her wearing makeup. Somehow, she knew he approved.

The audience applauded; folks began to exit. The couple walk hand in hand to the car. Time passed so quickly. Harriett did not want to go home but knew she must.

Eddy offered to take Harriett for some ice cream. The local drug store soda counter was where all the kids went after school and on dates. Harriett longed to be part of that crowd. She spent her entire childhood alone with her father and siblings. She so badly wanted to belong to a group. Tonight was her big chance as Eddy Kepler's date.

Reluctantly, Harriett thanked Eddy but announced that it was time to go home. Secretly, she was afraid to go someplace else with him. She planned her defensive strategy around being in a car and in a theater. Surprisingly, Harriett thought of her mother's human-ness and understood. Temptation is a challenge. She winced at the thought of her derogatory words. If there was a next date, which she hoped there would be, she would plan additional defensive strategy to fit that date to avoid temptation.

The couple spoke little on the short ride home, although Eddy still held her hand. Harriet willingly sat closer to Eddy's side of the car, leaving some space between them. Back at the Bailey's, Eddy pulled Harriett close to him and tried to kiss her on the mouth.

"No, Eddy. Not on the first date," was all she could whisper. Her willpower was failing, and she knew she needed to make her exit quickly. "Thank you. I had a wonderful time."

Having learned from the ride to the show, Eddy opened the door for Harriett and walked her to the back door. Again, he leaned in to kiss her. She moved away as she opened the door and slipped through the threshold.

"See you again?" asked Eddy.

"Yes. Maybe next weekend?" Harriett's heart was doing flip-flops. There would be a second date with Eddy Kepler!

Chapter 10

SUMMER FADED INTO AUTUMN. THE couple saw each other every week. Eddy found spending time with Harriett more pleasant than expected.

He did not know that Harriett was athletic. They went swimming every weekend. Harriett, a fish in the water, cut a beautiful feminine figure in her black one-piece bathing suit. Eddy watched as his buddies ogled her cute bottom with envy. Despite being double her size, Harriett's fluidity always won their races across the swimming hole.

Eddy bought her a used tennis racket. It only took three weeks for Harriett to begin winning matches. They rode bicycles over the country roads, sometimes stopping for either a picnic or a swim. Not owning his own, Eddy borrowed Harriett's brother Albert's bike.

Harriett quickly and easily fell for Eddy. She was in love. Her personality seemed to blossom. Even her boss, Mr. Roland, noticed that the quiet girl he hired was now a woman.

Eddy was getting pressure from Earl to move things along. However, he was enjoying having his first normal relationship with a woman. Finally giving into Earl, he bought a ring. He couldn't afford a large stone; however, he found a modest one-fourth carat round-cut diamond that was set surrounded by small chips. The illusion was a larger center diamond. It was darling, perfect for a petite finger.

The weekend after Labor Day, Eddy and Harriett spent Friday having ice cream at the drug store. The couple was no longer an oddity. Towns folks were used to seeing them together, although Harriett was frequently the recipient of nasty looks from Eddy's old girlfriends.

"Harriett, let's go to dinner in the city tomorrow night?" asked Eddy.

She looked up from her banana split and smiled. "In Madison?" Madison was the closest city to Campbellsville and the one in which she worked. She spent all week there and wasn't excited about returning over the weekend.

"No, not Madison. I was thinking Pittsburgh."

"Pittsburgh is at least a three-hour drive. Why there?" questioned Harriett.

"Earl went down last weekend and found a great Italian place. I thought we'd try it."

Harriett's exposure to Italian food was spaghetti and tomato sauce, with no idea of the kind of food offered on an Italian menu. She was skeptical that Eddy knew much more than she.

Curious but willing, she agreed. "If that's what you want to do, sure. Let's go. Tomorrow should be nice weather for a car ride." She hesitated then asked, "What are you up to?"

He just smiled back his infamous smile. "Never mind what I'm up to. I just feel like Italian food. Why don't you wear your cute blue and white dotted dress? The one you wore on our first date."

Harriett was amazed that Eddy remembered what she wore on their first date. She agreed to be picked up at three in the afternoon.

It was a warm evening, and the couple left the car at the Bailey's and walked to the drug store. As they walked home, they held hands. Harriett's stomach was jumping. She knew that Eddy was up to something. *They only dated for three months. He couldn't possibly want to propose, could he?* she wondered. "Don't even allow your mind to go there. You're setting yourself up for a huge disappointment." But Harriett couldn't help herself.

She kissed Eddy good night. Then lingered a little longer than usual. Eddy did not waste the opportunity for a long seductive kiss. Harriett slowly opened the door and blew a kiss as Eddy walked away.

Tabs was watching through the window. He winced when he realized that his little Janie was in love. He knew the day would come, but he had high hopes for his daughter. Eddy Kepler fell short of those hopes.

Harriett blissfully dreamt of what tomorrow might bring as she almost walked into her father.

"Oh, Papa, I didn't see you." Then realizing that her father may have witnessed their exchange, she asked. "How long have you been here in the kitchen?"

"Long enough, Janie. Are you sure he's the man for you? Oh, honey"—he moved to hug her—"I just want you to be happy. I want you to find a good man, one that will love you for the beautiful person you are."

Tears welled in her eyes. She loved her papa so much, but she was definitely in love with Eddy Kepler.

"I love him, Papa. God help me. I know who he was, but he's changed. I swear he has. And I love him!" Harriett hugged her father and burst into tears. "Please don't say a thing to mother. Not yet."

Tabs just held Janie tightly, wanting to protect her from the world and herself.

***

Eddy arrived at the prescribed time, dressed in navy blue gabardine trousers, white dress shirt, blue and white dotted tie, and white sports jacket. Harriett obligingly wore her blue and white dotted dress and white sweater, despite her apprehension of wearing white after Labor Day. Together, they looked like a Vaudeville act. Eddy beamed. He thought the couple was "the cat's meow."

As Harriett predicted, the day was a lovely early fall day, superb for a long drive to the city. The radio blasted Billboard's top hits, and Harriett sang along. She mused. Four months ago, she would have never considered singing in front of another person, especially not Eddy Kepler. Now they were harmonizing, however poorly, without embarrassment. She was comfortable around Eddy. Singing felt natural.

Eddy looked at Harriett, smiled, and fingered the small square box in his coat pocket. His heart was racing with anticipation. He forced his foot not to follow suit. He did not want to spoil this perfect day with a speeding ticket.

Dinner reservations were made for 6:30 p.m. at Tambellini's. Eddy knew nothing about Italian food, but he knew, through Earl, that Tambellini's was the most popular Italian restaurant in Pittsburgh. He was hoping to impress Harriett that he possessed worldly knowledge other than the knowledge of other women.

Earl took his girl, Lucy, there last weekend. She was from Chicago and liked the big city. Earl met her during the war, after Navy boot camp at Great Lakes, before he shipped out. The relationship sparked; therefore, the two remained in touch. Earl would probably propose marriage someday.

Earl was fond of Lucy and yielded to her request for city excitement by taking her to Pittsburgh for dinner. She raved to the Kepler family of the batter-coated, fried thin zucchini ribbons sprinkled with parmesan cheese and spritzed with fresh lemon juice. Eddy wasn't sure how zucchini tasted or even what it was. However, he was sure that if Lucy from Chicago praised the food, then Harriett from Campbellsville would likewise.

The hour was approaching five in the afternoon, and the car was approaching the eastern suburbs of the city when the wind picked up. Harriett's curls were blowing in her face despite the scarf she wrapped around her head. She looked forward and spotted the black rain cloud looming over the next hill. She raced to wind up the window. Eddy followed her lead, just managing to close the gap as the skies opened with a downpour of dingy gray water. It splattered over the light-colored car leaving dirty trails of run-off. The wiper blades swished back and forth, sweeping sheets of filthy water.

Pittsburgh's steel mills and factories spewed dark soot and waste daily into the skies. Hailing from a small town with fresh air, Eddy and Harriett were both startled to see pollution fall in the form of putrid rain water. They continued to drive for several miles. Every stoplight confirmed their fear that the rain would not clean the air but only bring more dirt back to earth.

Harriett looked at Eddy just as he too realized that they were both wearing white.

"How are we to exit the car without being drenched in this filth?" she questioned.

"I have no idea. And I don't dare get this jacket dirty. It's my father's and, well, he doesn't actually know that I borrowed it today. This is his, ah, lady killer coat," Eddy admitted, somewhat ashamed and embarrassed for his mother. "If I ruin this coat, I'm dead. Literally dead."

"Oh, Eddy, I can't risk ruining my dress. I don't own many dresses. And this is my sister Alice's sweater. If it got ruined, she wouldn't kill me, but she would be angry, and I don't want to buy a replacement."

"I can't buy a replacement!" protested Eddy, "I spent…" he broke off almost giving away his secret.

"Do you mind turning around? This is a nice idea, but I never liked big cities. Too many people, too much dirt. And I think Pittsburgh is dirtier than most. Please, can we turn back?"

Eddy slammed his fist on the dashboard and swore. "Son of a bitch! I want tonight to be perfect!"

His reaction stunned Harriett. "Eddy, if you are that heart set on eating at this Tambelli's, then we can go on. Maybe someone at the restaurant will have an umbrella? I hear these fancy places have guys to park your car, maybe they have umbrellas too?" Harriett said shakily.

"No, Harriett. I'm sorry. I didn't mean to scare you. I want today to be special, damn it. Damn it to hell!"

"It is special. We're on an adventure together. I just don't feel like a soggy adventure, do you?" She grinned. "If we turn around now, we may outrun the rain and make it home before it does. Our adventure can be to race the rain."

Eddy smiled gently at the simple idea. This really is a special woman. He turned the car around at the next intersection and the race began.

Halfway home, Eddy spotted a diner. It was close to seven in the evening, and they were both famished. He parked the car, and instead of proposing at a fancy Pittsburgh restaurant, he reached into his pocket, pulled out a small red box, got down on one knee, and proposed marriage over meatloaf, mashed potatoes, gravy, and lemon merengue pie.

Harriett burst into tears the minute she saw the ring. "Oh, Eddy, it's so beautiful. I never thought that I would own something this beautiful, not in a million years."

"The question still remains, my dear, will you be my wife?" Eddy asked for the second time.

"Oh yes, yes, of course, yes!" she answered.

Eddy slipped the tiny ring on the tiny finger. Exact fit. Harriett reciprocated gifts with a passionate forceful kiss.

The rain won the race. By the time they returned home, it was pouring clean water from the skies.

Chapter 11

HARRIETT AWOKE WITH A START. She was surprised that she fell asleep. She opened the bedroom window and inhaled a lungful of crisp autumn morning air. Only light fluffy clouds in the sky. Her wedding day was a bride's and a weatherman's dream day. Warm afternoon, no rain, light breeze, chilly evening requiring only sweaters. The morning alone reminding one that summer is over and winter soon to follow.

My wedding day, she thought. *That's an oxymoron! And yet it's today.* She stretched cat-like in her bed.

Through the kitchen window below, she could hear the bustle of activity. Her three sisters were already busy working. Their excited chatter filtered upward like the buzzing of bees. It sounded like Albert was also home helping Tabs with a project. Hammering, followed by a soft litany of cursing, as if a finger rather than a nail was a target.

She meticulously undid the bobby-pinned curls so that her hair could relax before she brushed it. "Please cooperate," she whispered to her unpredictable hair.

As if on cue, Harriett's sister Alice, matron of honor, appeared in the doorway with a cup of hot tea and a biscuit.

"Breakfast, darling?" Alice questioned.

Of all her siblings, Harriett was fondest of Alice. She was closest in age, next to Albert, and was always kind and tender. It was Alice's white sweater that Harriett borrowed all summer while dating.

Four years Harriett's senior, she was the person that explained a woman's monthly cycle to Harriett. Olive refused discussing such a topic with her girls. Poor Ester, the oldest daughter, was surprised by nature. When she questioned Olive, the explanation was "That's what happens to bad girls."

Luckily for Ester, close girlfriends helped her through the first couple of cycles. When the time came for each of the younger sisters, the sister immediately older assumed the responsibility of informing their junior sibling.

Today, Alice was organizing a celebration extraordinaire for her baby sister. First, she would stand as witness before the Justice of the Peace. Then she would orchestrate an outdoor reception, celebrating the nuptials.

Harriett greeted Alice's question with a robust embrace that almost made her spill her tray.

"Well, I see someone is excited," grinned Alice.

"I can't contain myself. Will you help me brush my hair and get dressed?"

"Yes, sweetie. Happy to attend you today, but first, eat or you'll be fainting before you say, 'I do.'" Alice placed her tray gently on Harriett's bed and quickly vanished. Chores awaited. Alice scurried down the stairs as Harriett continued to daydream.

The couple only waited three weeks to marry, just long enough to get their license. The ceremony was scheduled for 1:00 p.m. at the Justice of the Peace office in the courthouse. The JP was a friend of Edgar Sr. and returned a favor by working on a Saturday. It was a small wedding party consisting of bride; groom; Alice, matron of honor; Earl, best man; Olive and Tobias Bailey, parents of the bride; and Abigail and Edgar Sr., parents of the groom. The Keplers would drive the entire party, since the Baileys owned no vehicles. An outdoor picnic reception at the Bailey residence, planned by Alice, would end the day.

Alice was barking some instruction to her older sister June when Harriett entered the kitchen carrying her breakfast tray. Olive was nowhere in sight. Harriett was utterly amazed at the activity. The Hoosier was filled with bowls of potato salad, sliced cucumbers, tea sandwiches, fried chicken, cookies, lemonade, and a two-tiered wedding cake covered in white icing flowers and topped with a porcelain bridal couple.

"A cake!" she squealed. "A real white wedding cake with figurines on top!" She remembered the request for cake as a child, years earlier.

"Don't you start crying," warned Alice. "Can't have puffy eyes today." The sisters embraced again.

Outside, Albert and Tabs were nailing a string of electric lights around the grapevine. Extra Adirondack chairs and stools scattered the yard, most likely borrowed from neighbors or the Keplers'. A makeshift table of saw horses and plywood, covered with a bedsheet, would hold food. It was to be a party, the likes of which the Bailey's never hosted.

Albert and Tabs stopped to wish the guest of honor good morning with a hug. Albert patted his sister's back side with a tap.

"Last time I can do that without insulting another man's wife." He winked.

Tabs clung tightly to his Janie, not wanting to release her, "You're all grown-up. And after today, you will belong to another man." He sniffled.

"Papa, I will always be your little girl. No man will ever replace you in my heart. He may reside next to you, but *never* replace you."

"Watch those tears!" shouted a watchful Alice. "We want a clear-eyed beautiful bride!"

Kitchen under control, Alice and June scooted Harriett upstairs to begin the dressing ritual.

The girls invaded Olive's large front bedroom, minus the presence of Olive. A vanity with swivel mirrors was the room's prize furnishing. The sisters intended to use the full-length center mirror to review their final product.

Harriett, always practical, opted for a light blue brocade silk suit rather than a long white wedding gown. The suit collar rolled to lay slightly low on the shoulder. She purchased matching leather gloves to meet the three-quarter length jacket sleeves mid arm. Her hat was a simple blue band adorned with a small bow and matching blue netting. Her splurge was a pair of light blue pumps. The tiny figure looked darling, as usual.

Her sister brushed her hair, which decided to cooperate today. They applied cheek rouge, eyebrow pencil, and a soft pinkish-red lipstick. Pinning the hat in place, they pronounced the ordeal "finished." Harriett looked at herself in the mirror with amazement.

The reflection revealed that she would make a very respectable Mrs. Edgar Kepler, Jr.

She was shooed out of the room to meet her father and wait for Eddy.

"Don't worry about a thing. When you return, we'll be ready to celebrate," shouted June as Alice fell in line behind.

The Keplers' arrived driving three cars. Eddy was to take his bride. Edgar Sr. was to drive Abigail, Tabs and Olive. Earl was to drive Alice. The first car with bride and groom pulled out. Tabs called for Olive. She was not to be found. After searching ten minutes unsuccessfully, Tabs and Alice decided to go with Eddy's parents. Earl, lighting a cigarette, promised to wait another ten minutes to find Olive. The Bailey children went out in different directions searching for their mother. Finally, not wanting to delay the wedding any longer, Earl left without her.

Across town, Eddy opened the car door for Harriett, "You look absolutely beautiful. I am a lucky SOB." He handed her an orchid corsage. Eddy was wearing a navy-blue wool suit and a striped tie in different shades of blue. Boutonniere in his lapel, he cut a striking figure.

"You don't look so bad yourself," replied Harriett. "Will you do the honor of pinning this to my jacket?"

Eddy took the flowers out of their container and pinned them to Harriet's jacket. As he did so, he leaned over to kiss her.

"No way. Not until after the ceremony. My sisters worked hard to make me beautiful. I'll not ruin my makeup."

"Oh, but you are wrong. They had easy work. You came beautiful, they just put a ribbon on it." He meant it sincerely.

The JP met the couple at the courthouse door. He collected their paperwork and began to organize the proceedings.

"Are you bringing witnesses, or shall I fetch my wife and son?" he questioned.

Wondering why the other two cars were not right behind him, Eddy spoke first.

"Yes sir, our parents, her sister, and my brother will stand for us. They should be here already. I don't know what is taking so long?"

"Don't worry about it, son. We'll have a seat. They'll be by shortly."

The three sat in his office waiting and wondering. Harriett's mouth felt like cotton. She was terrified that something horrible would ruin her day. Fifteen minutes later, the Edgar's Sr., Tabs and Alice arrived. After another fifteen minutes, Earl drove in without Olive.

"Where's mother?" questioned Harriett, her voice shaking.

The group looked at each other, all wondering the same thing. What mother deliberately misses her own daughter's wedding?

"Honey, she's disappeared," explained Tabs.

"What do you mean disappeared? Has something happened to her? I don't understand?" Harriett was physically shaking.

"I don't understand either. But, Janie, do not let her ruin this day. This is your day. You pay her no mind!" ordered her father. He reached out, taking her by the hand, and walked her to Eddy's side.

"Sir, I believe you intend to wed my daughter today?"

Eddy almost giggled. "I certainly do!"

"Then please do so with both her parents' blessing." He kissed Janie on the cheek, knowing that she would never again be his little Janie, and gave her hand to Eddy.

Chapter 12

June was putting the finishing touches on the food table when guests began arriving. Today was a family affair; therefore, only spouses and children were yet to come. Her husband gently kissed her hand and then asked why her mother was walking down the street. June looked up. Sure enough, Olive was walking toward the house. Her head was wrapped in a bandana. She wore an old patched house dress covered by an apron. She looked a fright. As Olive neared the house, June ran to her and pulled her out of sight.

"What on earth are you doing?" June asked sternly. "You abandoned Harriett's wedding. You are not abandoning the reception also!"

"I'll do what I please, missy, and you'll remember that."

Ester, hearing the commotion, joined to rescue her sister.

"Mother, get inside right away and change your clothes. We'll not let you do this to Harriett. You have managed to embarrass, upstage, and belittle us your entire life. It *stops* today!" growled Ester.

June hid her smile. She never heard her sister so mad and speak so rudely to their mother. Olive grumbled a refusal, while her two daughters grabbed her arms and physically dragged her upstairs. June caught Albert's eye, who gave a thumbs-up, a sign that Albert would greet guests as they tended their stubborn mother.

Once upstairs, Olive squatted obstinately on the edge of her bed. "I'm not budging."

"Oh, but you are!" resounded the girls in unison. The daughters would have none of their mother's usual behavior today.

Ester removed the bandana and began brushing Olive's hair, making sure she tugged through any tangles. June pulled off the apron and managed, with resistance, to remove Olive's house dress.

She slapped her mother's hands several times as Olive fought back. June replaced the work frock with a lovely flowered print dress, suitable for Sunday service. Ester gave up on the hair, rolled it into a bun, and topped it with a flowered hat. Looking presentable enough, Olive was pulled back down the steps. Ushered outside, Olive was pushed into an Adirondack chair and ordered, "Do not move."

Albert gave his sisters an approving look. The three siblings gathered, vowed an oath not to let Tabs, Alice, and especially not Harriett, know how and when Olive showed up, then went on with the party.

The cake was on the end of the food table, and a separate table was erected just for gifts.

Mothers cautioned children to carefully avoid both tables, not wanting an upset.

Ceremony over, Mr. and Mrs. Edgar Kepler, Jr. exited the courtroom to find a "Just Married" sign and two rows of tin cans attached to the back of his car. Eddy's brothers, George, Bill, and Roy made a decorating stop before heading over to the Baileys. Eddy delighted in their creativity.

"We're going for a spin!" he shouted to parents as he kissed his new wife. Eddy hoisted Harriet into his arms and placed her into the passenger seat. He sped off, beeping his car horn as he went. Soon, the entire town was aware that Eddy Kepler was out of circulation.

Back at the Bailey's, most guests were assembled. Children were running tirelessly, in their Sunday best, throughout the yard. Several of the older children were playing catch in the road. Adults, in full regalia, occupied both front and back porch and under the grapevine arbor, looking for shade. A radio played music in the background. What a jovial afternoon! Olive was not big on family reunions, and this was the first time the entire Baileys were together in one place.

Not to be outdone, the Kepler brood was also out in full force. Although Abigail loved her family to gather, she missed no opportunity for yet another chance to be around her local sons and twelve grandchildren. The two families seemed to blend effortlessly. Abigail glowed with the knowledge of another daughter-in-law and, most likely, more grandchildren to follow.

Finally, the newlyweds arrived, invigorated by the beeping announcement of their nuptials.

Eddy carried Harriett out of the car and gently stood her in the circle of gathered guests.

"May I present to you, Mrs. Edgar Kepler, Jr.!" He kissed his wife, and the group exploded into applause.

Harriett blushed and then spotted her sitting mother. She approached Olive questioningly.

"Mother, where were you? How could you miss my wedding?"

Olive started to answer, "Well, all the money was spent on you! I had nothing left to buy my own—"

Tabs hurried over to his wife and interrupted mid-sentence.

"Dear wife, aren't you just a pretty picture? Well worth the wait." He leaned down and kissed her cheek. As he did so he whispered in her ear.

"If you say or do anything to ruin this day for Janie, you wicked, hateful, selfish woman, I swear I will slit you from neck to toe with my hunting knife and let you lay in your cold bed dying!"

Olive looked into her husband's eyes. They burned with the fire of anguish. She knew he was serious. She gave a nod of understanding and sat back. Tabs' body was close to convulsing. His life was emptiness until the blessed birth of Janie. She alone filled him with light that countered Olive's darkness. The other children were warm and kind, but Janie! Janie personified unconditional love. Tabs was devastated by his loss. He would lay down his life to ensure that Janie's wedding day was a bride's dream come true.

Laughter, music, and food transported afternoon into evening. Albert plugged in an electric extension cord, and suddenly, the grapevine twinkled with light. A collective "*Ah!*" went up from the group.

"Open your gifts," shouted one of the children.

"Kiss the bride," shouted one of the men. Eddy obliged.

"Cut the cake," chimed the women.

A chair was placed beside the gift table for Harriett. Alice, notepaper in hand, began handing her gifts to open. Most of the gifts were box-less, simply wrapped in white butcher paper. Some were wrapped in brown mailing paper, some in comic newsprint. There was one gift that outshone the rest. It was a rectangular box wrapped in white paper imprinted with silver bells, tied with a silk ribbon, and topped with a silk bow. Obviously, this gift did not come from Campbellsville. Several envelopes perched between the packages.

"Open the pretty one first!" urged another child.

Harriett allowed Alice to hand her gifts in random order.

The spoils of the evening included four drinking glasses from June; a set of embroidered pillow cases from Ester; five dollars from Albert; two each, Fiesta ware, plates, mugs, and bowls from Alice; a mixing bowl from Bill; a frying pan from George; a bottle of whiskey from Roy; a knotted bed patchwork quilt from Abigail and Edgar Sr.; ten dollars from Eddy's collective Detroit siblings; and five more dollars from Olive's cousin, Mrs. Jethro Westchester. The beautifully boxed gift, something wrapped in comic strips, and one envelope remained.

"Harriett, it's time to choose. Which one next?" asked Alice.

In a daze from the generosity, Harriett flicked her hand in dismissal, allowing Alice to continue selecting. Alice picked up the envelope and slid out the card. Harriett read the outside verse and then opened the card. She gasped.

"What is it, dear?" questioned Tabs, still in defensive mode.

"It's from Mr. Roland, my boss at Dugan & Co. It's fifty dollars!" exclaimed Harriett.

Eddy broke out in a verse of "We're in the money!"

"The card reads, 'Congratulations and Best wishes on your wedding. May this small token of my appreciation help you establish a loving home. Sincerely, Thomas Roland.' I am flabbergasted," said Harriett. "This will be deposited into my—I mean, our savings account immediately."

The crowd murmured its approval. The beautiful box was next in line. Harriett gently untied the ribbon. It would be saved for use in her hair. She also carefully unwrapped the paper, smoothing and folding it for future use. The outside of the box read "Marshall Fields."

"Where is Marshall Fields?" asked Alice.

"In Chicago," responded Earl.

Harriett turned her head in the direction of Earl's voice, "How did you get something delivered from Chicago so quickly?"

"Lucy bought it for me. She brought it on the train when she visited last month."

"Last month? But we only got engaged three weeks ago? How did she—?" Harriett broke off and looked at Eddy, who was grinning ear to ear. "You planned this in advance!"

"Guilty as accused!" The handsome man beamed.

Taking off the lid and carefully turning back the delicate tissue paper revealed a beautiful white silk chiffon negligée. Harriett held up the gown. The bodice was French lace. The skirt was sheer white silk. A silk ribbon adorned the neckline. The matching robe was made entirely of sheer white silk chiffon. Worn together, the outline of the body beneath would be visible without divulging detail.

"Wow, brother. That's a stunner," thanked Eddy.

"I wanted something sexy for you, my little brother, but something that provided some modesty for my sweet new sister," Earl smiled at Harriett, who again blushed. "Mission accomplished?"

Both nodded in agreement.

The last package left to open was wrapped in comic paper. Harriett did a quick inventory in her head and figured that this gift was from her parents. She opened it more quickly than the last gift. A four-fox stole lay inside. She held it up for her family to see the head of the fox biting his tail. Tabs was now the one smiling.

"Papa, did you make this for me?"

"Yes, Janie. You are no longer a little girl, rather, a woman of the community, and you must look the part. I hope you like it?" faltered Tabs.

Harriett ran to embrace her father. As she threw her arms around his neck, they heard a muffled "Harrumph" coming from a distant chair. No one cared that Olive was not pleased.

Alice interrupted the intimate moment between father and daughter. "You better cut the cake soon. Eddy wants to be on the road. The entire group contributed money to buy this wedding cake, I know they all want a piece!"

Harriett moved away from Tabs, who commenced carrying gifts up to her room. The cake was purchased from Campbellsville bakery. The bottom tier was two layers of white almond cake filled with a strawberry glaze. Both top and bottom of this tier was encircled in white icing roses. The sides looked like a woven icing basket. The top tier was small, meant for the bride and groom to save for their first anniversary. It was covered entirely with icing roses. A porcelain bride and groom finial completed the marvel.

"I am overwhelmed," Harriett whispered to Alice. "You have all been so generous. I am afforded a wonderful nest egg with which to begin housekeeping. I am so lucky."

"Do not question, honey. You are a sweet, loving sister. I'm so happy that you found someone deserving of your love and who loves you in return. By the way, I'm happy to wrap the top layer and keep it in my deep freeze for your first anniversary, or at least until you get your own Frigidaire. It will be here before you know it!"

With the addition of better chilling compounds, electric ice boxes with a deep freeze compartment became more common in Campbellsville. Olive and Tabs still owned an icebox; however, Alice and her siblings owned the electric style.

Harriett took a large knife and made the first cut into the bottom tier. Eddy followed her example. Alice carved two small pieces and handed one each to the bride and groom. Harriett lovingly fed the delicacy to her love. Eddy took a non-gentlemanly approach and smeared his slice all over Harriett's face. Surprised by a face covered in icing and strawberry ooze, she smiled, grabbed Eddy's face, kissed him hard and shared the mess. Everyone laughed, even Olive.

"I hate to break up the party, but we really do need to hit the road," shouted Eddy. "I have an hour drive before I can be properly introduced to my new wife."

The family laughed. Harriett continued her new habit of blushing. The couple began their "goodbyes."

Finally, Eddy picked her up gently in his arms and, once again, lifted her into his car. As he pulled away, the couple waved vigorously while Eddy beeped his horn. The group, including Olive, threw rice at the car and waved goodbye, except for Tabs. Tabs sat on the edge of Harriett's bed with his face buried in his hands. He wept as the horn faded into the distance.

Chapter 13

"Umm," Harriett manage to moan as she snuggled closer to Eddy. In a drunken stupor of sleep and the afterglow of the night before, Harriett was content to not move all day.

"Well, good morning, Mrs. Kepler," greeted Eddy.

Harriett purred another, "Umm."

If there had been any question of Harriett's love for Eddy, the discovery of physical intimacy sealed her fate. There was no going back. The point of no return was crossed around midnight the previous evening.

"Wake up, sleepyhead," insisted Eddy. "We have at least five hours to drive today before we get to Niagara Falls."

"Oh, but I want to just stay here," she said, snuggling closer to her husband.

Eddy laughed heartily. "If we hit the road now, we'll get there before bedtime tonight. I promise to cuddle you again."

By the time the couple had showered and dressed, the sun indicated noon.

"Come on, slowpoke. We'll miss check-out time and have to pay for another night."

Harriett was glowing. Alice warned that she might experience physical pain at first. However, Eddy, an experienced lover, tenderly and patiently attended his wife. The minimal pain gave way to total emotional bond. Eddy owned Harriett; body, mind and soul.

The drive through the Pennsylvania countryside was lovely on the sunny autumn day. The oranges, reds, and yellows of the trees ignited the hillsides with color. Harriett sat nestled under Eddy's arm as he drove.

Only thirty minutes into the drive, their comfortable silence was broken. Harriett blurted, "Eddy, I'm famished! May we eat breakfast before we continue?"

Laughing hysterically, Eddy looked at his tiny wife. "Of course. Although I think I did most of the work last night."

"Aren't you famished too?"

"Come to think of it, I am," as his stomach let out a big grumble.

They arrived at the Canadian border around five o'clock. Eddy showed his driver's license to the patrol. Harriett did not drive; however, she carried a copy of her birth certificate and their marriage license. They were granted passage.

"I can't believe I'm in a foreign country," she marveled as she looked out the window.

"I can't believe I'm married," answered Eddy with a grin.

Eddy booked a room in a small hotel several blocks from the falls. It was much less expensive than the rooms on the water. "We can walk!" frugal Harriett agreed. The room held a double bed draped with a factory-made striped bedspread. The window draperies were the same stripe. A small television sat on a mirrored dresser. Eddy splurged to book a room with a private bath. The in-suite consisted of a pedestal sink, toilet, and large soaking tub. Eddy eyed the tub and made mental plans for after dinner.

"Good gosh, we have a TV!" Harriett exclaimed. "Can we watch it tonight?"

About half of the Campbellsville population owned televisions. The Keplers and Baileys were members of the half who "did not."

"For a little bit. I have other plans for you this evening," answered Eddy.

Harriett continued blushing. "First, let's take a walk, grab some dinner, and then stroll back and see what we can find to occupy our time," suggested Eddy.

Harriett's entire body flushed red.

Walking hand in hand down the street, they heard first a rumble, and then the roar of water. Both were astonished by the size and power of the falls. Naïvely, they envisioned a river with a slight drop in water level. Never did they imagine the force or sheer energy generated by Niagara's rushing water. They sat for an hour on a park bench in awe, watching the magnificence. Beautiful manicured flower gardens scented the park. Horse drawn carriages, occupied by lovers, drove past. A tour boat was making its way back to the dock.

"Harriett, look over there." He pointed to a sign across the water. It read "Maid of The Mist." "I think we can take a boat ride on the river below. What a thrill!"

Finally satiated with the beauty before them, they left to satiate their bellies.

"Harriett," asked Eddy as they searched for an inexpensive restaurant for dinner, "Do you think we could spend some extra money tomorrow to ride the boat? It may go up to the falls? What fun!"

Neither love bird imagined boat tours to the falls nor a wondrous new wax museum they just passed on the way to dinner. The honeymooners were visiting the falls three nights. Their intent was to walk around during the day, eat dinner, and then retreat to their room each evening. That first walk changed their minds. Luckily, Harriett grabbed some of their wedding money.

"Yes, Eddy, I do. I brought extra money. We need to spend prudently, but we must take advantage of attractions. We may never return. If we eat carefully, we may splurge on a couple of tours. This is the first of many adventures of our married life."

Eddy squeezed her hand, without the realization that he just designated Harriett household financial manager.

Chapter 14

"OH, IT WAS AMAZING," HARRIETT said as they prepared Harriett's room for the couple. The sisters giggled. "I mean the falls, except for when I slipped on the rocks. See, I hit my head." Harriett showed Alice the resulting lump on her forehead.

The mishap occurred while they were on the "Maid of the Mist" boat tour. The group disembarked to climb up the side of the waterfalls. Usually surefooted, Harriett uncharacteristically lost her balance, slid sideways, and hit her head on a protruding rock. It left Harriett embarrassed, with a large contusion.

"But the other was pretty amazing too. Since you brought it up," Harriett said with a blush, "I never realized there could be such happiness in my life. For the first time ever, I feel whole. Is that crazy? Eddy completes me. I love him so much. And when I am in his arms, my soul is entwined with his."

Alice observed her sister's face. Harriett was radiant. Alice knew her sister spoke from her heart. "Honey, I am so happy for you. Too few couples find a love so pure." Alice neglected to caution Harriett; with love so strong came the risk of pain equally strong. She kissed her sister on the cheek, smiled, and picked up the next gift to put away.

Eddy was already working. Harriett did not return to work until Monday.

Three adventurous days followed by three blissful nights ended much too quickly. The couple explored hand in hand both day and night. Harriett's experience was near spiritual. Her commitment to Eddy was sealed for eternity. She would love him "'til death do us part." In three days, Eddy became her life. She dedicated every breath to him.

The sisters continued to ready Harriett's old room. The newly-weds would live with the Baileys until more suitable affordable lodgings were found.

A voice called to them from outside.

"Harriett, it's Earl. Some mail arrived for Eddy yesterday. I wanted to bring it right away."

Harriett hurried down the stairs and gave her brother-in-law a hug. He handed her the letter saying, "You may not want to hug me after I deliver this."

She looked at the envelope addressed to Eddy from The Department of Selective Services. Harriett's knees buckled. She steadied herself on the grape arbor. "Oh my! Alice, please stay with me today until Eddy gets home?"

Alice agreed as her sister's face drained of all color. Brought together by the wedding events, the sisters cultivated a closeness that did not previously exist between the siblings.

"Alice, I am grateful that you are my friend. I never had a close girlfriend. I always spent time with Papa. I was too young to be close to you, June, and Ester."

"I know, honey. Four years is a big difference, especially between seven and eleven, or thirteen and seventeen. I'm glad too. Family is precious."

The sisters finished their work and then sat quietly on the bed, holding hands. Alice left at the sound of Eddy's car door.

He bounded up the staircase, anticipating a kiss from his wife. Instead, he was met with an extended hand.

"Eddy, what does this mean?" Harriett questioned as she handed Eddy the letter. Her voice ready to break, she took his hand and squeezed.

Eddy's hands shook in hers as he ripped open the top of the envelope and pulled out the letter. This wasn't supposed to happen. He was married. Did he notify them too late?

"Edgar G. Kepler, Jr...you are hereby ordered to report..."

"I did it for nothing," mumbled Eddy. "All for nothing! What a damn farce."

"What are you talking about?" Harriett looked questioningly into his eyes.

"Nothing," he said feebly. "Forget it. It's not important, at least not now."

Harriett ignored the comment and fell into Eddy's arms.

"Eddy, I'm scared." She buried her head into his chest. "I don't want you to go."

"I don't want to go either," murmured Eddy.

"Promise me that you will come back to me. I need you. I need you more than life itself." Earnestly clinging to her husband, Harriett pleaded. "Please Eddy!"

He stroked his wife's hair, twirling it around his finger. His idea of life and future destroyed by one single letter.

"Eddy, be faithful and never leave me. I couldn't bear it if you left me." Harriett's tears flowed freely. She trembled, remembering the Eddy Kepler of old, the Eddy Kepler with women lined up to just get a look.

"Harriett, I love you, I really do," convincing himself as much as Harriett. "You are my wife, and I vowed to always be true to you."

She leaned up and kissed his mouth as she choked back her tears.

"I promise, I am yours and yours alone," he vowed a second time.

The next day, fall yielded to winter with blowing freezing rain. Two weeks later, Eddy was gone.

Part Two

Chapter 15

Trieste Italy 1950

THE BOAT DOCKED IN ITALY and the new recruits disembarked after a rough couple of weeks trekking on land and sea. The ocean could be rough any time of year, but a December crossing was always tough. Eddy Kepler suffered seasickness across the entire Atlantic. Swinging back and forth in a close quarter hammock, Eddy's daily spewing of his stomach left him ten pounds lighter and weak as a newborn colt. Dragging his duffel down the gangplank and over to the awaiting fleet of jeeps, Eddy tossed the bag into the first vehicle and collapsed into the seat beside it.

"Who the hell do you think you are, private?" questioned the surly corporal behind the wheel.

"This vehicle is for officers only. Noncoms queue over there for truck transport." The driver took a closer look at Eddy, whose face was literally green, eyes sunken encircled by black rings.

"Okay, buddy. Let's get you over to sick bay straight away." His tone softer. Eddy couldn't speak. The smells of the dock wafted over him. He closed his eyes and tried not to puke as the jeep drove off.

"Doc, I got a ripe one just off the boat," yelled the driver.

Two corpsmen wheeling a gurney lifted the dry heaving private from the jeep.

"Take it easy, fellow. I'll be back around to collect you in a couple hours after your head stops floating," laughed Corporal Walter Stuart as he pulled away to pick up his next set of passengers.

***

Eddy and Walter became immediate friends. Wally showed the greenhorn the ropes of working the army's system, legally; for the most part. It wasn't long before Eddy procured an assignment as assistant to the supply sargeant.

Eddy always seemed to be at the right place at the right time. The previous supply assistant, Corporal Mason, was due to rotate out. Being friendly, Eddy already made connections at the docks and with local merchants. One day, Eddy and Walter were outside the supply office when they overheard Sarge looking for a special perfume for a visiting dignitary. Next day, perfume in hand, Eddy arrived at the supply office. Garnering "Sarge points," he was immediately assigned replacement duty as supply assistant. Corporal Mason mentored the private for the next two weeks and then boarded a ship and headed home. Eddy was left to his own creative devices.

Wheeling and dealing came second nature to Eddy. It wasn't long before he was known on base as the "Go-to Guy." Having a friend in the motor pool helped. Walter and Eddy formed an industrious collaboration.

The two friends joked about their enterprising Stuart/Kepler Acquisitions, which generated extra pocket funds. Walter, as CFO, managed all monies, knowing Eddy's temptation to squander. Eddy, as COO, obtained the necessary network of product.

***

"Kepler, hand me the file on available supplies. I need to know how many blankets were issued last week."

"Twenty-seven, Sarge," answered Eddy. "Fifteen to Alpha and twelve to Delta. We have one hundred thirty-seven in reserve. Need anything else?"

"You know that without looking?" asked the Sargeant.

"Yes, sir! I know most of what goes in and out, officially and unofficially," laughed Eddy.

Eddy was never much for school; however, he was great with managing inventory and ensuring proper distribution. Having a personal stake in S/K Acq. helped to enhance these skills. Sarge, recognizing his value, recommended Eddy's promotion to corporal, making it the fastest promotion in base history.

Wanting to impress his wife, Eddy proudly wrote in one of his weekly letters to Harriett of his new position. Instead of the usual half pay, he enclosed an extra five dollars.

Leisure time was easier to arrange now that Eddy and Walter were the same rank. Walter took him to the hot spots and helped him find girls. Although married and determined to remain faithful to Harriett, Eddy rationalized that he still needed physical satisfaction. He would not look at a woman for anything other than a "quick fix." His resolve lasted for exactly one month.

Eddy and Walter were at the Piazza della Borsa when he spotted her. He was hit with a thunderbolt. Never in his life had a girl cast a spell over the carefree cad. That is, until now. She took his breath away.

Beautiful, petite, long black hair; the sparkling green-eyed teen, looked like an angel. Eddy was mesmerized. His legs refused to move as he gawked, mouth open at the girl.

"Eddy! Hey, old man. She's just a kid. That stuff will land you in jail," warned Walter.

"Let's get moving. Sully told me about a new bar. It's just down the street past the Torre." Walter looked at his friend who was still entranced with the black-haired teenager.

Eddy stood in silence, staring.

"Eddy. She's off limits. Everyone on base knows it. That's Rosa the untouchable." Walter's warning morphed into threat. "You're scaring me. Be smart, man. You're married, for Christ's sake. Think about your wife back in the States."

"I'll catch up with you later," Eddy said calmly as he walked toward the exquisite girl. He was totally bewitched.

"Hi. I'm Eddy. Care to walk with me?" He greeted her with a wide smile.

Now it was Walter's turn to stare open mouthed. Rosa, the untouchable took Eddy by the arm and said, "*Sì.*"

Rosa was equally taken with the tall blonde GI with strappingly broad shoulders, bulging muscles, and the face of a Norse god. Only sixteen, her parents cautioned her about commiserating with soldiers. Until today, she had shunned every advance, earning the nickname of "untouchable." One look at Eddy Kepler, and she forgot all warnings.

They strolled the Barcola, arm in arm. Rosa wore embroidered yellow silk draped from her shoulder that fell to wrap her thin hips. As she walked, the movement of the silk accentuated her tiny form. Loosely braided hair secured with green ribbon exposed a long graceful neck garnished with a stunning string of matching 6 mm cultured pearls. Red toenails peaked through the front of a green stacked heel shoe. She looked more adult than child. Every GI they passed stopped to look in amazement at the starry-eyed, handsome couple of Rosa the "untouchable" and Eddy the "Go-to Guy."

Rosa's was a privileged family. She was educated in private schools. English was her second language. Dressed in the latest fashion, she commanded the attention of all the local boys and most of the soldiers on base. In addition to her reputation of rejecting all invitations, she was also labeled "off limits" due to her father's position in local government. None of this deterred Eddy; he was completely smitten.

Their mutual attraction was immediate. Completely oblivious to the world around them, they walked. The pungent smell of the waterfront created an exotic backdrop to the early bloom of honeysuckle and Rosa's sweet perfume, causing heads to swoon.

Completely lost in time, the church bells pealed curfew. Wrapping his strong arm around her waist, Eddy pulled her close. After a brief hesitation, Eddy stole his first kiss. Her lips were warm and salty. His lips were eager for more. Both bodies trembled with excitement and arousal. The base curfew siren blew. Reluctantly, he turned to go, dazed and in love. Rosa coaxed him back, whispering in his ear.

"Meet me again tomorrow? Same place?" With a smile she blew him a kiss goodbye. "Buona notte" and walked into the night.

***

The next day at work, Eddy was in elated spirits thinking about the girl. Midday, his thoughts were interrupted by a surprise visitor. An important-looking man, wearing a slightly gaudy tailored suit, sauntered through the supply office door.

"Are you the young man seen with my daughter Rosa last night?" barked a baritone voice.

"How the hell did you get in here?" asked Eddy. "And who the hell are you? This office is for army personnel only. Leave or I'll call the MP's."

"I am Magistrato Giovani Romano. As a high city official, I have an arrangement with your commanding officer allowing free access to this base. Now, I'll ask you one more time. Are you the insolent GI who was seen kissing my daughter last night? Answer the question before '*I*' call the MPs!" demanded Romano.

"Yes, and I happen to be in love with your daughter."

"You wear a wedding band, yet you dare tell me that you love Rosa. You know her one night then you proclaim *love*? I'll have your insubordinate ass court-martialed if you don't stay away from her!"

At that, the sargeant appeared, investigating the shouting coming from Eddy's office.

"Woah there, *signor*. No one is court-martialing anyone in my office," declared the Sarge.

"Eddy, go back to your barracks. You're done for today. I'll sort things out with mister magistrate here. That's an order, son!"

"Yes, sir!" Eddy made a hasty exit.

***

"Walter, I need a favor, buddy."

"If it has anything to do with a black-haired enchantress, count me out! I'll not be part of your felonious behavior. Think of your wife!"

"Come on, man! I can't meet Rosa outright. But I need to get a message to her. Please! Give her this note, then wait five minutes. I'll break it off tonight."

"I'm not bailing your ass out of the brig, man. But just this once, if you promise to break it off."

Walter drove into town, approached Rosa, handed her the note, and waited. She read it, smiled, and then slapped Walter across the face.

"What the hell?"

"My father has spies. That slap will keep you safe," she said with a beguiling smile. Then she turned and walked off to meet her GI in the alley behind San Giusto church.

Eddy and Rosa met at every possible chance, but in secret because of her family's objection. Acting as a reluctant signal man, Walter would drive past Piazza della Borsa every night to a waiting Rosa. Honking the jeep horn the prescribed number of times according to Eddy's code, he transmitted that night's place of rendezvous. Rosa and Eddy were able to meet undetected by her father's scouts.

They sat in secluded grottos, drank wine, and ate cheese. Sometimes they would meet at a borrowed boat. Eddy usually skipped mess to spend supper hour thus more time with Rosa. The alley behind San Giusto was a favorite. Spreading his army blanket on the ground, the couple lounged, ate, drank, and kissed. Rosa dressed in elegant affluence; never without her pearls.

Rosa taught Eddy some Italian. They giggled at his American pronunciations. Some nights, they spent hours just gazing into each other's eyes; always ending the evening with kisses.

It didn't take long for their kisses to ignite a deeper passion. Eddy was already past the bursting point. He wanted Rosa so badly. Every muscle in his body ached for her when they were together. He tried to take it slow; but it took only two weeks after first meeting this beauty for his willpower to drain.

His desire culminated one night on one of the borrowed boats.

"My God, you are so beautiful. Come here," he pulled her close. "You know I love you, don't you? Even though"—he pointed to his ring finger—"I love you."

She shuddered as he touched her; her own desires exposed.

"Yes, Edwardo. I love you also. You will leave her, I know you will."

Although young, Rosa knew the power she held over Eddy. She felt his hardness against her body. She was sure that he would renounce his American wife and marry her. With that conviction, Rosa accepted Eddy's advancements. As he tenderly lifted Rosa to a kiss, Eddy ignored his vow to Harriett and hungrily took Rosa and her childhood to his bed. Not as a "quick fix," but as his endeared love.

Chapter 16

"Mamma!" Rosa called out after losing her breakfast for the second consecutive day. "Please call Doctor Borkey. I think I have the flu."

The teen looked pale. Perspiration clung to her neck and wrists. Sofia Romano complied by sending a house servant to fetch the doctor. Cases of flu were not to be trifled with. The elderly and children continued to die from the disease.

A general practitioner, Dr. Georg Borkey was the Romano's family physician for many years. Although babies were usually delivered by midwives; Giovani Romano insisted that his wife Sofia's baby be delivered by a physician. Therefore, Georg Borkey knew Rosa from birth.

"In here, please," Mrs. Romano escorted Borkey to Rosa's bedroom. "Shall I stay?"

"No," replied the doctor. "I'll call after I examine the child."

Sofia reluctantly turned to leave and then spun around to challenge the order.

"Sofia, please allow me to examine her in private. She is a modest young woman and should be afforded some privacy. I promise to bring you in when I am finished."

Sofia withdrew to the drawing room and ordered tea, wringing her hands as she waited.

***

"Rosa, I need to ask you to undress and to don your dressing gown," requested the doctor.

After changing, Rosa climbed back onto her bed and nervously awaited her examination. She heard of people dying from the flu and she was scared.

Dr. Borkey was thorough with his exam; checking heart, lungs, kidneys, temperature, blood pressure, and pulse. He asked Rosa numerous unrelated questions, ending with a very personal question that led to a different kind of exam.

"Sofia, you may enter now," called out Borkey.

Scampering down the hall, he heard a sense of urgency in Sofia's footsteps. She entered the room to find Rosa sobbing in her bed.

"Oh my dear! What is it?" she questioned, running to comfort her daughter.

"Please have a seat, Mrs. Romano," continued the doctor. "I'm afraid I have some disturbing news."

"Is my Rosa going to die?" Sofia burst into tears.

The doctor tried to stifle a chuckle. "There is nothing wrong with Rosa that nine months won't cure," he finished, "I'm afraid your daughter is pregnant."

A gasp and then a hush filled the room. Sofia looked at her daughter with distain and disgust.

No longer crying, *Signora* Romano sneered, "How dare you disgrace your father and me with this behavior? Our family is an important, respected pillar of this city. It has been eminent since before the first war!"

It was Rosa's turn to burst into tears.

"Sofia, she's as upset as you. These things happen. There are solutions," offered the doctor.

"The only acceptable solution is to terminate the pregnancy!" shouted Sofia.

This statement sent Rosa into hysterics.

"I'll not kill my baby! That is a sin." Rosa gulped. "I am in love with his father, and he will marry me!"

Chapter 17

AFTER THE ANNOUNCEMENT OF PREGNANCY, her prominent parents, Magistrato Romano e la signora, disowned their only daughter.

"You shall neither inherit nor live in Villa Romano," roared Giovani Romano as he escorted her to the door.

Rosa, at a loss and needing advice and shelter, gathered clothing, a few belongings, caught a train, and escaped to her grandmother.

Embarrassed by her daughter and son-in-law's eviction of Rosa, Isabela Cortina took pity on her granddaughter. Rosa's maternal grandmother, residing comfortably in Santa Croce, hid Rosa in her small alpine cottage. Cortina family property since the mid-1700s, the cottage witnessed several wars, the change of sovereign countries, and multiple family dramas.

It was the perfect location to hide the shame of this latest family trauma.

Isabela and her husband, Joseph, supplied the cottage with canned food and dried fruits and meats as best they could for their granddaughter and great-grandchild. *Nonna* Cortina, wanting to do more, resisted, fearing the wrath of her pompous daughter and son-in law. She feared retaliation if discovered helping the poor young lovers.

She arranged to send word to Eddy of Rosa's pregnancy. Rosa wanted to tell Eddy herself, but Isabela insisted that it was best to get her out of Trieste as soon as possible.

***

"Kepler," the mail clerk called.

Eddy usually received one daily letter from Harriett. Today, there were two letters delivered. Looking at the postmarks, he opened the one from Harriett first. Containing the usual gossip from town, report of her work, list of accomplishments for their home, and pledge of everlasting love; Eddy read quickly and pocketed the letter.

Eddy was nervous, not seeing Rosa the past four nights. She was nowhere to be found. None of his cronies could find her. Eddy even tried making an appointment with Magistrato Giovani Romano, only to rudely be turned away with a threat to "Never return—or else!"

The second letter had an Italian post mark from Santa Croce. Not knowing anyone from Santa Croce, he tore at the envelope and began to read.

> Dear Corporal Kepler.
>
> Allow me to introduce myself. My name is Isabela Cortina. I am Rosa Romano's grandmother. Rosa is now living under my care in our alpine cottage located outside Villa Opicina. Rosa is carrying your child and will stay at the cottage while in confinement until the baby is born.
>
> Sadly, her parents, my daughter, have disowned the child; family disgrace being unacceptable. Rosa is on her own. My husband and I are helping her; however, we must tread carefully. My son-in-law is a vengeful man.
>
> If you truly love her, please contact me via return post and I shall arrange for you to meet Rosa at the cottage.
>
> Sincerely,
> Isabela Cortina

Staring at the letter, Eddy let its message sink in and then collapsed to the floor.

"Call the medic!" cried a voice.

"Christ, Eddy, wake up. It's Wally," he said as he picked up his friend's head and cradled it on his lap. "You all right, man? What was in that letter?"

Wally read the letter as Eddy regained his senses.

"What am I going to do now?" Eddy asked, totally lost.

"Well, I can't say I'm surprised. I hate to say, 'I told you so', but… I did!" chided Wally.

"Get this man some water," Wally commanded. "We'll think of something, buddy. Right now, you need to decide if you want anything to do with this baby. You have an out. Do you want to take it?"

***

For once in his life, Eddy chose not to take the easy way out. He accepted responsibility for Rosa and the baby. Eddy went to the cottage whenever he could get off. Sarge agreed to cover every other weekend for him so that he could leave Friday night to make the trip to the cottage. Weeks that Eddy stayed on base, he worked Monday through Saturday 0800 to 1700 hours and 0900 to 1400 on Sunday. Sarge gave him a couple of bucks occasionally, for "working long hours." Although, Sarge just wanted to help him. Eddy quit sending half of his soldier's salary back to the states. He needed every cent to provide for his newfound family. However, Wally drew the line; S/K Acq. money was off limits, to be saved for use once discharged.

Nonna Cortina smuggled in scraps of fabric, yarn, and fruits and vegetables from her abundant garden. Rosa spent her lonely weeks sewing clothes for herself and the baby-to-be and preserving food for winter. To fill the time, she taught herself how to knit and crochet. She knitted a scarf for Eddy that she tucked away as a Christmas present. Next try was a sweater.

After about three months' time, Rosa tried to return to Villa Romano. *Nonno* Cortina's automobile was granted passage through the front gates; however, when the guard at the house spotted Rosa, she was turned away. Isabela exited the car and demanded entrance to her daughter's house. Sofia met her mother in the front courtyard.

They argued loudly. When Isabela tried to retrieve some of Rosa's possessions, Sofia slapped her across the face; Isabela and Rosa now both ostracized.

Shunned by Sofia and no longer afraid of reproach; Isabella visited Rosa most weeks, bringing her bottles of wine, salt, flour, butter, and sugar.

Rosa thankfully welcomed her *Nonna's* visits but longed for weekends with her lover. She dedicated her life, no matter how challenging, to Eddy. The couple walked hand in hand through the alpine foothills, picking either wildflowers, mushrooms, or berries. Rosa kept a wine bottle filled with wildflowers on the window sill. It reminded her of home and Eddy.

Spring turned to summer as Rosa's belly began to sprout. Eddy was amazed how much larger she grew every two weeks.

"Rosa, can you feel the baby kick yet?" asked Eddy on a June visit.

Rosa giggled. "It has been kicking all week. Here, feel." She grabbed Eddy's hand and placed it on her stretching stomach. He waited patiently and then it happened. A punch from either a hand or a foot. Eddy jerked back his hand in surprise. Rosa giggled again.

As Rosa's belly expanded, *Nonna* brought her three maternity dresses. They would have to last the remainder of her pregnancy.

Summer sped by quickly. With the approach of fall came the approach of the birth. If she conceived the first night, the baby should arrive late October. The fall mountain view was spectacular. The cabin provided shelter from the chilly night air, her parents, and Eddy's unit.

As her time drew near, Eddy found it harder to leave. The love he felt for Rosa caused an ache in his heart every time he left her. She occupied his every thought and he hers.

Rosa, in return, was lethargic when not with her GI. She needed Eddy with every ounce of her being.

By the time September ended, Eddy's nerves were frazzled. Although he stopped writing to her, not knowing the status of her husband, Harriett faithfully wrote to him every day. He felt guilty about betraying Harriett, but she would never change his decision to be with Rosa.

***

Also, by September's end, *Nonna* Cortina decided that Rosa should live with her in Santa Croce until the birth. Rosa reluctantly agreed, although it meant that she would not see Eddy for at least a month. She wanted Eddy to be present when the child was born.

Life was much more luxurious in Santa Croce. Rosa ate nutritious meals, took walks on even ground, and sat in the sun. There was no worry of collecting firewood or building fires. The bed was soft and feathery, not hard and lumpy. She tried not to grow accustomed to her surroundings; knowing that, if she were to stay with Eddy, life would go back to hardship.

No worry of that. Her first week at Santa Croce, she awoke to a warm gush of water between her legs. Then the pains started. She tossed her shawl around her shoulders and waddled down the hall to her grandparent's bedroom.

"*Nonna, Nonna,*" she whispered through the door, not wanting to disturb her grandfather. "I think it's time. Please call the midwife."

Midwife dispatched, Isabela sent word to Eddy that he would soon be able to greet his baby.

Labor lasted thirty-six hours. All present were exhausted from waiting. Finally, a loud cry erupted as the baby boy announced his arrival.

"He's so beautiful," said a yawning Rosa. "He looks just like his papa."

The midwife took the infant from his mother's arms, wrapped him tightly in a blanket, and let Rosa sleep. He did look like Eddy; blonde hair, fair skinned. He was a large baby, especially for the size of his mother; nine pounds/ eleven ounces, twenty-two inches long. The resemblance ended with his bright green eyes; those were Rosa's.

***

Already stressed, Eddy found it intolerable to have no word from Rosa.

"Did the baby come? Is it healthy? Is Rosa okay? When will I be able to see them?"

These thoughts constantly filled his mind. Insomnia plagued his nights. Tired in the daytime, his work suffered.

The Sarge issued two weeks of KP duty as punishment due to his lack of concentration. Finally, the dispatch from Santa Croce arrived.

> Dear Corporal Kepler,
>
> You have a son. Mother and child are both well. They shall remain at Santa Croce until after the baby's Christening.
>
> Please feel free to attend mass at noon on Sunday, October 14, Sant'Andrea della Zirada. Giovani and Sofia Romano neither know of the birth nor shall attend his baptism. You are free from reproach from my husband and me.
>
> Sincerely,
> Isabela Cortina
>
> P.S. Rosa sends her love.

"Wally!" Eddy shouted as he ran across camp to the Motor Pool. "It's a boy! I have a son!"

Cheers erupted. It was no secret about Rosa and Eddy. It seemed the entire camp was waiting for the same news.

"Sarge, I'm a daddy!" He ran into Sarge's office and gave him a bear hug. The Sarge responded with a laugh. "Is it okay if I take off next Sunday? I need to baptize my baby boy!"

October fourteen was warm and sunny as Wally and Eddy drove to Santa Croce. Clothed in dress uniforms, the corporals made a handsome entrance. Eddy needed every ounce of strength not to run to Rosa. Although he did not attend church in Pennsylvania, he was aware of church decorum.

The men removed their hats, walked slowly to join the family, and sat down. It was Eddy's first look at his son. Decorum or not, he burst into tears.

"Eddy, my love. Here, hold your son," whispered Rosa, beaming with joy to be reunited with her lover.

"Have you named him yet?"

"No, darling. We should do that now. I would like to name him Joseph, for my grandfather," said Rosa, looking appreciatively at the man and woman who took her in when her parents threw her out.

Eddy smiled. "I agree." Joining her look of appreciation for her grandparents. "Would it be okay if we named him Joseph Earl Kepler? I don't want you to have a bastard son. I want him to have my last name."

Misty eyed, Rosa leaned over and kissed Eddy. "When you get out of the army, you must return home to divorce your wife so that we can be married. Yes?"

"Yes. Absolutely. Yes!" agreed Eddy as the organ began to play.

***

Rosa moved back to the cottage with supplies for about six weeks. With the onset of winter, *Nonna* would not be able to make the trip in from Villa Opicino. She must rely on Eddy.

Concentration returned, Sarge removed Eddy's KP duties. He resumed an "every other weekend off" schedule.

Eddy made the trip to the cottage twice. Joey was now six weeks old. He hated to leave his family. Despite improved conditions at base and two years left until discharge, Eddy grew more anxious every day. Living without his family; he finally broke. He could no longer tolerate the pain in his heart.

Thus, the fateful night when Eddy yelled, "Wally, go. Go now before I chicken out! *Go!*" The night he decided not to return to base, to abandon all creature comforts, family, and country for this beautiful young girl and infant and to go AWOL.

Chapter 18

"*Due* pounds pig's feet, *uno* pound soup bones, *E una metà* pound ground pork?" repeated Eddy to the customer in his best Italian translation. Having studied "English as a foreign language" in high school, Eddy now earnestly tried speaking Italian, German, and Slovenian.

"*Si, signore.*"

Easily finding employment, Eddy worked as a butcher, using the skills learned in high school, in the small town of Plave, Slovenia. The train line through the Alps offered a means of transport. He found Plave to be secluded, off the beaten path of army traffic. A two-hour ride from Villa Opicina, the closest stop to the alpine cottage he and Rosa shared. From Villa Opicina, in mild weather, it was a thirty-minute foot trek to their hideaway. Because of the distance and the risk of riding the train, Eddy stayed all week in Plave, renting a bed in a small third-floor room. He only ventured exposure over the weekend; Rosa needed fuel for heat and money to buy food for herself and the baby.

Gaining two visits each month was worth the price of desertion. Weekends in their cottage were blissful. The chubby-cheeked baby looked just like his daddy. He was a pleasant baby; growing quickly, always smiling. Eddy loved his time with Rosa and Joey. Eddy pulled Joey on a rickety two-wheeled cart that he converted with broken skis to a makeshift sled for the winter. Joey delighted in the cart rides with Daddy. The dirt path was stone-covered, resulting in a bumpy carnival-like ride. The baby giggled tirelessly, urging "another ride" with a grunt. The couple roamed the mountainside hand in hand, baby on Daddy's back.

Money was tight; without army salary and *Nonna's* weekly donations. However, they were in love. Although used to finery, Rosa neither worried nor cared. Her baby was a sheer joy. She was in love with a handsome blonde ex-GI and his precious son. Despite parental ostracization, life was fulfilling. Worldly goods were no longer a requirement.

It was winter; the foothills could be harsh. The fireplace was the only heat for the two rooms. Eddy labored tirelessly to ensure Rosa had plenty of fuel for the week while Rosa, toting Joey, collected kindling.

The butcher shop owner generously sent Eddy home with small cuts of meat and bones. Rosa preserved the meat with salt, made delicious soups and stews, and baked aromatic hearth breads. After the work was done, the family luxuriated all evening and night; three, close together on the single bed, only stirring to stoke the fire or tend to the baby.

This was the simple life of Eddy, Rosa, and Joseph Kepler every weekend for the four months following his desertion from the United States Army Corp.

Chapter 19

"EDWARDO, I WISH TO SPEAK to you," requested the butcher.

"*Si. Si*," replied Eddy, as he washed his hands and turned away from the counter. "Is everything okay?"

"My family is taking a ski trip tomorrow. Would you like to join us? You have been working very hard, and I think you deserve a treat," proclaimed the butcher in a fatherly tone.

"Who will watch the shop?"

"My brother. He broke his leg in the last war and can no longer ski. How about it? It's a weekday. You will not miss your weekend home to visit your sweet Rosa."

Eddy smiled broadly, he needed a break. It was not his nature to work so hard for so long; although he did gladly for the love of Rosa. However, he was used to having fun. This sounded like the perfect opportunity.

"Sure, why not? Sounds great. Yes, I'll go." Remembering his manners, he added, "Oh, and thank you very much."

That night, Eddy slept soundly, as usual, but with an excited anticipation of the pending adventure. Daylight came quickly, and Eddy arose to dress. He wore his army issued thermals under a thin pair of trousers. His clothing was not sufficient to keep him warm, but the adventure was worth a little cold.

His scarf was one of Rosa's knitting projects; his Christmas gift. Bulky, it kept him warm. Eddy, always resourceful, bought Rosa a small graduated string of pearls for Christmas to replace the beauties she abandoned at the villa. Eddy wrapped the scarf tightly around his neck, tucking the ends into his belt. As he did, he noticed something in his pocket. Reaching in, he pulled out Rosa's Christmas pearls.

"How in the name of God did those get into my pants pocket?" he wondered. Then he remembered Joey reaching for them. Rosa cherished her new pearls. She removed them and put them in Eddy's pants pocket, preventing the strong little guy from breaking the strand. He shoved them back into his pocket.

Eddy met the butcher, Luigi, and the Rizzo family toting skis, boots, and poles at the train station at 0600 hours. Luigi handed Eddy a set of skis.

"They belong to my brother. The boots might be a little tight. Try them. Paulo has the biggest feet in our family."

"Thanks, man. I was hoping to not have to rent skis!"

The ride to the closest ski resort was forty-five minutes. Once aboard the train, Luigi's wife, Carmella, gave each member of the travel party a generous slice of bread and some cheese to break their fast. Luigi followed with a flask of wine. All were jovial and laughing by the time the group reached the ski resort.

Luigi purchased lift tickets for all, handing one to Eddy, who accepted hesitantly but graciously.

The mountaintop was cold. The wind cut through Eddy's thin clothing and chilled him. Breakfast wine did not help the situation. Undeterred, Eddy was the first to head down the mountain.

Natural athlete that he was, balance and agility came easily. Eddy flew down the mountain, passing trees and other skiers. Unguarded, he briefly thought, *Harriett would love this. We'll have to ski when I return home.* A gust of wind sucked out his breath and returned his thoughts back to reality as he remembered Joey and Rosa. There would be no returning home to Harriett.

Eddy traversed the mountain three times over multiple trails before Carmella descended one time.

"Gather everyone," she yelled over the noise of the crowds and the wind. "It's time for lunch."

The family headed for the shelter of a small warming hut where Carmella proceeded to distribute meat pies and dried fruit. Luigi offered more wine. They all ate and drank hungrily, especially Eddy. He was compensating for expended energy and lost body heat. Exhilarated from the exercise, cold, and comradery, the Rizzos bragged loudly about their skiing prowess as they stuffed their faces.

The laughter of the hut was interrupted by the entrance of several American uniformed officers. Also seeking warmth after enjoying the slopes, they paid little attention to the Italian family.

Taking a quick second glance, one lieutenant noticed the oddity of a tall blonde man in the middle of seven short dark-haired people. Eddy simultaneously recognized his squad commander and turned his head away from the Americans.

Approaching his ranking officer, the lieutenant pulled him outside and whispered, "I think that tall blonde with that Italian family is my AWOL corporal, Edgar Kepler. Do you remember, he jumped several months ago? Over a girl, I think. Shall I check it out?"

"Damn straight! I'll not have our men deserting without consequence," was the reply.

"Corporal Kepler!" the lieutenant boomed.

Despite himself, Eddy turned in reply.

"Sergeant, place this man under arrest. Corporal Edgar Kepler is AWOL. He deserted my squad of the 351st infantry; 88th Army Division."

Without hesitation, Eddy darted for the door. The sargeant was closer to the threshold and stopped his retreat. He threw Eddy against the wall, grabbed his arms behind his back, and tied them. Eddy, trying to salvage a dire situation, decided not to fight back. He turned willingly, following the officers. For the sheer fun of it, the sargeant picked up a nearby log. Cracking Eddy on the side of the head, he fell unconscious into a lump of snow.

Chapter 20

EDDY AWOKE WITH A GROAN. "Geez man, why the hell did you whack me? I was coming peacefully!" he said to the guilty sargeant sitting guard in the back of the jeep.

"God!" Eddy said rubbing his head. "That hurts!"

The sargeant just grunted in response.

"That's enough," interjected the lieutenant. "Sargeant Hill, you owe Kepler an apology. He was following on his own accord."

"Sorry, Lieutenant."

"Not to me! To Kepler."

"Uh...sorry, Kepler."

The remainder of the journey was traveled in silence.

Back on base, Eddy was processed and then deposited in the brig. Alone, with no way to contact Rosa, he panicked. He started pacing back and forth in his cell and then he yelled hysterically.

"Rosa! Rosa. Oh my God, Rosa. I need to find Rosa." His screams continued for the next sixty minutes until his voice went hoarse. Exhausted, he slumped into a corner and sobbed. Finally, an MP investigated the lack of commotion.

"Hey, Go-to Guy, what are you doing here? I thought you went AWOL over Untouchable?" asked the MP.

Somewhat relieved, Eddy tried to dry his eyes as he whispered to the MP. "Get Wally Stuart."

"Sorry, buster. No can do. You are not to have visitors for the next three weeks. Didn't they tell you when you processed in?"

"I wasn't listening," mumbled a despondent Eddy. "Oh God!"

The MP continued, "Wish I could help you, buddy, being the Go-to Guy and all, but my hands are tied."

The news of Eddy's arrest traveled quickly. However, there was no deviation to his sentence of no visitors. By the time Wally got in to see him, three weekends passed, with no one going to the cottage.

"You got to go out to the cottage and check on Rosa and Joey," pleaded Eddy. "I won't rest until I know they are safe and they know what's happened to me."

"Eddy, you really push a friendship."

"Well, there's more. I need you to take some of my S/K Acq. money to her. She's out there in the middle of nowhere, in the middle of winter, on her own. She needs firewood, money, and food. Oh God! What have I done to her?"

Walter agreed and headed to the cottage on Saturday supplied with money, food, wood, and milk. To his surprise, the front door was ajar. The place was deserted for some time. There were no tracks or footprints. The fireplace was cold—no sign of recent burning. As Wally entered the cottage, a small rodent scampered across the empty shelf. Supplies, blanket, and duffel—all gone.

Now it was time for Walter to panic. He didn't condone Eddy's behavior; however, he didn't wish ill on Rosa or Joey. Where could they have gone? He left the milk and supplies on the stoop and drove off in search of Kepler's family.

Back in Trieste, Walter stopped at city hall. Closed on Saturdays, the building was locked. Next, he decided to brave and try Villa Romano. He drove to the front gate and was immediately stopped.

"Hey, chief, I don't need to go in, I just need some information. Have you seen Romano's daughter and grandbaby around here? Maybe they showed up several weeks ago?"

"Are you asking about Rosa?" questioned the guard.

"Yes, yes," replied Wally, feeling hopeful.

"She has not been seen at Villa Romano since last March. The magistrate has forbidden her entrance. She has been disowned."

"Holy shit! Cold-hearted bastard! Isn't he?" Wally was shocked that a father could be so cruel to his only child.

The guard refused comment. He knew firsthand that Magistrate Romano was ruthless, cruel, and unforgiving.

Having no luck, Wally headed back to base to tell Eddy the bad news.

"Wow, back so soon? I thought you might spend some time with Rosa to keep her company. I know she gets lonely out there all alone," asked Eddy.

"Eddy, sit down. You're not going to like this."

Wally's foreboding face frightened Eddy, so he sat.

"She's gone. No trace of her or Joey."

"What are you saying to me? Gone? Gone where?"

"Well, if I knew that, it wouldn't be bad news, would it!" piped Wally. "Look, sorry, man, I'm frustrated and scared too. I went to the courthouse—closed—so then over to the Romano house. She's nowhere to be found."

Eddy hyperventilated. "Tomorrow, go to Santa Croce, please! I have to find her."

"Buddy, we don't know where her grandmother lives. We were only at the church."

"Isabella's last name is…shit! Why can't I remember her last name!?" By now, Eddy was desperate. He buried his head in his hands and wept.

Neither man thought to look for Isabela's last name on her two correspondences; that is, if Eddy kept them. This was not a time for rational thought.

On Sunday, Walter made the trip to Santa Croce but without success. The city was larger than either Eddy or Walter expected and close to other major metropolitan areas. Without a last name, it was impossible to find "Isabela and Joseph."

Eddy tried again. He wrote Rosa a letter explaining his arrest, enclosed some money, and sent it in care of her parents to Villa Romano. Hopefully, they would forward it to her so that she knew she and Joey were not abandoned.

"Lieutenant, what's to happen to me?" asked Eddy when he got an unexpected visit from his company commander.

"Son, you have been stripped rank back to private, you have been given solitary time to think, you will serve an additional six weeks behind bars, then you will be transferred to Korea."

The light sentence was due in part to Eddy's regular supply of reasonably priced bourbon to those officers in charge of his fate. A supply which Wally guaranteed through S/K Acq. during Eddy's incarceration.

The lieutenant continued, "The supply sargeant spoke highly of you. He has intervened on your behalf. You will not be court-martialed. You remain eligible for army pay and an honorable discharge, provided you don't screw up again!"

Eddy just stared straight ahead. *Goddamn Korea!* he thought. *I had it made. A cake assignment that was safe. What a FUBAR! I knocked up the girl of my dreams, I deserted my company, my wife, my son, my love, and now I'm going to God damn Korea.*

"Do you have anything to say for yourself?"

"Yes, sir. Thank you, sir. I am sorry I left my post. I wasn't thinking clearly, sir. My girl was pregnant. She bore a son. I forgot my responsibility to my post and only thought of my responsibility to my family, sir," recited Eddy. Wally rehearsed Eddy on this response many times, knowing that someday, he would have to own up to his mistake.

The next six weeks passed quickly. Wally continued to search for Rosa and Joey. Eddy continued to write her letters, send money, and post them to Villa Romano thinking if he pestered them enough, they may forward them to her.

As he climbed into the transport truck, Wally yelled after Eddy.

"Keep in touch, you sorry-ass jerk! I promise to keep looking for your family. Don't forget, after the war, we must distribute S/K Acq. funds."

"Yeah. Whatever, man. Thanks for your friendship. I mean it!"

"Keep your head down!" Wally waved as the truck pulled away.

Part Three

Chapter 21

Campbellsville, 1952

"Harriett, are you eating with us tonight?" yelled Tabs up the stairs to his daughter.

"No, Papa. I stopped to grab a sandwich before my appointment. I didn't want to be distracted by a growling tummy. I am so excited."

"Okay, honey. Have a good night." Tabs left his daughter in the privacy of her room; the room she should be sharing with her husband.

She sat down on her bed and began writing her nightly letter to Eddy.

My Dearest Darling Eddy,

I desperately miss you. I hope you are safe and well. It is torture not hearing from you. I pray every morning and evening for your wellbeing.

My college classes are going well. A few of my Associate Degree credits count. It won't be too many years until I have my bachelor's degree. I am making high marks. Currently I enrolled in one class per week, however, next semester I shall increase to two.

I am so happy that your mother introduced me to Jesus. He gives me comfort in your absence. I enjoy my Sunday's with Abigail. I hope you realize what a wonderful woman she is.

I found us a house. It is the big red brick house on the street above my parent's; the old Songer house. I'm sure you remember which one I mean. It is the one that displayed single blue Christmas candles in each window every holiday. I got a fair price and it doesn't need too much work; at least not at first.

Please write! Please, and let me know what you think about buying this house. I don't want to miss the opportunity.

God's Speed.

All my deepest love to you my dear.

Love,
Harriett

Eddy was gone seventeen months. The first five months Eddy dutifully wrote his wife once a week. He neither wrote nor sent money the last twelve months. Harriett missed her husband dreadfully. His silence terrified her. Fearful of the worst but hopeful for the best, she channeled her pain and loss into her work. The super energy overachiever became "super woman." Thomas Roland, her boss, promoted Harriett to Office General Manager; June past. She now earned as much as she and Eddy together before he deployed.

Her new responsibilities included overseeing staff functions for payroll, personnel, secretarial pool, accounts payable, and accounts receivable. A huge responsibility for a woman; she performed her duties better than most men.

Still saving money, Harriett was ready to take the plunge to buy a house. Living with her parents cut household costs, but living with Olive was growing tiresome. At almost twenty-two, she was ready to live in a different building; preferably with her husband. If only Eddy would answer her letters!

In possession of Eddy's car, Harriett solicited Earl for driving lessons soon after Eddy's departure. No surprise: she was a quick understudy. Harriett continued to ride the bus to work rather than spend money on gas; however, she capitalized on her newfound freedom by driving to visit her mother-in-law.

Abagail welcomed the young woman into her circle. A caring and generous Christian woman, Abigail demonstrated unconditional love; something Olive, her own mother, was incapable of comprehending. Abagail invited Harriett to join her every Sunday for church services. Lonely, Harriett agreed.

Edgar Sr. gladly relinquished the duty of Sunday chauffer to his new daughter-in-law. Soon, Harriett was attending Sunday school, Sunday services, and Wednesday night Bible study. She accepted Jesus as her Savior by baptism on Easter Sunday, 1951.

Christian faith gave Harriett strength to endure the pain of Eddy's absence and silence. Her daily prayer offered comfort and hope.

Stopping on her way home from work to collect the keys, Harriett walked up the hill to her new house. She would rely on her family to help her move her meager possessions over the weekend. Her only furniture was her bedroom suite that she purchased from Olive and a small table with one chair. She would furnish the dining room, parlor, kitchen, and three other bedrooms later. For the time being, she needed nothing—that, is except Eddy.

Harriett found a bargain. The passing of Mrs. Songer caused family turmoil. The Songer children all moved either out of town or out of state. Disagreement on distribution of property left the house unoccupied. Eventually, the siblings came to terms. Deciding to sell as quickly as possible and divide the proceeds equally, the house went on the market.

Harriett, earning more than most family units in town, had the available funds to move fast.

Making an equitable purchase offer, lower than the asking price, Harriett made a significant down payment. Loan secured with minimum monthly mortgage payments, the sellers agreed to her terms.

Although having more to spend, she saved a sizable reserve to buy furniture and to make repairs, if needed.

The Songer house was a stately large structure high on a hill, overlooking the town, valley, and river below. A steep, wide-walled, gray stone staircase, with multiple terraces, climbed the hill leading to the white pillars framing the front porch entrance. The center terrace was extended on both ends and enclosed with carved concrete benches. In time past, pots of flowers and vines lined the walls and terraces, giving it the look of an English country manor house.

Paneled wood double doors emptied into the foyer. Nine-and-a-half-foot ceilings made the rooms look huge. A beautiful blue crystal chandelier hung in the center of the entryway. Casting shimmering silhouettes of light, it beckoned the visitor to enter and be awed.

A formal parlor was on the left and the dining room on the right. A wood paneled office, a butler's pantry, and a powder room divided the front of the house from the large kitchen in the back. Two spacious pantries completed the kitchen that emptied onto a sprawling covered porch. The house was much larger and newer than Olive's; of course, she was jealous.

Two staircases; a beautifully carved curved wood one arching from the foyer, the second plainer leading from the kitchen, floated to the second story. Upstairs boasted three bedrooms, a complete bathroom, plus a master room with in-suite bath and large cedar-lined walk-in closet. The entire house was floored in beautiful hardwoods.

A third narrower staircase led to the upper-floor attic, which featured built-in storage drawers and shelves, a large oak work table, and a second cedar-lined full closet. Discarded items formed a pile on the rear side of the attic space.

The house windows were made of beveled leaded glass framed in dark-stained mahogany. A stained-glass transom topped the front door, casting rainbows on the inside walls.

The new Kepler residence was easily the largest, grandest home in Campbellsville. Once again owned by a company executive; this time, by a woman.

Harriett unlocked the brass fixture and walked through the threshold. Her elation of home ownership was soon overpowered by her worry over Eddy. The polished wood entrance floor, although dusty, reflected her solitary form. Seeing herself alone, she lay down on the floor, broke down, and wept.

Back at her parent's that night, she wrote:

Dear beloved husband,

> I pray you are safe. I miss you terribly. Take care of yourself wherever you are.
>
> Your mother sends her love. She and I continue to pray for you daily. I hope that you will join us at Sunday service when you return home to me.
>
> I have wonderful news. I bought us a house. I waited for your approval, but you continue not to write. I took some of our savings and bought the Songer house. It will be a joyful home when you return. We do not own furniture, other than our bedroom set. I will only buy a few necessary items. I want to wait to furnish our new home together.
>
> Eddy, dear, please be safe and stay out of danger. I love you so much! I can't wait to make this house our home. Please write.
>
> With all my everlasting love,
> Harriett.

Placing her pen on the nightstand, she resumed packing their wedding gifts and her limited clothing for transport. Albert borrowed a truck for tomorrow's move. One trip would conclude the move, giving Harriett plenty of time to unpack before Monday.

Eddy elected not to move his clothing over to the Bailey house after receiving his draft notice. Earl boxed Eddy's clothes and property for the move.

Move over and unpacking underway, Harriett eagerly made space in the closet for Eddy's articles. Having his things around her made her feel a little less alone.

Before going to sleep in her new home, she wrote:

Dearest love,

You are constantly in my thoughts and prayers. I pray that God keep you safe and return you to me soon.

Today was moving day. Earl and Albert made short work of the task. All your clothes now hang in our closet. I love having your smell close to me; although I confess it makes me miss you even more. I know you will love our new home. There is a garage for your car with a bench for your workshop. The kitchen needs to be updated eventually, but I need to learn to cook first. I promise to master that task before you return. I am anxious to prepare delicious food for you.

My sister Alice is pregnant. This is her third child. I am so excited for her.

Please come home soon so that we may start our own family. You are my love and my life. I miss you with all my heart. I wish I knew why you do not write. Please write.

Your devoted loving wife,
Harriett

Chapter 22

"ABIGAIL, TELL ME TRUTHFULLY, HAVE you heard anything from Eddy?" tested Harriett at church on Sunday. She didn't think her mother-in-law would keep information from her, but she wanted to ask.

"Darling Harriett, I would never hide anything from you."

This is exactly why Eddy did not write to his mother, father, or brothers. He knew one of them would slip and Harriett would find out about his transgression. However, he should tell someone how to contact him, now that he was in Korea. Wally sent him a stack of mail last week that was delivered to Italy.

"Honey, why don't you stay for dinner today? You need to learn to cook now that you are living alone. I can teach you," added Abigail.

Harriet jumped at the chance to acquire cooking skills. "Of course, thank you for your kindness."

All members of the Kepler family managed to visit Abigail and Edgar Sr. every Sunday. Total chaos ensued, to Abigail's delight. Harriett, slightly overwhelmed, lagged in the kitchen, with her pencil and notebook documenting every step of meal preparation.

The next four weeks were a continuation of her cooking education until Earl approached her, questioning, "Why are you taking so many notes?"

"Abigail is teaching me how to cook."

"My mother is teaching you to cook? No wonder Eddy isn't writing!" retorted Earl.

"What are you talking about?" Infuriated that Earl threw Eddy's lack of communication in her face, Harriett clenched her fists and glared, her face flushing bright red, verging on magenta.

"Woah, Harriett. I am not ridiculing you. It's just…" Earl broke off.

"Our mother is a terrible cook," chimed all four Kepler boys in unison.

The family laughed, including Harriett. It felt good to laugh. *This family makes me happy. Eddy makes me happy. I am so blessed.* she thought.

***

Harriett opted to ask Alice for cooking lessons on the Kepler brother's advice. It was good to spend one night a week with her sister. The girls grew even closer as they talked about Alice's growing belly, children, cooking, baking, sewing, and married/ family life in general. As expected, Harriet learned quickly, with one exception; she was a terrible cook. Her baking was exceptional, she developed sewing skills, but a major weakness was finally exposed; no cooking talent.

Several weeks after working with Alice, Harriett decided to make pork chops, mashed potatoes, and glazed carrots for supper. She knew Eddy loved pork, so her effort was earnest. Worrying about trichinosis, the thin chops were so overcooked that they could have been used as shoe leather. Her potatoes were lumpy and watery, verging on wallpaper paste, and the carrots burned in the saucepan. It was so bad that the neighbor's dog refused to eat a bite. Reluctantly admitting defeat, she resorted to canned soup and sandwiches for her evening meals.

Despite trying, her cooking skills never improved. But the woman could bake! Harriett's mastery of yeast was impressive. She baked delicious breads, cakes, pies, and her cinnamon rolls became legendary. She was soon earning extra cash selling the delicious breakfast treats.

When not baking, Harriett spent her lonely nights and weekends either studying or working on the house. Tabs taught her carpentry "how-to."

Enclosed by six-foot high fences, once-beautiful gardens surrounded the house and filled the property. An arched gate led to the woodlands behind the house. Slightly neglected and overgrown, Harriett took advantage of warm summer temps to tidy the flower beds populated with exotic plant life.

"Papa, what is the name of this tree?" Harriett asked one Saturday. Tabs was more than happy to get away from Olive and could frequently be found with his daughter.

"That is a Japanese maple. The leaves are a feathery red. The tree naturally grows in Japan, China, and Korea," Tabs knowingly responded. "I think this is the only one of its kind in Campbellsville."

"How do you know that?" asked Harriett.

"Old man Songer was a boss at the factory. He loved strange things and used to brag about his travels and purchases from foreign countries. Talk of that tree bored the entire production floor for two weeks after Songer planted it. He made lots of money, and from the stories I heard, spent it also. I bet you'll find some hidden treasures in this house if you look," Tabs continued.

"Do you think so, Papa? I'll start looking. I certainly have enough time on my hands. Want to help?" Trying to entice her father to spend more time with her, Harriett smiled coyly at him.

"Of course, Janie. It will be an adventure."

Harriett thought to herself, *I would rather do this with Eddy, it will be fun to explore our new house together, but Papa is good company.*

Before he left for the evening, Tabs asked, "Janie, I have a favor to ask of you?"

"What's that, Papa? Is everything all right?"

"Nothing is wrong, but it's not really right. Will you take me to church with you on Sunday? Do you think it would look unseemly if I went with you and Abigail?"

"Oh, Papa! I would love to take you to church. I'll pick you up tomorrow at 9:00 a.m." Harriett delighted as she kissed her father goodbye. She hoped that church and faith would fill the void left by despicable Olive.

That night, her letter read:

Dear sweet husband,

    My Papa helped me in the gardens today. We have a red feathery Japanese maple tree! It is the only one in Campbellsville. Imagine that. I wish you were here so that we could explore our new home together. You will love our house. It is very special.

    Papa is going to church with me tomorrow. I'm so happy that he wants to learn about The Lord. Papa is wonderful company. I'm not as lonely when Papa is around, but I would rather spend my time with you.

    I baked a red cake this evening. I'll take it over to your parent's house tomorrow after church. I want to keep my figure, but I do like to bake. You may gain weight when you come home. You most likely can stand to add a few pounds after being in the service. I pray you are not seeing any action of war. I imagine not; being in Trieste. Are you still in Trieste?

    Please come back to me! I miss you terribly. Eddy darling, I don't understand why you can't or won't write? Please write as soon as you are able. Your mother sends her love.

    I try not to think the worst. Sweetie, I pray for your safety.

With everlasting love,
Harriett

Chapter 23

Summer and fall passed quickly. The gardens were once again manicured show pieces; thanks to Harriet and Tabs' arduous work and a rebuilt gas lawn mower.

During inclement weather Harriett worked inside, rubbing and polishing the floors and wood molding until it gleamed. The house was regaining grandeur lost; with the absence of furniture.

Harriett added a suitable kitchen table and four chairs. She purchased baking and cooking equipment, along with a few other kitchen items to fill her pantry shelves. Despite having plenty of income, she frugally shopped at tag sales, consignment and second-hand shops. She found a beautiful room size woven wool Karastan rug to protect the parlor floor.

Her most exciting find was an oversized green leather wing chair and a floor light. Positioned next to the wood-burning fireplace, she imagined chilly winter nights, fire burning, reading to their children who were gathered at her feet. In the meantime, the chair was a comfortable respite after long days of work and study.

The remaining house was void of furniture, apart from window blinds in her bedroom. Harriett was determined to share decorating activities with Eddy.

Harriett spent Thanksgiving dinner with the Kepler's. The noise and chaos of the motley crew no longer alarmed her. She enjoyed the camaraderie of Eddy's family; delighting in their acceptance of her.

The approach of Christmas threatened Harriett's composure. She managed Christmas number one without Eddy since their marriage was new and he was still writing. Christmas, 1951, was more difficult; however, she was living with her parents. Olive never a comfort; Tabs always a delight! This Christmas, 1952, would be the first in her new home, the first spent truly alone.

Eddy, you should be here. This should be a magical time for us! Where are you? she thought. Her hope was starting to wane despite the holiday. Or was it due to the holiday?

After Sunday school and church, Harriett asked, "Papa, will you help me cut down a tree?"

"Why, yes. Are you sure you want one?" questioned the gentle old man. "They can be dirty when the needles drop. You worked so hard buffing your floors."

"Yes and no. I love Christmas. Now that I understand its meaning, I want to celebrate the birth of my Savior. But I surely do miss Eddy. Being apart makes me so sad." Tears trickled down her cheeks.

"Sure, Janie. We'll go this afternoon. I'll get my bowsaw."

Harriett found an old throw rug left behind in one of the pantries and placed it on the floor in the parlor. She hoped it would collect most of the lost pine needles. Tabs found a beautiful Scotch pine growing in the woods behind her house. Quick work, and the seven-foot tree was in a tub of water centered in the front window. Tabs made a makeshift stand to hold it upright.

"Looks pretty good. What do you think?" Tabs asked as he squeezed his daughter's waist. "Do you have any decorations to hang on it?"

"It's beautiful," she sighed. "I will buy some lights and a star next week. I think I'll make the rest. I want to pick out our permanent trimmings with Eddy."

Tabs heart broke again. Every time he saw Janie hurt by Eddy, a little piece inside him died. *Damn that Kepler boy! I knew he was bad news!*

Next day after work, Harriet made a visit to Gimbels Department store. Decked in red and green from ceiling to floor, it was hard to not feel the wonder of Christmas.

She made her way to the holiday sections. Shelves were filled with beautiful hand-blown glass ornaments. Other shelves held tree skirts made of silk or embroidered felt. A quick look at the price tags sent Harriett's head spinning. She would settle on looking for a star top but buy her lights and other ornaments at Murphy's Five and Dime.

Made of Bohemian-cut glass, the star was a masterpiece. Harriet knew, as soon as she spotted it, that she must buy that star. Without looking at the price, she gathered a boxed piece and proceeded to pay. She managed not to gasp when the clerk asked for twenty dollars.

Murphy's was two doors down the street. She found a pack of construction paper, rubber cement, heavy duty thread, a large needle, two strands of 9C UL tested multicolored lights, silver tinsel, and a bag of un-popped popping corn. Total cost: five dollars. Feeling better, she ran for the bus, clutching the star tightly under her arm.

That night, Harriett lit a fire and sat down with a bowl of popcorn. Threading the needle, she began stringing. Developing the rhythm of "thread two, eat one," it took all night to finish her popcorn garlands. She decided to call it a night and finish decorating the tree tomorrow.

Before sleep, pen and paper in hand, she began to write.

Dear Eddy,

Now that Christmas is in the air, I miss you even more, if that is possible. I am sad thinking about spending yet a third Christmas without you.

I decided to decorate a tree. It looks good in front of the parlor window. Our children will enjoy running down the staircase Christmas mornings to see Santa's packages. They can hang their stockings from the mantle. What a glorious thought; you and I with our own loving little ones opening presents Christmas morning. Is this a mere fantasy or a dream that can come true?

I did not buy expensive tree trimmings. I want us to collect them together to commemorate events and travels of our life. This year I am stringing popcorn and making construction paper garlands.

I will be eating Christmas dinner with your family. They are delightful. I love Abigail. She is the loving mother I never had. You are so lucky. You treat her poorly with your silence.

I'm not sure when you will get this letter. With Christmas only a week away, I shall wish you a safe and blessed Christmas. I can't wait until I can tell you that in person and seal my wish with a kiss.

I have enclosed several boxes of cookies and cinnamon rolls. They may be stale when they arrive, but dip them in coffee to eat. I sent enough for you to share with your friends.

I adore you my love. What a wonderful gift it would be to get a letter from you. Please give me the gift of communication! I need to know where you are and why you do not write,

Merry Christmas,
Harriett

Placing the star at the top of the tree concluded her first decorating ritual. Thinking to herself, *Next year I shall hang wreaths on the door and windows.*

She plugged in the lights and inhaled at the beauty of the star. Refracted light shone in every corner of the room. Harriett envisioned it to be as beautiful as the Christ Star.

The holidays were passed with her papa and at the Kepler's. She gave and received gifts from the clan; two were special gifts. Abigail crocheted her a warm afghan to use in the green wing chair. Dearest Tabs carved a wooden replica of the pillars, front porch, and doors to the house. He painted it corresponding colors and wrote "1952 New House" on the back of the doors and signed it "Papa." It was her only hanging ornament, and Harriett cherished it.

Christmas night, alone in the big house, Harriett cried herself to sleep. The act replicated each following night that week. The year

1952 brutally assaulted Harriett. Her faith no longer enough to sustain her mood; her spirit broken.

***

The New Year brought challenging work followed by success at the office. Tom Roland was promoted to CEO after old man Dugan retired. Tom moved to the large corner office vacated by Dugan. Harriett was at the head of a shortlist for Roland's replacement as CFO. Due to her previous experience as Roland's executive assistant and her success as general manager, deliberation was quick. Harriett's exceptional work and pending degree, landed her an executive position—in a man's world. Offered a salary double that of the average family, it was still only seventy-five percent of her male counterparts. She negotiated for an additional five percent higher.

She was moved into the other corner office; also, with windows on two sides. A big desk centered on a bookcase. It held vast numbers of notebooks filled with Dugan & Co. financial information. Her secretary, Miss White, having worked with her when general manager, sat in the cube outside her office. Miss White came as part of her promotion bargaining process. She was about the same age as Harriett, with equal motivation. Miss White looked at Harriett as a mentor, the trailblazer of the path to executive positions for women.

Harriett bought a large houseplant to brighten up the window corner. A small conference table and four chairs occupied the other side of the room. Trying to add more color, she purchased a large oil painting, already framed, from the consignment store. The room remained predominately masculine; a result of male dominated business world.

The excitement of her promotion to company executive vice president, CFO, and personnel manager was diminished by the fact that she experienced it without her husband. Tabs and Abigail shared in her success without truly understanding the significance of it. Sweet Alice bought her a new hat to commemorate the event.

This successful woman executive needed nothing—nothing but her Eddy.

Chapter 24

January, February, and March 1953 were harsh and cold. Snowfall being average, it seemed to be overly wet and rainy; always on the verge of freezing, but without forming flakes. Harriett found the weather intolerable. She wasn't sure if it was due to more miserable weather conditions or a more frustrated attitude.

Eddy remained silent. Harriett struggled to be positive and optimistic. She mistakenly spent less time with Abigail, feigning work but fearful her desperation would be contagious. She wanted her mother-in-law to continue to hope for her son.

Convinced that her husband was a fleeting fantasy of the past, Harriett opened bank savings and checking accounts in her name only. Bills were paid out of the joint account, although she contributed all of the funds.

Her second action, after accepting that she was abandoned or widowed, was the sale of Eddy's prized sports car. Tom Roland, company CEO, was selling his 1946 Buick Super, a four-door sedan, for a new model. Deciding an executive needed a more appropriate car, she purchased the Buick and sold Eddy's Ford coupe to an ecstatic high-schooler who would own the "infamous Eddy Kepler chick mobile."

Tired of waiting and tired of living alone, Harriett went in search of furniture. She abandoned her quest of decorating with Eddy. True to her frugal nature, she searched personal ads to find a mahogany table with three leaves, six side chairs, two captain chairs, and matching breakfront for a fraction of full retail price. Albert and Earl transported her purchase. It complimented the hand-painted oriental silk wallpaper of the dining room; one of the house's special treasures.

Having furniture brightened her spirits somewhat. The house began to feel like a home, despite being a home for a single woman. She worked hard, and it was becoming her personal retreat.

She also found antique bedroom furniture. Tackling a new project, she stripped the wallpaper, patched the walls, and applied a fresh new floral print. The double size iron bed was covered with an antique red work stitched quilt, found among Olive's Westchester family treasures. A marble-topped, three-mirrored vanity, a wash stand, pitcher with basin, and embroidered linen hand towels added ambiance. Furniture concluded with a small white stuffed chair. Red and white striped ruffled drapes, a crystal bedside lamp, and a white wool rug completed the room. A guest room fit for a queen. To no one's surprise, Harriett showed a knack for decorating.

April offered a break from the rain. Satisfied with her progress inside, Harriett began work once again on her gardens. Winter clean up would take several weeks, if the weather held. She was delighted to see spring bulbs poking through the ground. To Harriett's surprise, daffodils and narcissus lined the front stairs and walls. Tulip leaves peeped up, interspersed among the daffodils and hyacinths, and ensured the continuation of a beautiful colorful display.

Forsythia, azaleas, and rhododendrons layered colorful texture to the pink and white tree blossoms. The spring burst of color was breathtaking.

Harriett's overall mood deteriorated from the winter and caused her to struggle with her thoughts of Eddy. Her letters decreased from every night to once a week.

After a long stressful week working at the office and in the garden, she decided to pick up her pen to write. Her frustration showed. Her meaning was clear.

Dear Eddy,

I can't help but wonder what it is that I have done to keep you from writing? Our house is a colorful display of spring. Yet, I am unable to enjoy it because I do not understand why you continue to ignore me.

Are you hurt? Are you in a hospital? Or are you dead? What is it? Why?

If you are dead, surely the army would notify me. Are you a prisoner?

I have done nothing but support and love you. Your mother is heartbroken that you do not write. I am heartbroken, but I am also angry.

Now that I am making good money as an executive, I can support myself, if necessary, and in luxury.

Do you intend to stay away forever? Did you find someone else?

Well, then tell me so. I need to know if I should continue to hope or if I should find happiness someplace else.

I still love you very much. If you love me even a little; if you ever loved me, then at least write to admit the truth. WHY the silence?

You have broken my heart. Come home to me and patch it back together again!

Harriett

Chapter 25

DUE TO HER EXECUTIVE POSITION, Harriett installed a home telephone. She opted for the extra cost of a private line. Any company conversation needed to remain between Harriett and the party on the other end of the line. Wanting a place for the phone, Harriett furnished the office as her work space.

The room was relatively large for a home office. A set of French doors, flanked with electric carriage lights, led to a stone-walled terrace that overlooked the valley below and opposite hillside. The spring and fall views from this spot boasted sheer beauty. Harriett envisioned many enjoyable evenings spent on this terrace with Eddy and their children. She envisioned them buying comfortable stuffed patio furniture for this space, Eddy's participation mandatory in the purchase.

The walls of the office were stunning exotic acacia wood paneling, with built-in walnut bookcases to match a darker tone. Topped with hand-carved cornices, the built-ins revealed another house gem. A small assortment of manuscripts, purchased with the house, lined a top shelf. Harriett began collecting books other than her college textbooks. She purchased a large wood executive desk, carved to match the cornice, and a tall-backed red leather swivel desk chair. Resisting the temptation of a masculine dominance, she made use of a bright yellow desk lamp shade. The wood floor was covered with a red and yellow Aubusson rug. A yellow floral Chintz chase offered comfortable reading space.

A covered Remington typewriter sat at the ready, close to the desk. Harriett had Miss White, her own secretary at work; however, she practiced to retain her typing skill of sixty words per minute.

Harriett ran from the kitchen to answer the ringing phone. *I really need to splurge on a second phone for the kitchen*, she thought. *This house is too big for just one phone.*

"Good afternoon, Harriett Kepler speaking," she said as she placed the receiver to her ear.

"Mrs. Kepler, this is Doctor Paulson. I'm afraid I have some unwelcome news. I need you to come to my office immediately," said the voice on the other end. "Your mother is here."

Harriett interrupted. "Is my mother all right?"

"Well, yes, just a little shaken."

"Then what's the problem? My mother is always shaken," Harriett interjected.

"I'm sorry, if you'll only allow me to finish. Your mother is here, she is shaken. It's your father. I'm afraid your father suffered a terrible accident. He fell from a ladder and broke his neck. I need you to identify the body and assist your mother with funeral arrangements," the doctor concluded.

Harriett dropped the phone and collapsed into the desk chair. "*No!*" she screamed. "You are wrong! It is not my father." Then she fainted.

She awoke to the sound of a muffled voice saying, "Mrs. Kepler. Mrs. Kepler. Are you there?"

Regaining consciousness, she picked up the phone and answered, "Yes, I am here. I'll be right over. Thank you, Doctor."

Sitting in the chair in disbelief, Harriett took a few minutes to compose herself. Heading across the hall to the powder room, she splashed water on her face. The reflection staring back at her was pale, with dark circled eyes. She managed to comb her hair and put on fresh lipstick before leaving the house.

Alice lived on the same street, four blocks away. Harriett stopped on her way to the doctor's office to tell her the dreadful news.

"Oh, honey, please let me come with you," Alice demanded.

"You can't drag three children, one of them an infant, along to see their dead grandfather! It will scare them for the rest of their life.

"You are probably right, but you can't be alone," insisted Alice.

"This is mine and mine alone to do," maintained Harriett. "I was closest to Papa. I shall do this. Will you tell Albert, Ester, and June?"

"Of course. Remember, we are family, don't forget that. You are not alone."

"With the exception of Olive," Harriett mumbled. She kissed her sister, tears streaming down her face, and left to claim the body of her beloved papa.

***

The body of Tobias Bailey lay lifeless on the examination table. Harriett approached slowly. Olive reached to grab her hand as she walked past, Harriett shook free. She turned to stare at her mother, who returned a glare at her daughter.

Dr. Paulson drew back the sheet covering the body.

Tenderly touching her father's shoulder, Harriett sobbed, "Oh, Papa. What were you doing climbing on a ladder? Why? How can you be gone?"

Paulson pulled over a chair for Harriett to sit beside the body. She continued as if alone with her beloved father.

"Papa, you can't leave me now. I need you. How can I possibly live without you and Eddy? The only men I ever loved, both gone!" Harriett, on the verge of panic, cried ardently.

Olive's grunt was ignored.

Harriett kissed her father's cheek, lips lingering on the cold skin. She pulled a cotton hanky from her purse and wiped the tears from her face. "Goodbye, beloved Papa. Your Janie loves you very much!"

Chapter 26

Torrents of rain poured from the sky the day of the funeral. A service of Christian burial was held at St. Martins; Abigail, Harriet, and Tobias' church. Pastor Klinghoffer spoke of Tobias' accolades. His love for nature. His knowledge of native plant and animal life. How he never failed to provide for his family during the Depression. How he loved his children. And how later in life, he found his Savior. Tobias was relieved of earthly strife. "We celebrate that he now enjoys the splendor of Heaven." Despite her faith, Harriett did not celebrate his passing.

The more intrepid mourners trudged to the grave site. The local veterans bestowed a full Military Honors grave side ceremony on their fallen comrade, including a twenty-one-gun salute and coronet "Taps."

Holding hands, the Bailey sisters flinched with each pull of the trigger. The beautiful, moving, regard for a World War I veteran left the Bailey friends and family emotionally drained.

Harriett catered a funeral luncheon at one of the local veteran's clubs. She kept the menu simple, which consisted of fried chicken, potato salad, homemade baked beans, and chocolate cake, in honor of her simple father.

The Keplers, Mr. Roland, several work associates, including Miss White, the entire Bailey brood, Campbellsville merchants, local veterans, and a host of friends attended, offering sympathy and condolences.

The circulating undertone was, "Why was Tabs on a roof-height ladder in the first place?'

Tired of hearing the question whispered, Harriett probed her mother.

"Mother, what was Papa doing on a ladder?" demanded Harriett. "We all want to know. The man is—was—in his sixties. He has no business climbing ladders."

Olive glowered at her distraught daughter. "He is *my* husband! He should be helping me, not you," she jeered at Harriett. "He was cleaning out the rain gutters."

"On a three-story house!" burst Harriett.

"Your husband abandoned you," continued Olive. "You do not have the right to take my husband away to do all of your work. I have work that needs to be done too! My husband never abandoned me!" screamed Olive.

"Oh my god! This happened all because you are a selfish, jealous, wicked bitch? Papa spent time with me because he couldn't stand being around you." Harriett was now hysterical, eyes flashing unfathomable hatred.

"Yes, you are correct—I do not know the whereabouts of my husband. He may have abandoned me, he may be a prisoner of war, he may be dead. I do not know. But I do know that you killed my father to spite me! It is obvious to everyone that you never cared for him. He was an honorable man who married a loose pregnant hussy. He maintained your dignity, and in thanks, you tortured him."

"I am done with you. Do you hear me? I never want to see you again," bawled a frenzied Harriett. "I shall never speak to you again. You are dead to me!"

The stunned crowd hushed; most wandered away from the mother-daughter catfight.

Furious at her public exposure, Olive decided her future was more important than her past. She was physically concerned for her well-being. Assuming Harriett, possessing the money, would take care of her in her old age, she now worried.

"Now, Harriett, you don't mean that," Olive attempted placation. "I'm your mother, after all. Doesn't that count for something?"

"The only time you were my mother was either when it suited you or when you received personal gain. Your game is over. You lose! You shall die an old woman—alone."

Non-family members began a hastened departure, too embarrassed to witness the interfamily strife. Within thirty minutes, the only grievers left were the Baileys and the Keplers.

Recent prognostications realized, Harriet was surrounded by both families trying their best to comfort her loss of Tabs and the unknown whereabouts of Eddy. Olive sat alone, gagging on a piece of chicken and potato salad.

Harriett flashed her a vile look. "I hope you choke." At that moment, Harriett erased every thought and memory of her mother. In Harriett's mind, Olive Bailey never existed.

***

Crying in inconsolable grief over her father, that night, she decided to try Eddy one last time.

Eddy,

Words cannot explain the pain and agony I endure. I am beyond despair. Today I buried my beloved Papa. I shall spare you details of his death; your entire family was witness to despicable ugliness.

I need to tell you, I am at wits end. The bottom line for us is this; either you are in my life or you are out of my life? If you are gone, I need to know now so that I may purge myself of the pain of losing both men I adore. I cannot do this twice. It is now or never. If you intend to come back to me, tell me now.

Otherwise, I shall assume you are no longer part of my life and I shall look for happiness elsewhere.

Giving you the benefit of the doubt; our new address is 400 Vista Drive, Campbellsville, Pa. Write NOW if you wish to save our marriage.

I have always loved you, enough to give you up.

Harriett

After a fitful night, eluding sleep, Harriett showered, dressed, and drove to the office, stopping to post the letter. If Eddy was still in Italy, she may have a response within four weeks. However, if he was in Korea, it may take six weeks or more. She must hold strong for another two months, and then let go.

***

Without the companionship of papa, Harriett lost interest in working on the house. She immersed herself into her work. She often worked ten hours at the office and another four at home, developing fierce leadership skills.

Refusing to allow the property to decay, she hired a local boy to maintain. However, she contributed nothing to enhance. Harriett even stopped producing delicious baked goods, much to her families' dismay.

Alice tried to offer distraction by visiting with the children. Harriett loved their company but remained dejected.

On such a visit in early August, 1953, Alice and Harriett enjoyed a glass of ice tea on the back patio. A large back porch wrapped the right side of the house and then emptied via a set of wide stairs to a flagstone patio in the back of the house. Planted pots dotted the space for a splash of seasonal color. The grounds of the Songer house were designed for executive entertaining. Harriett hoped that, someday, she and Eddy would experience such entertaining.

The children played while the sisters chatted as Harriett opened her mail. Harriett looked up from the mail, face ghostly white.

"Harriett? What's the matter?" Alice grabbed the letter from her sister. Harriett offered no resistance.

"Girls! Be quiet!" Alice shouted at her children. "Get Aunt Harriett a pillow and a glass of water," she commanded as she read.

Dear Harriett,

I am not sure where to begin, so let me just say that I am coming home. I ran into some trouble in Trieste and spent some time in the stockade. Then they sent me to Korea. I am fine, alive, and I am to be discharged.

Can you pick me up at Fort Indian Town Gap on September 10th? Thanks. I will look for you there.

Eddy

The succinct note slipped out of Alice's hand. She looked stunned at her sister.

"Are you going to get him?" she asked.

Harriett exhaled a long sigh. For three years she awaited this letter, anticipating feelings of euphoria. Neither euphoric nor excited, Harriett sat dumbfounded. Harriett read and reread the letter. Happy that he was alive but confused that he offered minimal information. She was most wounded by no mention of "love."

"No excuse, no explanation, no apology. Where was he? Why the communication boycott?" Harriett was truly astonished.

She shook her head, "No. I do not think I shall get him. Until he decides to elaborate on his disappearance the past three years, I shall not be eager to forgive."

"No. I'm not driving to Harrisburg. I'll ask Earl to go in my place."

The next day she went to the bank to transfer half of the money in their joint account into her private account.

Chapter 27

THE BUS PULLED INTO THE designated meeting place. Anxious families were waiting to be rejoined with their loved ones. One by one, the GIs disembarked, running to embrace either mother, girlfriend, or wife. As Eddy hit the pavement, he began the search for his car. Not seeing it, he switched to searching for Harriett. Still no luck, he walked over to a bench and dumped his duffel.

Serves you right. You are a real asshole, he thought. Just then, he heard a male voice calling.

"Kepler, you son-of-a-bitch brother. Over here. Ready to get into some civvies?" yelled Earl. He looked at his brother who was already in civilian clothing. "Didn't take you long to transition out!"

Eddy ran to his brother, boxing his ears and shoulders in place of a hug.

"Where's Harriett?"

"God, you really are an ass. You ignore her for three years and you expect her to be here waiting with open arms? You'll be lucky if she lets you into her house."

"What do you mean 'her house?'"

"I thought you'd grow up in the army, but I was wrong. Did you contribute any money to buy the place?"

"Well, a little. Not much."

"Yeah, right. My point–her house!"

"But she's my wife!"

"Really? And how many other wives do you have?"

"Just one. Is it that bad?"

"Hopeless bastard. You deserve whatever she dishes out," finished Earl. "She is a real peach of a woman. Far too good for a prick like you. Get in the car. You disgust me!"

Earl turned to Eddy and gave him a big bear hug. "Good to see you, little brother! Even if you are a jerk!"

The radio played top forty hits, but the brothers remained silent the first half of the ride home. Eddy struggled with his decision on how much of his shenanigans to disclose to Harriett. He wrote three letters in July; first to Harriett, second to Wally Stuart, and third to John Williams, his Trieste supply sarge, giving them his new address; assuming Harriett took him back. He wanted to maintain old contacts for the sake of S/K Acq.

From the sounds of her letters, she was doing very well financially. Harriett certainly did not need Eddy as a provider. She had every right to turn him away.

What choice did she have, you never provided anything to her, thought Eddy.

Eddy broke the quiet. "Earl, please turn down the radio. We need to talk."

"Damn right, we do! What the hell were you thinking not writing to Harriett and Mom? They were both worried sick over your sorry ass!"

"I really screwed up."

"Care to share? We know from the brief communication to Harriett that you spent some time behind bars. The whole time? What the hell did you do?"

"Well, I was AWOL," Eddy replied sheepishly, afraid of Earl's response. Eddy was more afraid of disappointing Earl than of disappointing Harriett.

"You stupid brat. Let me guess? Over a girl?"

"Yes, and my son."

"Christ, man! You got some local whore pregnant! You have a bastard son?"

At that, Eddy went ballistic. "She is not a whore. My son is not a bastard. I gave them both my name. Oh God, I love her with all my heart and soul. She makes me happy, she makes me whole. When they arrested me, I died a thousand times over."

"I couldn't find them. I sent my buddies out looking for them. I searched two years. They just disappeared," sobbed Eddy, recognizably distraught. "I spent last month seeking them. I was discharged in April. For a month, I looked all over northern Italy, southern Austria, and western Yugoslavia without any luck. I still have people looking for them. I'll search until my dying day!"

Earl pulled off the road and looked at his brother.

"Okay, kiddo, let's go to that diner and have a cup of coffee. You can tell me the whole story."

Chapter 28

HARRIETT WINCED AT THE KNOCK on the door. Several weeks was insufficient time to prepare herself for meeting her estranged husband. How well did she really know this man? Obviously not well enough. They dated over the summer, were married for four weeks, and then separated without communication for three years. He was a total stranger that stole her heart.

She opened the double door to see a beautiful Adonis holding a bouquet of flowers. He looked tentatively at her, and then he spoke.

"Hello, Harriett darling. These are for you. Any chance you can welcome your prodigal husband back into the fold?" Then he smiled the infamous Eddy Kepler smile.

She stared in disbelief. *That was it? Some cheap flowers and a cheesy smile and he expects all to be forgiven?*

"Why, it's really you. My missing husband," she answered sarcastically. "I think it would be better for everyone involved if you stay with your parents. We need time to reacquaint ourselves. And I need to hear your story before I am willing to let you back into my life. It will take more than your smile to mend my heart."

Eddy leaned in to kiss her. Harriett recoiled and then resumed speaking, sternly.

"Besides, your mother is heartsick and misses you terribly. You should spend some time with her. Perhaps, perhaps not, if we start dating again, we may be able to rekindle what we had before you left for the army."

"I'm sorry you feel that way," Eddy answered with caution. "But if that's what you want, okay. Just give me my car and I'll be off. Would you like to have dinner tomorrow night?"

"No, on both accounts. I have class tomorrow night. As I wrote in my many letters, I am finishing my BS and shall graduate in December. I traded your juvenile car for a more respectable vehicle. It is registered in my name only. I'm afraid you are without a ride." She added, "Dear," with a sneer.

"You what? Spiteful bi—"

"Be careful. I have already seen an attorney. Trust when I say I have ample grounds for a divorce based on desertion." Regaining her confidence and composure. "I'll drive you home. You may call me at 555-4789 if you care to talk."

Reception by the Keplers' was more welcoming than by Harriett. Abigail rushed to her son, threw her arms around his neck, she kissed his forehead. Then she backed away and slapped him smartly across the face.

"That's for making Harriett and me worry so much!"

Harriett smiled at her mother-in-law. She deeply loved Abigail and the rest of the Kepler crew. However, she wasn't sure she loved the youngest son, her husband.

"Are you children staying for dinner?" Abigail asked, tears of joy running down her face.

"Yes, I'll stay."

It was Harriett who answered, "However, Eddy shall be staying indefinitely. I need to clear my head. Eddy and I need to reacquaint ourselves before he moves into our house. I packed a small bag of his things. Are you okay with this, mother?"

Abigail nodded her head approvingly. "Of course, darling. You two barely know each other. His silence is unforgivable, except for a mother's love. As a wife, it takes longer to accept and forgive transgressions. That I know." She flashed a look at both son and husband. "I'll pray for you, precious Harriett." Then she slapped Eddy across the face again.

Harriett and Abigail embraced. Eddy recognized that he was outnumbered, with an uphill climb in front of him.

***

Eddy waited three days before calling Harriett. He enjoyed the time spent with his mother. She spoiled and babied him. She made his favorite meals, washed and ironed his clothes, and caught him up on all the local gossip. To Eddy's surprise, Abigail somehow knew the whereabouts and status of most of his old girlfriends. Some were happily married, some unhappily married, some not married with children, but all were anxious to hear of the return of Eddy Kepler.

Eddy knew that if Harriett took him back, there would be no doting on her part. The couple agree to meet for a late dinner that Thursday. Required to work late to prepare her staff for inventory, Harriett was not available until after eight.

Eddy took advantage of the wait to find the boy who bought his car, make an offer he couldn't refuse, and buy back his Ford; never thinking about the effect this may have on Harriett. Eddy then borrowed Earl's car for the date. His pride prohibited him from neither showing the recovered Ford to Harriett nor allowing her to drive her Buick.

The restaurant was quiet on a Thursday evening, allowing the couple the luxury to speak to each other in hushed tones.

Harriett started, "Do you intend to tell me what went on the past three years? I was terribly worried. Why were you so cruel in not writing? Both my attorney and I are curious."

Eddy, intending to tell the truth; at least most of the truth, lost his nerve when he heard the word "attorney." He opted to take advantage of what he did best—charm his way out of trouble.

"I stopped writing you when I was arrested. I was not permitted to get or send mail while behind bars. Then they sent me to Korea."

"Oh my god! You were in Korea? I had no idea." Forgetting to ask the reason for his arrest.

"Yes, I was wounded there in the fighting. It was horrible! Here, look at my leg." Eddy rolled up his pant leg and showed Harriett a nasty looking scar where a bullet entered the front of his calf and exited the back. It left him with a slight limp.

"The bone was shattered. It took many months to recover. As you can expect, army mail is not very efficient. It never followed me to the hospital. Then, when I recovered, as if being wounded wasn't enough, I was sent out on a special secret mission. The mission was so secret that, once again, I could not send or get mail. It wasn't until the fighting was over that I got your last letter."

Harriett looked down at her trembling hands. Did she believe him? She fumbled with the rings on her finger. They meant so much to her; declaration of everlasting love, guarantee of unwavering fidelity. What did these rings mean to Eddy?

Psychologically stunned, she thought of her father. His loss still raw, she ached from loneliness. Tabs' loyalty and devotion left a cavernous void that needed to be filled.

"Tell me the truth. Is this really what happened? You were off fighting secret missions, keeping our country safe, while I was ungratefully chastising you for not writing?"

"Yes, dear." He lied deliberately to his wife. "I thought by your last letter that you were angry. I knew you were angry when Earl came to pick me up."

"Eddy, did you keep your promises to me?" she pried shyly.

Eddy tried to look injured, "Are you really asking this question? Yes, darling, of course. How could I behave otherwise? I made you a promise!"

"Geez, I was off fighting a war, taking bullets to keep you free. There was no time to do anything but try to stay alive." He was now laying it on thick.

She thought of her father's warning of Eddy's character. Unfortunately, the thought vanished as quickly as it formed. Protection from her emotional wall began to crack. A seed of denial took root in her mind. Her love for Eddy was firmly rooted in her psyche. She was rendered defenseless.

After a few minutes, she answered, "Eddy, I'm so sorry." It was Harriett, not Eddy, who was expressing remorse.

Eddy lit a cigarette, flashing his infamous smile at her. "Can you ever forgive me? I brought you something."

He pulled a modest strand of graduated sized pearls from his pocket.

"Here. I hope you like these. I couldn't afford much, but it's the thought that counts."

Harriett took the pearls, tears welling in her eyes. To her surprise, a flash of the infamous Eddy Kepler smile *was* all that was needed to mend her heart.

"Will you put them on? They are beautiful," she said, softening and falling once again, despite her better judgement, hopelessly in love with Eddy Kepler.

Eddy buckled the clasp and gently laid the pearls on Harriett's neck.

"They suit you," he said. Whispering in her ear, "Can I come home and be your husband?"

Harriett shivered. The smell of his aftershave and his nearness rekindled her burning desires; their physical connection fervently recalled.

Three years ago, she devoted herself, heart and soul, to this man. For three years, she longed for his return. Emotionally depleted, she was defenseless against him.

Thinking it would take more than one dinner and a petite strand of pearls, Eddy was shocked when Harriett answered.

"Oh yes, Eddy. I have always loved you. I still love you. I can't tolerate the loneliness. Please come home."

Chapter 29

FRIDAY INDICATED THE END OF the workweek and the beginning of the Kepler's second try at marriage. Eddy moved his freshly laundered clothing into their closet. Harriet was alarmed at the lack of military uniforms and the abundance of civilian clothing. Was Eddy returning home from a war zone or a party zone? The astute CFO instinctively identified the inaccuracy; however, she defensively denounced the discrepancy. Denial filed more unpleasant data into the dark recesses of her mind.

Harriett insisted their reintroduction move slowly. However awkward, she refused him access to her bed, for sleep or otherwise. Eddy was not the least bit pleased. It was three weeks since his last encounter with a woman. He was annoyed at the delay of bedding Harriett. Tempted to seek out an old flame, he decided it too risky with his marriage so unstable.

Harriett sought to introduce Eddy to her new life and her new home. His attentiveness waned. He cared not for bank accounts, stocks and bonds, investments, *art d'objet*, college degrees, or the finances of a small local corporation. His priority was directed to pleasures of the flesh. She timidly refused his advances, except for an occasional passionate kiss.

About five weeks after his return, Harriet shocked him when she asked him to buy a bottle of champagne. Eddy assumed the chore of cooking; both agreed life would be more palatable if Eddy cooked and Harriett baked.

Their modest dinner of macaroni and cheese over, dishes washed, Harriett excused herself. Eddy expected yet another night of his wife working late in her office. On those nights, Eddy usually could be found at one of the Veterans clubs, drinking and cohorting with his old high school friends.

She reappeared wearing the white negligee worn on their wedding night.

"Wow, you look fabulous! Shall I open the champagne?" Eddy asked expectantly.

"That's perfect," Harriett responded.

"Does this mean the iceberg is thawing?" Immediately wishing a different choice of words.

"The tip of the iceberg is thawing. Good behavior will alleviate some of the deep freeze. Speaking of deep freeze, I retrieved the top from our wedding cake from Alice. The pastry, plated, was on display. Do you have any idea the occasion?" she questioned.

Eddy thought for a minute and then went back to October three years prior. "Shit, it's our anniversary!"

"Correct. Our actual third anniversary, although the first one we can celebrate," continued Harriett. "I have a gift for you."

Eddy was clueless to the occasion and clueless for the need of a gift.

She handed him a box wrapped in foil paper tied with a ribbon. Thinking it was a neck tie, due to the shape of the box, Eddy was amazed to find a leather document satchel embossed E. G. K., for Edgar Gregor Kepler. Eddy was named after his distant relative, Gregor Campbell, the town's founder. Inside the satchel, he found five separate but identical documents.

"Are you divorcing me dressed in that?" Eddy asked with actual fear in his voice.

"No, silly! First anniversary is paper. Third is leather. I filled the leather satchel with one hundred shares of General Electric stock, in twenty share lots." She smiled at her cleverness. "These shares are yours. You may do with them as you please. I bought myself one thousand shares," she added as an afterthought, wanting him to know she controlled the money.

Eddy didn't know much about the Dow Jones or stock indices, but he was smart enough to realize that Harriett would make value purchases. He kissed her a note of thanks.

"But I don't have anything for you." Noticeably disappointed with himself, he frowned.

"There is always next year," said Harriett with equal disappointment. "Shall we retire for the evening?"

Harriett grabbed Eddy by the hand and led him to her bedroom.

"It's time that we share this space," she said, quickly forgetting the letdown of his lack of a gift. Then she kissed him with reckless abandon. Ignoring her feelings and memories of the honeymoon was no longer an option. He complied to her unspoken invitation and finally joined her in ecstasy as husband and wife.

Chapter 30

HARRIETT FINISHED COURSE REQUIREMENT FOR her BS and commenced classes in the master's program. Because of her current position as CFO and corporate officer, she was able to apply practical experience and test out several degree requirement courses in finance.

Joined by fifty other students receiving degrees on Friday, December 4, 1953, Harriett proudly wore the honor cords of summa cum laude. Alice and husband, Earl, Abigail and Edgar Sr., Eddy, and Albert attended graduation ceremony. Earl treated the group to dinner afterward. Harriett neither told nor invited Olive to participate. When Albert happened to mention Harriett's success to Olive, she spat on his face.

To the party's delight, Earl chose a steakhouse in Madison, near the college. The aroma of searing meat started the festivities with olfactory stimulation. Bellies growling, the troupe zealously ordered their meals. Earl selected a bottle of cabernet sauvignon with a hefty price tag. Eyebrows went up around the group.

"Let's raise our glasses to toast the first college graduate of both families," said Earl. "To my beautiful, intelligent, talented sister-in-law. Having no idea of the meaning of 'summa cum laude' until she remarkably achieves the honor, I commend you on a job well done and wish you much success in the future! To Harriett!" bragged Earl.

"To Harriett," chimed the group. Followed by, "this wine is fabulous!"

Eddy, perplexed that he should also toast his wife, sat silent: nothing came to mind.

"Ok, my turn," said Abigail after their hunger was sated. "I have something for you Harriett."

"Mother, that's not necessary," Harriett protested, although she was very pleased with the toast and a gift. She worked hard, and it made her happy to know others recognized her efforts.

Handing Harriett a package, Abigail beamed, "Open it, honey."

Harriett opened the package to find a knitted cashmere scarf in her college school colors of red and white.

"Mother, it is beautiful. I shall wear it proudly. You know I am pursuing my PhD, so I am still a student! Besides, it matches my new plaid coat perfectly!" She hugged her mother-in-law. "You are so loving. I am so lucky to have you as a mother."

"Me next," declared Alice as she handed Harriett another wrapped gift.

"I am embarrassed. So much fussing over me!" Blushing as she unwrapped the second gift, she opened a small box to expose a beautiful gold pen engraved with her initials HBK. "I thought you would like to use Bailey as your middle name."

Harriet was in tears. "You are so kind. I am so blessed to have you as my sister."

"Don't think you are finished yet," added Albert, handing Harriett yet another gift.

Albert's present was a silver business card holder, again engraved HBK. Lastly, Earl handed her a large wrapped box.

"But Earl…you have picked up the tab tonight. Surely you did not buy a gift."

"Open it sweetie," Earl requested as Eddy scowled at his brother for using a term of endearment. Harriett lifted the lid and spread open the tissue paper to display a stylish tan, leather attaché.

"Earl. It's breathtaking," she said as she kissed her brother-in-law on the forehead.

"Mrs. Executive should set an example." Earl grinned as he squeezed Harriett's hand.

"Oh, but I do." She giggled as she flung the fox stole always worn around her neck.

Laughing, the group collectively looked at Eddy, thinking him next to present his wife with the recognition of a graduation gift.

Feeling peer pressure and knowing he fell short, Eddy handed Harriett a bunch of mixed flowers. He did not bother to buy red roses or orchids, his money spent on the purchase of his old car. He presented a generic bouquet.

Harriett smiled and graciously accepted the flowers; however, she could not help but be disappointed. She was showered with stunning gifts to celebrate a most special occasion from everyone she loved, except her husband.

***

"Eddy, I know I make plenty of money, but don't you think it's time for you to find a job?" she asked tenderly, a few days after graduation. "I would like to cut back a little so that I can finish my PhD within the next two years."

"I'll look in the New Year. The past three years of war were so traumatic, I just want to enjoy being with you."

Smiling in agreement, she kissed him again. "Very well. Let's enjoy this holiday. I do love Christmas! And I do love you."

Eddy smugly reaffirmed that, although he may not oversee her money, he oversaw her emotions.

Chapter 31

"Today, we should choose our Christmas tree," declared Harriett as she handed Eddy a cup of coffee. A week passed since graduation. Eddy made no amends to his lack of generosity.

"Sure," he said, taking a big gulp. Harriett did not cook, but she made drinkable coffee. "Where do we look?"

"Why, our backyard." She motioned out the kitchen window with her hand. "We own five acres of those woods! There is a beautiful stand of pine trees and plenty of ground pine for weaving garlands. What do you say? Let's do it up properly!"

Eddy complied, wolfed down a biscuit, and donned his hat and coat. Harriett quickly packed a few sandwiches, filled a thermos, and then grabbed a jacket and hat.

The couple spent a relaxed afternoon together walking in the woods. The first time both partners felt comfortable since Eddy's return; Harriett hopefully prayed for improvement in the relationship. Dragging the tree behind them, on the way home, they sang Christmas songs and munched on cookies.

They collapsed, arm in arm, on the Chintz chaise, exhausted from the day's frolicking.

Harriett was honestly happy.

***

"Please hand me those lights," she said over her shoulder. Eddy complied, reaching up with a strand of Christmas bubble lights. "I have mixed feelings about this Christmas."

She climbed down the ladder and hugged Eddy, stretching to gently kiss his mouth.

"Last year, Papa helped me decorate my tree. I miss him so much! I wish he were here to celebrate with us." Eddy returned her kiss as she continued. "Thank God my life is no longer empty now that you have returned."

The couple took respite from tree decorating to sit on their newly purchased living room furniture. The wing chair and floor lamp remained beside the fireplace; however, modern furnishings, of low sleek lines filled the rest of the room. Although the house was Victorian, the new style complimented the architecture, in an eclectic kind of way.

Again, motivated to nest in her own space, Harriet and Eddy took some of Harriett's savings and furnished the remainder of the house. Eddy contributed minimal funds, having spent most of his service pay while in Korea and Italy. The past three months found the couple lovingly attentive to each other, apart from the reintroduction of Eddy's Ford.

"Why did you buy that childish car? Are you so desperate to relive your glory days? I thought we were past this!" Harriett, irritated, found it remarkably immature of Eddy purchasing such a foolish item. Unaware that he spent his entire savings to buy it back, Eddy would otherwise be living in the car.

The Kepler tree was dressed in strands of bubble lights, three dozen Shiny Brite reflecting indented balls, garlands of strung popcorn and cranberries, clove studded oranges, peppermint candy canes, and a wooden copy of the house's front doors. Tabs' handy work of last year, occupied a place of honor, center front of the tree. The crystal star's glowing elegance signified a home of wealth and community status.

Harriett used her sewing skills to construct a beautiful multicolored tree skirt. Two matching stockings hung from the fireplace. Eddy laced together chopped pine boughs and ground pine to frame the double front doors. Paired wreaths; adorned with berries, pine cones, fruit, and nuts, hung from lush red velvet ribbon on each front door.

In five days, all Keplers and Baileys, minus Olive, would descend on the stately meticulously decorated home for 1953 Christmas dinner. To her sibling's amusement, Harriet declared no memory of her mother and, therefore, extended no invitation to join the family. No resistance came from her siblings. They wanted to spend the day in the extravagant house without incident. Olive, again, found herself ostracized by her family.

Alice, June, and two Kepler sister-in laws were providing the meal while Harriett was responsible for cookies, cakes, and pies. Albert and another two Kepler brothers were bringing ribbon candy, fudge, and coconut bonbons. A glorious feast planned to celebrate the return home of Eddy and the Birth of Christ.

Harriett was exploring the attic for stray decorations, searching through the pile of "inherited" items when she squealed in delight.

"Eddy. Eddy. Come here. Look what I just found."

Eddy lazily ascended the three flights of stairs at his wife's request. Harriett met him, grinning ear to ear. Holding up her hand, she produced electric window candles outfitted with blue bulbs; the same exquisite blue that matched the entrance chandelier and that made the Songer Christmas décor so special.

"The house will be resplendent with a blue light in each window," she exclaimed with excitement. "What a wonderful find. Our beautiful home is now restored to its old splendor."

Eddy's climb was rewarded with a tight squeeze and a lingering kiss. The couple grabbed the weighted candoliers and began placing them in each window. They were sturdy and stood easily in the marble window sills. To their amazement, an electrical outlet was strategically placed to the right side of every window in the house. All but three of the bulbs lit.

"Babe, I'll go to the hardware store and get a few more blue bulbs," said Eddy.

"Wonderful, I'll clean up the house."

Eddy really needed an excuse to be alone so that he could mail a letter to Wally and a package to Italy.

Returning home within the hour, Eddy called, "Honey, I'm home. I replaced the bulbs. Let's go outside and look at our work."

Harriett ran outside with just a shawl around her shoulders. She anxiously wanted to share an intimate moment involving their home with Eddy.

The house looked like a giant music box. The blue candles cast light shadows of bluish hues on the red brick. Green boughs surrounded the doors toting duel wreaths. A spotlight shown on the entranceway.

"Oh, Eddy, on Christmas Eve, we'll place luminaria along both sides of the front staircase and on the top of the side terrace walls. It is, and will be, perfect."

That night in bed, Harriett wore her white negligee again. She snuggled into her husband's arm. Her nose nuzzled his neck. "I am completely happy and satisfied," she said as she nibbled his ear. "I'm so glad you are home. I need you terribly."

Eddy returned the kiss but not the sentiment. He deeply missed and worried about Rosa and Joey, especially over the holiday. He wondered how long he could live in deceit.

Chapter 32

"Stop running," Alice shouted at her youngest child. Harriett and the other women sat in the parlor, the men in the office; children were everywhere dressed in their Christmas best. The holiday began at six in the morning, opening presents from Santa, continued with morning church services, and then directly to Harriett's for the feast of the season.

"I can't remember a better Christmas," exclaimed June. "Just perfect. From the food to the decoration—and the company, just perfect."

Harriett looked sadly at the carved ornament of her front door hanging on the tree, "The only thing missing is Papa." She shed a tear, wiped her face with her apron, and turned back to her guests smiling.

"Shall we tackle dessert?"

A collective groan went up from all the stuffed bellies.

"In fifteen minutes?" asked Ester. "The older I get, the less I can eat. I intend to enjoy your treats, but my stomach needs more time."

All chuckled in agreement.

Brightly wrapped gifts piled under the Christmas tree. The corner of the parlor was overrun with Tannenbaum. More than one set of inquisitive eyes stopped to inspect the colored mound. Several of the older children decided to intercede on their own behalf before the adults started napping.

"It's time," they squealed.

Children, equal in number to the adults, permitted each adult to draw the name of one child for the gift exchange. A price limit of five dollars per gift was set. Anticipation was high.

"How shall we begin?" asked Harriett. She was as eager as the children to get on with the evening events.

"Why don't we start with the youngest and work our way to the oldest," suggested Abigail, who sat in a place of honor, right in the middle of the parlor. Even though Olive's grandchildren were not blood relatives of Abigail, they all called her Grandmama. How could they resist? Olive cared for no one but herself. Abigail cared for everyone but herself.

It was decided that each child would take a turn sitting on Grandmama Abigail's lap and then be given their gift by the gift giver. Even the older children loved this arrangement. The process took ninety minutes to complete. When it was over, Abigail, not the least bit tired, looked at Harriett and said, "Let's eat dessert."

Cheers erupted as a mad dash headed in the direction of the dining room.

Lavish desserts and pastries disappeared at record speed. The devouring of the last powdered-sugar treat signaled the end of a memorable, enjoyable family holiday.

The couple kissed their guests goodnight. Unanimous agreement decided every Christmas shall be celebrated like this Christmas.

It was past midnight by the time Eddy and Harriett finally found their pillows. She turned to him in a sweet "good night" kiss but stopped short of touching his lips.

"Don't be stingy," Eddy protested.

"Oh, I'm not." Harriett handed Eddy a gift box saying, "Merry Christmas, darling."

"What's this?"

"It's our first Christmas together. Gift exchange is in order," she decreed. Eddy tore off the paper. To his amazement, writing on the outside of the box was written in German.

"What is this? Why are you patronizing Nazis?" questioned Eddy.

"Silly boy. It's Swiss. Open it," she persuaded.

Inside the box was a Heuer "Auto-Graph" watch.

"It has amazing features—a hand especially for drivers," she pointed out. "And also a feature, for golfing, if you care to learn?" Harriett was pleased with her choice. "It is the latest thing in Swiss watches," she concluded.

Eddy was happy with the extraordinary gift. He leaned over and kissed his wife. "You are such a kind, generous woman. I don't deserve you."

Hesitating, he handed Harriett a gift. She was visually ecstatic to be given a gift by her husband on their first Christmas together. She anticipated this moment thousands of time over the past three years, knowing it would be a special lifelong memory. Giddily, she tore into the paper to reveal a box of drug store brand chocolate-covered cherries.

She thanked and kissed her husband, silently agreeing with his assessment that he did not deserve her love. Then she cried herself to sleep.

Chapter 33

THE GARAGE DOOR WENT UP. Harriett was home. Eddy turned from his cooking. When he heard footsteps on the staircase, he yelled, "Harriett, did you remember to buy the wine?"

Eddy procured a job as a supply manager in January 1954. Three years securely into the job, his day comfortably started at nine in the morning and ended promptly at five; leaving him ample time to prepare the evening meal before Harriett's return home, usually at six-thirty.

The successful executive was concluding her thesis research. She hoped to complete her dissertation within the next four months. She chose to write on *The Financial Effect of Korea's non-war on The U.S. Economy* for her PhD in finance. The subject, currently noteworthy, impressed her professors that a woman chose war as a thesis topic. It also gave her access to recent non-classified military records.

The kitchen table was set for a typical weeknight meal. Eddy removed a tuna casserole from the oven. Not a nightly indulgence, Eddy felt like wine tonight.

Harriett handed the wine to Eddy, who opened and began to pour. "None for me," she said casually.

"I know you don't drink much, but why none?"

She smiled. "Sit down, let's eat. We can talk over dinner."

"Okay, now you have my full attention. What's going on with you?"

Harriett was giggling. "I stopped by Dr. Paulson's office yesterday evening, before class. I have some news."

"Are you sick?" asked Eddy, slightly hopeful, immediately followed by guilt.

"No, no. Not at all. Oh Eddy, I am so excited!" She handed him a package.

It was a book to record life events. Looking questioningly at her he asked impatiently, "Come on, out with it. What's up?"

"Oh Eddy, I am so excited. I am going to have a baby. We are going to start our family! This book is to keep record of my pregnancy and the baby's birth, growth, and milestones."

Harriett ran over to Eddy and jumped onto his lap. Arms encircling his neck, she squeezed and began smothering him with kisses. Eddy tried not to show his shock and disappointment. He worried daily about little Joey. Did he survive being abandoned? Was he five or six? Could another child give him the same pleasure? Was his delight in his son a result of his love for the mother or the child or both?

"That's wonderful," he finally managed a response.

Harriett was so excited that she never noticed his hesitation. She was too involved with discussion of converting the smallest bedroom to a nursery and how she would fit the pregnancy into her work schedule. Potential names for either a boy or a girl. When the baby would be born in relationship to finishing her thesis. Decidedly thrilled, Harriett was planning the next eighteen months. Eddy was dreading them.

***

Pregnancy became Harriett. Her petite form only gained weight in a protruding front belly. From behind, she still looked like a size two, but turn sideways, she looked like she was carrying a whale.

The couple discussed potential names. If it was a boy, Eddy was adamant; Joseph Edgar Kepler. Harriett preferred Edgar Tobias Kepler. For a girl, Eddy stood firmly with Rosa Isabella Kepler; Harriett's choice; Shelby Abigail Kepler. When asked for an explanation of such unusual non-family names, Eddy argued that he liked the sound of the Italian language. No one in the family, except Earl, understood his resolve.

The forth and smallest bedroom was converted into the nursery. Although small, it was the perfect room for a baby. Facing the privacy of the back of the house, a large window remained without curtains to admit natural light in the daytime and starlight for midnight feedings. Eddy spent several weekends scrubbing the woodwork and painting the walls a pale green and yellow.

Harriett found a slightly used crib and highchair which Eddy also meticulously scrubbed and polished. A small chest of drawers; to be used as a changing table and holding bin for clothes, diapers, and other baby supplies; was painted yellow. A rocking chair painted white was placed beside the large window. Abagail knitted a soft green nursing blanket that hung over the back of the chair. The crib blanket was handed down from Alice. It was a beautiful patchwork flower-garden quilt with scalloped edges. Harriett hung a mobile of stuffed zoo animals over the crib. Some animals made noise when squeezed, some animals jingled.

The room was finished with a green and white washable cotton rug, just in case of accidents. The Kepler baby was to be introduced to luxury, beginning day one.

Mr. Roland hoped that Harriett would continue to work after the baby's birth. To entice her, a lucrative maternity leave was established for the company's first female executive. She would be given full pay for the first six weeks' leave. If she wished to take additional leave, she may do so at half pay for up to another six weeks. The agreement hinged on her promise to return to her former executive position as CFO, after a maximum leave of three months. This was a very generous benefit for a female employee of the 1950s. However, few women held male executive roles. The benefit was modest for a male executive of the 1950s. Harriett approved by signing the contract to return to work.

With only three weeks before her scheduled delivery date, Harriett frantically worked to finish her thesis before the baby was born. One day, at the military library, while hoping to complete the last bit of her research, Harriett decided to see if she could find any record of her husband.

Taking a side journey, she looked at army rosters for both locations of Trieste and Korea, 1950 to 1953. Trieste was easier to research due to limited troop occupation. After about thirty minutes searching, she found what she was looking for.

Kepler, Edgar Gregor. Campbellsville, PA
Rank: Corporal
Assignment: supply department. Trieste, Italy
Immediate supervisor: Sargeant John Williams.
    Toledo Ohio
Misconduct: AWOL. Served three weeks solitary
    confinement. Followed by six weeks regular
    confinement.
Reinstatement: At Sgt. Williams recommenda-
    tion, reinstated with demotion to rank of
    private.
Reassigned: Soul, South Korea.
Rank: Private
Active duty injury: Hospitalized for gun shot
    through right calf. Broken bone. Hill 266.
Transferred to MASH 8076 for recovery.
Reassigned: MASH 8076: supply department.
Immediate supervisor: Corporal Anthony
    Zarnecky
Camp Commander: Colonel Charles Bowers
Discharge: Honorable: April 01, 1953

Harriett was all too familiar with discrepancies in Eddy's stories. However, this information was not a discrepancy, it was an absolute contradiction. Charged with going AWOL!

"Oh my god!" Harriett slumped into a chair. "Is it all a lie?" She copied the information exactly as it was recorded from the military records. Eddy needed to do some explaining.

Chapter 34

"IT DOESN'T MAKE ANY SENSE. Don't lie to me! I am not an idiot," Harriett screamed at her husband. "Our whole life is a lie. Why? Why? I don't understand any of this!" Harriett's face was the color of a ripe tomato.

"Please calm down, Harriett. Your closeness to delivery makes you extra sensitive." Eddy tried to quiet her.

"You were AWOL! Whatever possessed you to act so stupidly?"

"I can explain," said Eddy, trying to interrupt her ranting.

"Secret missions in Korea! I actually wept over the danger. I anguished thinking of the horrors you must have experienced. Yet you worked in a hospital unit as a supply person. And don't tell me that those hospitals couldn't get mail. You ignored me. You prick! I suffered for two years while you frolicked as 'playboy soldier.' While you outright ignored me! I saw the clothes you brought home from the army. Looked like clothes for socializing to me," she yelled at the top of her lungs.

Before the argument continued, Harriett let out a bloodcurdling squeal. She suddenly doubled over in pain. Clutching her bulging belly, she let out another scream. Then she looked horrified at the wet floor beneath her chair.

"Oh my god. The baby is coming. Get me to the hospital, you bastard."

Eddy never heard Harriett swear. He grabbed her overnight bag, her car keys, and helped her into the Buick. He sped into the night to the music of intermittent moans and shrieks.

***

"Mrs. Kepler. Mrs. Kepler. You have a beautiful baby girl. Would you care to hold her?"

Harriett, still dozing from the anesthesia, managed to open her eyes. She looked up to see a nurse holding a swaddled baby.

"Is that my baby?" she asked. "Is it healthy? It's three weeks early. I didn't hurt it, did I?"

"Why, my dear, you may stop calling the baby 'it.' Use 'she' instead," said the nurse.

Harriett reach for the bundle and began unwrapping it. She inspected toes, fingers, ears, nose, mouth, tummy, head, and bum. Finally, the tiny package objected to the probe with a loud continuous squawk.

The nurse took the baby away from Harriett. "She's perfect in every way. She is totally complete, and with a good set of lungs."

Harriett smiled and drifted back into her dream, "Shelby Abigail, my baby girl."

Eddy, Abigail, Earl, Alice, and June were all anxiously waiting the outcome of the delivery. Terrified the prematurity might suffer some deformity, Eddy paced up and down the hall, knowing he was the reason for early labor.

"Why am I such a coward? Why didn't I tell her? At least some of it," he asked Earl as they stood at the opposite end of the hall waiting.

"You mean you told her nothing?" asked Earl.

"Big fat *zero*. I lied my way into her life from the very beginning. Then I lied my way back into her life. I'm damned to hell."

"Can't say damnation isn't deserved," was Earl's response.

"Thanks for nothing."

"Little brother. You better be careful and stop the self-pity. This mess is totally of your own making. Harriett is a fabulous woman. Smart, sweet, loving, and loyal. I don't think anyone has ever described you using those words, have they? You are a selfish, ego-centric, immature, scoundrel. Harriett deserves so much more than your sorry ass." Earl looked repulsed at his brother.

"Sounds like you have fallen in love with my wife," said Eddy accusingly.

At that, Earl curled his hand into a fist and hit Eddy squarely with a strong upper cut. Eddy stumbled backward but remained upright.

"I have always had a special place in my heart for you, little brother," Earl sputtered. "That place is gone. I respect your wife too much to even think of such a betrayal of your marriage. Too bad you don't have the same respect for her."

Earl managed another hard slap across Eddy's face and then returned to family. He leaned down and kissed Abigail, Alice, and June on the forehead. "I'll be back to see mother and child after the 'father' has gone home. Alice, do you mind taking my mother home?"

"Not at all, Earl. I'll be happy to see her home," said Alice, wondering what just happened at the end of the hall.

Before Earl could leave, the nurse appeared in the viewing window, proudly displaying the youngest Kepler.

The baby's face was round and pink, with father's features: blue eyes and blonde hair. Clearly, this child was the offspring of Eddy Kepler. The family would learn later that little Shelby inherited her mother's intelligence and ambition.

All spectators "oohed and awed" over the infant wrapped in pink.

"She's so tiny," said Earl, as he made goofy faces at the window.

Looking at her wristband, Alice said, "Not so tiny for three weeks premature. Look, she is seven pounds, nine ounces, and twenty-one inches long. She'll be big like her daddy."

"My boys were that size," added Abigail, not knowing that she was the baby's namesake. "Pretty big baby for a woman Harriett's small size."

As the group gazed through the window, Eddy stared at his daughter, tears pouring down his face. His heart filled with love and pride.

Chapter 35

ANXIOUS TO SEE BOTH WIFE and daughter, he paced the halls, carrying a wrapped box for Harriett and a stuffed bunny for his daughter. Harriett refused to see Eddy the night of the birth. He impatiently waited again.

Harriett was feeding Shelby when Eddy arrived. Her private room was already filled with flowers. Dugan & Co., Tom Roland, Earl, and joint siblings sent arrangements that filled the room with the aroma of spring.

"Mr. Kepler, you may now visit your wife," announced the nurse. Hearing an invitation, Eddy turned and walked hesitantly toward Harriett's room. He doubted she would permit entrance, but he hoped she would at least let him hold the baby.

He poked his head slowly into the room. He waited to be greeted by a flying missile before crossing the threshold. Eddy whispered, "Harriett darling, how are you feeling?"

Harriett lay cuddling her baby, both mother and child satiated after the feeding. She looked up at her visitor. "Hello," she said without emotion.

"May I come in?" Eddy knew he treaded on thin ice. Harriett was entitled to banish him from her life. The thought of losing yet another child sent Eddy into a panic attack.

"Oh, Harriett, I'm so sorry. Please forgive me. You are right. I ignored your letters. I am selfish, greedy, and immature. I don't deserve you. Please!" was his plea.

"Hush. Shelby is sleeping."

"You named her already?"

"Yes, this is my little girl! Her name is Shelby Abigail"—she hesitated—"Kepler"

"Will her father live with her?" he ventured.

"That depends. Does her father have more secrets?"

"No, he does not. I took a direct hit during the fighting. As you saw, my leg was pretty badly shot up. I did stay in the hospital recovery for a long time. But then they discovered my knack for 'finding' things, so I was transferred permanently to the MASH unit. I got every one of your letters. I still have them. I never answered because"—Eddy paused—"I just wasn't sure I wanted to be married."

Harriett winced at his last statement.

"You weren't sure you wanted to be married?" She clung tighter to her daughter and rolled onto her side, away from Eddy.

Eddy began to speak, but Harriett held her hand up for silence.

"Leave us alone. I am too tired to talk about this right now."

"But Harriett, please let me hold my daughter! I need to touch her, count her fingers and toes. She is so beautiful."

"Of course you think she is beautiful! She's the spitting image of you. A constant reminder to me of my folly in life!"

Now Eddy was crying. "Harriett! Please! Just let me hold her," he whimpered.

Shocked at Eddy's emotional reaction, Harriett reluctantly rolled over and handed Eddy the baby. Shelby started to cry as she was passed to strange arms.

"Shh. Shh. Little Shelby. I am your daddy, and I promise to protect you the rest of my life!" It was a solemn, heartfelt, sincere promise. Shelby quieted immediately.

The nurse entered the room. "Time for her bath. May I take her, Mr. Kepler?"

Unwillingly, fearing he may never hold her again, Eddy delayed giving the nurse the baby.

"Please, Mr. Kepler. I really must bathe her now," insisted the nurse.

Eddy relinquished his possession.

"Harriett, this is for you." Handing her the box, "And this is for Shelby." Tossing the bunny on the bed.

Harriett picked up the bunny, squeezed it, and smiled. "It's so soft. The eyes are sewn on with thread. Well done, Eddy. There is nothing for the baby to accidently swallow. Who helped you choose this?"

"I picked it out myself," replied Eddy, hiding the fact that he knew what could choke an infant. "Open your gift."

Harriett turned her head. She was in no mood to be bought with some trinket. Eddy had a terrible track record of choosing gifts. She had a terrible track record of being disappointed by his thoughtlessness; however, she mollified him. Ripping off the paper, she uncovered a bottle of White Shoulders Perfume. Her favorite scent. *How did Eddy know to buy this?* she thought.

"Thank you. My favorite. But how do you know?" she asked.

"I checked with Alice yesterday."

"Always full of surprises, aren't you? I prefer knowing things in advance. Makes life easier."

"But knowing can be boring, right?" he questioned and flashed the infamous Eddy Kepler smile.

Damned that smile. And damned my weakness when it comes to this man. I need him. I'll never be able to shake him. It's as if the devil himself owns my soul. And there's the small matter of Shelby needing a father, she thought.

"We shall be in the hospital another three or four days. If I give you my list, can you make arrangements for our return home?" she asked. "The diaper service is waiting for a call to begin delivery, and—" Harriett went on and on with her plans and preparations, the consummate manager.

Eddy listened with a smile. Upon leaving the hospital, Eddy stopped at the tobacco shop and bought a big box of cigars. Each cigar was wrapped in pink paper that read "It's a Girl." His next stops were two of his usual veterans' haunts. He passed out cigars and drank to the many toasts made to his daughter.

"May she be beautiful," "May she marry rich," "May she take care of her father in his old age." Not one of the predominantly male crowd mentioned "intelligence," "success," or "ambition."

Eddy stumbled into the beautiful red brick house and fell into the parlor wing chair.

You lucky son-of-a-bitch! You did it again, he thought as he drifted into a drunken slumber.

By some act of divine grace, an always blundering Eddy remained part of Harriett's world!

Chapter 36

EARL, THE GODFATHER, MADE THE trip to Chicago himself to purchase the beautiful pure white Dupioni silk gown. It was fifty inches long, twice Shelby's length, and boasting rows of stitched pin tucks, hand-embroidered angels, and yards of inserted French lace. An antique bonnet, crocheted by Abigail's grandmother, and embroidered booties made of matching white silk completed her royal attire. A Swiss cotton slip, worn under the gown, was embroidered "Shelby Abigail Kepler October 15, 1958," an heirloom for Harriett to use for other children and then pass on to her grandchildren.

"I baptize you, Shelby Abigail Kepler, in the name of the Father,"—first splash of water hit the baby's head—"and of the Son,"—second splash of water—"and of the Holy Ghost. Amen,"—third splash of water—said Pastor Klinghoffer of St. Martin's Lutheran Church.

Alice held her goddaughter who behaved like a perfect angel, that is, until the third splash of water. Shelby objected to the rain showers and let the entire church know her displeasure. Eddy reached for the baby, taking her from Alice.

"There, there, little one," he said softly, his big hands encompassing the tiny form. "Daddy is here. You are safe."

Shelby hushed immediately. Harriett rolled her eyes in disbelief. "Did this man have the same effect on every living female?"

The Keplers baptized Shelby at age four weeks. Until then, mother and child remained in the Kepler house, primarily the nursery, bonding. Harriett was at peace; she glowed in motherhood. Holding and feeding her baby gave her unimaginable pleasures. The pain of childbirth long forgotten, Harriett bathed in spiritual and physical harmony.

Concluding the worship service, Pastor Klinghoffer invited the congregation to celebrate God's love through the gift of the child at the Kepler home.

Harriett served a formal afternoon tea with finger sandwiches, scones, clotted cream, fresh homemade jams, and various pastries. The dining room table was clothed in a hand-crocheted antique dating back to the glory days of her Great-great-grandmother Westchester. Not owning a sterling tea service, she cleverly used various porcelain tea pots with mismatched sets of china cups and saucers found at local thrift and antique shops. Her center piece included remnants of garden greenery and potted mums stacked on cloth-covered boxes. Hydrangeas in shades of blue, white, green, with pure white silk ribbons and bows balanced the composition.

Many of their guests were not in the house since Mr. Songer's death. The house and grounds sparkled. They marveled at the charming mixture of old and new. The home displayed an elegant but inviting aura. One that said, "I am a very special place" but "please come in and make yourself comfortable."

The wide double doors regally opened to frame Eddy, across the room, proudly holding Shelby on display. Her eight pounds was immeasurable for a sustained lift. Guest came and went, leaving cards and small packages for their newest neighbor.

Halfway through the day, Ester, her husband, children, grandchildren, and Olive appeared. Seeing Eddy, they made their way across the room to greet Shelby. Googling over the baby, Olive suddenly said, "Can I hold her?"

Not knowing about the rift between Harriett and Olive, Eddy handed Olive her granddaughter. Harriett spotted the exchange and bounded across the room.

"Who is this woman holding my baby?" she demanded.

Ester and Eddy looked at Harriett in puzzlement. Ester braved the answer, "This is our mother, Shelby's grandmother."

"I do not know this woman. She is not my mother. Give me back my baby immediately and kindly exit my house!" ordered Harriett.

Looking at Eddy, Harriett continued, "Eddy, take back our baby. I do not want this stranger touching her!"

Confused and hurt, Olive handed Shelby back to her father.

"*Now* get out! Whoever you are—you are not welcome in my house!"

Olive snorted, turned on her heel, and muttered profanity as she left alone.

"Ester, why would you bring a stranger to this event?" Harriett was calmer once the offender removed herself.

"Harriett dear, I think you need to rest. Alice, June, and I will clean up after your guests are gone," suggested Ester.

"Harriett," added Eddy, "I have Shelby, and I shall keep her safe. Please go up and take a nap. You must be exhausted."

Eddy looked at Earl, who gently aided his sister-in-law. Harriett thanked her guests, excused herself, and with Earl's help, climbed the stairs. She immediately fell asleep on her bed.

Below, her siblings murmured hushed concern over their sister's non-recollection of their mother. Alice relayed to Eddy the terrible confrontation during Tobias' funeral luncheon. They concluded that Harriett truly erased Olive from her memory; filed her someplace deep and non-retrievable in her brain.

Taking Shelby so that Eddy could tend to his wife, Earl lovingly enjoyed a tender moment with his sleeping goddaughter. He softly sang a lullaby, concluding with, "Uncle Earl will always be your safe haven, should you or Mommy ever need one." Bewildered by his own thought, recognizing that Eddy could be a continued source of pain, Earl wanted to protect both Shelby and Harriett.

When most guests were gone, the sisters began gathering stray cups and plates. Pastor Klinghoffer was one of the last to depart. Before leaving, the pastor approached Eddy, who was, once again, snuggling Shelby in the crook of his arm.

"Son, I have a request of you. Your wife and mother are—and your father-in-law was—loyal members of my congregation. However, your wife has not joined the church. She is waiting to do so as a family. Now that you have a child, don't you think it's time to settle down and plant some Christian roots?"

If Eddy was intrigued by what he considered a brazen request, he was astonished when he heard himself answer, "Yes, Pastor. I agree.

That is a great idea. Please begin the paperwork. I'll tell Harriett when she is rejuvenated," he said with contriteness.

"Will you be attending services next Sunday?"

"Of course. All three of us will be there. Thank you for inviting me to join." Eddy's full intention was to honor Harriett with the truth, moving-forward truth. There was past truth that must remain hidden.

With that, Eddy, Harriett, and Shelby Kepler became members of a broader family—a Christian community. And with that, Eddy began his daily morning vigil of prayer. He prayed for forgiveness of abandonment, for forgiveness of betrayal, for forgiveness of deceit, and for forgiveness of his transgressions; that his soul may not rot in hell for eternity.

Chapter 37

KEPLER FAMILY LIFE STABILIZED. EDDY completely devoted himself to Shelby and, surprisingly, supported Harriett.

Harriett published her thesis, completing her PhD, once again wearing the cord of summa cum laude at graduation ceremony. Refusing to be fussed over, Harriett chose a quiet evening of coffee and pastries at home.

"No gifts!" she protested, when Earl suggested the purchase of a cashmere coat. "You are too generous with us. I know Eddy is your favorite, but enough is enough. Please save your money and enjoy a simple celebration with us," she requested. "If you really want to honor me, read my thesis."

"Good grief!" exclaimed Earl. "I wouldn't understand a word."

"After reading it, I'm amazed that I understand it," confessed Harriett. "My advisor was shocked that I chose to analyze the financial effect of war. Fighting is usually a male subject, but then again, so is CFO." Proud of her work, she bragged just a bit.

A small assembly of family gathered in the parlor. Harriett made her famous sticky cinnamon buns. The adults drank coffee and ate the gooey treat. Shelby, at seven months, was indicating the need to walk but not the coordination to do so.

"It won't be long until she is off and running," said Eddy proudly of his daughter. "She is so determined. Just like someone else I know."

Looking at his wife, he smiled. He handed her a wrapped gift. "I hope this makes amends for my insensitivity. I owe you for our first anniversary, your first college graduation, and our first Christmas," he said guiltily.

"Eddy, I thought I said no gifts."

"You did, but this is long overdue. I neglected you for too long," he insisted. "Open it please." Since Shelby's birth, Eddy truly motivated himself to be more attentive to Harriett.

Inside the box, she found a beautiful gold Rolex watch with diamonds on the face to indicate the hours.

"My god. This is beautiful!" Harriett gasped, truly stunned. "You know I always wear a watch."

"Yes, I do know that," chortled Eddy.

"This'll be beautiful on my wrist," said Harriett, as she passed the box for her family to inspect.

Kissing her husband, she never felt closer. He was coming around. Although the past disappointments hurt deeply, this was an effort to atone.

Appreciative of Eddy's effort, in bed that night, Harriett asked, "Eddy, I was thinking, we both used to be active athletes, but work, school, babies"—she smiled—"have kept us rather stationary. Why don't we join the Madison Country Club and learn to play golf? They have a swimming pool. I assume you can swim with your injury?"

"Really, are you sure we can afford it?" asked Eddy, more excited than he expected to be.

"Yes, I do think we can afford it, if we don't replace our home as our primary entertaining site. We both need more exercise. I think it's a grand idea!" Harriett concluded.

Eddy concurred. "You are a well-educated, extremely successful executive, I am a flourishing supply manager—we can mingle with the 'hoity toity' heads held high!"

That night, the couple slept wrapped in each other's bodies, thoughts, and spirits; Harriett content.

The next day, she applied for a full family membership to the Madison Country Club.

Chapter 38

THE GARAGE DOOR OPENED, AND Harriett drove in. Eddy's car occupied the back space since Harriett was usually first out and last in.

"Did you remember to pick up a bottle of red?" he yelled to his wife, as she climbed the stairs from the basement.

Eddy placed a record on the hi-fi. The couple enjoyed jazz, Sinatra, Cole, Gillespie, and Count Basie, to name a few. Tonight's choice was Mel Torme', the Velvet Fog. Five-year-old Shelby was home from kindergarten, fed, bathed, and watching television in the parlor. A good eater, Shelby usually ate with her parents. Tonight, Eddy wanted time alone with Harriett.

Although the Keplers were one of the few families in town able to afford multiple television sets, Harriett refused their placement in the bedrooms or the office. She insisted bedroom was for sleep; office was to work or read.

The dining room table was set, complete with tablecloth, cloth napkins, candles, and wine glasses; special for a weeknight. *Veal Osso Buco*, a dish Eddy discovered while in Italy, smelled heavenly. Harriett walked into the kitchen, handed Eddy the wine, and kissed his cheek.

"We're eating in the dining room tonight? What's the occasion?" she asked. "By the way, wonderful aroma. I'll be right back, I want to say hello and kiss Shelby."

Although reformed, Eddy was never without an agenda.

"Bug's fed," he shouted after her. "No special reason, just wanted alone time."

"Come on, Eddy, you're like a little boy. Geez, one thing I've learned from thirteen years of marriage is that you are always up to something!" Harriett rolled her eyes, a habit she repeated frequently. She leaned down to kiss Shelby, who eagerly returned a sloppy kiss.

"Hi, Mama. I already ate. A hotdog, on a bun! I'm watching *The Flintstones*," she said gleefully as she hugged her mother.

"Why, Bug, isn't that a fun night! Mama's going to eat with Daddy, I'll check on you later."

"Okay, Mama. I promised Daddy I'd be a good girl."

"Harriett. Come on! Dinner is ready. We'll eat first. We can talk over wine," he said, grinning at his wife, not the least bit offended. "I can't pull much over on you."

"If only that were the truth." Eyes rolling once again, as she entered the dining room.

Terms between Eddy and Harriett significantly improved. Although Harriett was completely in love with him, she did not totally trust him, making it difficult for a completely fulfilling relationship. Eddy, on the other hand, grew to admire, perhaps love, Harriett; however, it was his daughter that possessed his entire being. He adored Shelby a.k.a. the Bug. Daddy's little curious girl, constantly playing with insects, who was given nickname Bug, and who happened to look just like Daddy. Shelby adored them both.

Dinner was delicious. Harriett admitted that Eddy was a great cook. His cooking skills were equal to her baking skills. Together, they could become quite plump if they didn't watch out.

"Okay, what do you want?"

"One of my good army buddies wrote to me." Omitting that they remained in contact since their discharge. "He asked if he could come for a visit."

"Of course, he may visit us. Why would you go to all this trouble for such a simple request? I'm happy to entertain your friend."

"Well, it's not just a day visit. I told him he could stay with us. Actually, he's recently divorced and without a home right now, so he may be staying a while. I think he may want to settle in the area."

"How long is a while? You know my work schedule is crazy. Between my responsibilities at Dugan & Co., I am teaching one class this semester at Madison College. I'll have very little extra time."

"In fact, that may work out okay. We have a lot of catching up to do. He is a really good friend, the kind that helped me out of tough spots. The weather is nice, maybe we can play nine holes a few nights?"

Eddy poured them each a second glass of wine. Harriett waved him off, still a light drinker. One glass of wine was usually her limit. Eddy habitually finished the bottle.

"Okay, as long as he doesn't stay too long. And if my work time is uninterrupted, so consider Shelby if you are out nights. He may visit. Does he have a name?"

"Thanks, babe, you really are the best. Walter Stuart. Wally for short."

"Let's keep Wally's visit to two weeks max!" She qualified the approval. "I am serious about my work. Besides, you have responsibilities at your job. I don't want this guy having unsupervised run of the house. There are some really special objects in this house, and then there is Shelby to think of."

"Wait a minute. Are you insinuating that Wally is a potential thief or child molester?" Eddy was indignant. "Wally was my business partner and saved my skin more than once. I owe him."

Eddy continued, "If he wants to stay, then he stays. Besides, he would never do anything to hurt Shelby! I'll ensure that. I'd kill him or anyone else who considered hurting her."

Harriett looked with bewilderment at her husband. *What other secrets are you keeping? Business partner? I thought this was over.* Suspicion rapidly growing, denial reached up, and grabbed the negative thoughts to file in her mind, close to her files of Olive.

"Ah… I didn't mean to imply," she stumbled over her words. *How was Eddy able to make me feel like I'm in the wrong?*

"I'll leave it to your discretion, with the caveat that I may not be available every night for dinner. When is he expected?"

"Week after next," answered Eddy, smug in his absolute control over such a strong woman.

***

Walter Stuart, of S/K Acquisitions arrived on September 25, 1964. It was eleven years since Eddy and Wally were together; however, they wrote to each other frequently. Wally maintained contacts in Italy so that S/K Acquisitions remained a viable enterprise. Eddy maintained contacts in the Far East. According to the books, they were very profitable, although Eddy had no idea how profitable. He never withdrew any of his money apart from the money used to search for Rosa after his imprisonment. Money distribution was one of the reasons for Wally's visit. He insisted that Eddy assume his profits before it became a liability with the IRS.

"You son-of-a-bitch. Look at you!" said Wally as Eddy picked him up at the bus station.

"Gotta watch the swearing. Can't have Shelby hearing foul language," Eddy retorted and then warmly embraced his friend. "Good to see you man! Let me grab your bags. My car is over here." Eddy pointed to a new Cadillac.

"Life's treating you okay, I see. Wearing a suit, driving a luxury car."

The men jumped into the car and Eddy drove home. As they ascended the hill to the red brick manner house, Wally let out, "Good god, man. Who are you married to? I know you said Harriett was in business, but does she own fucking AT&T?"

"Wally, watch the mouth. We are not in the army. Harriett will be appalled, and I care not for Shelby to overhear such vile profanity."

The mailbox read Mr. and Dr. Edgar Kepler, 400 Vista Drive.

"Dr. Kepler?" asked Wally.

"Yes, she's a smart cookie. Has her PhD in finance. She's the CFO of Dugan & Co., and she's teaching a class at Madison College this fall—assistant professor."

"Why are you even working? Sounds like she makes enough for five people."

"She does, but she keeps her own accounts. We both contribute a set amount of funds to both a joint checking and savings account. Then whatever is left over we can spend as we please. Don't get the wrong idea, I usually don't have too much excess."

"That's a nice little arrangement. Don't have to try to sneak money for booze."

"Booze comes out of the house budget! She keeps the bar stocked with respectable brands. Not top shelf, but certainly not house brand!"

"Sounds like a perfect wife!" approved Wally.

"For our third anniversary, she gave me one-hundred shares of General Electric in a monogramed leather satchel. Paper/Leather. I don't know what her portfolio is worth, but I'm sure it is a very large number."

"You lucky bastard. Oops—sorry. You continuously manage to fall into shit and come out smelling like a rose. You don't need your S/K Acq. payout. You already have a stash."

Eddy was silent. "You are wrong friend. I pay dearly, every day. Let's go inside."

The two men made themselves comfortable in the office, now library. The Chintz chaise removed to a guest bedroom, was replaced with two overstuffed red leather chairs and matching ottoman. Harriett assembled an extensive collection of books, mostly purchased secondhand from tag sales or consignment shops. Some of her most prized possessions were on the library shelves. Harriett valued intellectual wealth over material wealth. Shelby was encouraged to enjoy the large selection of children's books.

Pouring whiskies, Eddy motioned for Wally to have a seat. "On the rocks or neat? So what's on your mind Wally? Why the visit?"

"Rocks. Well, I do need to get rid of this money, but I also wanted to talk about a proposition?"

Ice bucket supplied in anticipation of the visit, Eddy reached for several cubes.

"Woah, buddy, just because I live in a beautiful house and drive a fancy car doesn't mean I have money. I already told you how Harriett manages household finances," objected Eddy, taking the chair beside Wally.

"I don't think we need more than what we already have. And the GI Bill may afford us to borrow at a lower rate, if we need to."

"You have my interest," interrupted Eddy. "What's the proposition?"

Wally explained in detail his plans to open an import/export business using their current and old contacts. The main products would be luxury items such as wine, fine fabrics, perfumes, watches, exotic teas, and so on. The goal was to select less bulky items that would be less expensive to ship and to store but would appeal to the growing middle class in America. Eddy listened to his friend opine for an easy forty-five minutes before asking a question.

"From what you are explaining, you really need a financial partner to get the business started, is that correct? It doesn't seem like there is much workload for both of us outside of making the initial contacts and contracts," commented Eddy. "At least, not until the business grows. Then you still wouldn't need me—rather, a clerical or additional bookkeeper is most appropriate."

"Exactly. I could run the business, provided you invest and introduce me to your people. If you need the security of your current job, I'm cool with a semi-silent partnership," concluded Wally. "Although I may call on you from time to time to tap into your operational skills."

"I belong to Madison Country Club, good for networking," threw in Eddy. Walter smiled, knowing Eddy was "all ahead go."

"How much money do we have, and how much money do we need?"

"Eddy, old boy, we did really well in the army. Then I invested most of the money in stocks. We have about fifteen thousand each. Thirty thousand should be enough to set us up."

"You sound like my wife!" interjected Eddy with a chuckle. "She has stock in General Motors, Standard Oil, US Steel, General Electric, AT&T, Westinghouse, and others that I can't remember. She watches every penny that goes in and out of this house. We may look like we spend lots of money, but frugal Harriett is a smart consumer and a smarter investor!"

"You're starting to sound like you went to college." Wally laughed.

"You can't help but pick up a word or two when you live with a PhD and CFO, she's a special lady."

The friends laughed, and Eddy poured each another drink.

"Not to change the subject but have you ever found Rosa and Joey? How old would Joey be now—nine, ten?" asked Wally, still laughing at Eddy's previous comment.

Laughter and the clink of ice camouflaged the footsteps. Neither man saw Harriett standing in the doorway of the office. She stopped home, on her way before class, to welcome her husband's friend.

Eddy was answering Wally's question, "No, I think closer to twelve. God!"

Both men were startled to hear a woman's voice saying, "Who are Rosa and Joey?"

Eddy gasped, looking up to see his wife, hands on her hips, face reddening.

"I asked a question! Who are Rosa and Joey?" she demanded, now tapping her foot in irritation.

Eddy and Wally exchanged terrified looks. Wally sat down his drink, Eddy gulped the entire contents of his. Finally, Wally said, "Good god, man, you didn't tell her?"

"Tell me what? Who are Rosa and Joey! Eddy…tell me right now!"

Eddy tried to explain his relationship with the Italian teen and the resulting child; however, Harriett was not listening past the phrase "wife and son." Her head was spinning, ears were ringing, and she was dizzy. She vomited just before she passed out.

Eddy saw her swoon, jumped up from his chair, and managed to catch Harriett before she hit the floor.

"Don't just sit there, call an ambulance," Eddy yelled at Wally.

Wally walked to the desk, picked up the phone, dialed emergency, and then turned to Eddy, saying, "Looks like things never change with you. I am always bailing your ass out of trouble."

Eddy, carrying Harriett securely in his arms, looked at Wally with disdain. "If you didn't open your big mouth, I wouldn't be in this fix!"

"Wrong! If you wouldn't have opened your pants fly, you wouldn't be in this fix or any of your previous fixes! I'll go, man. If you want to talk business, we can talk after your wife recovers the shock of meeting her real husband. You may need a place to stay. A warehouse might be suitable." Wally let himself out the front door, calling, "I'll be in touch. You are one sorry-ass fool!" With that, he started down the hill on his way back to the bus station.

"Wally, wait!" Eddy was still holding Harriett. "Stay, we need to talk. But right now, help me with her!"

Just then, the ambulance, sirens blaring, pulled in front of the house. Taking two steps at a time despite an injured leg, Eddy quickly carried Harriet down the massive front stairs to a waiting gurney. Throwing the car keys to Wally, he yelled, "I'll go with her, follow in the car."

The two men waited nervously in the waiting room. Eddy managed to call Alice, asking if she would get Shelby from school and keep her overnight, promising to call back as soon as he knew Harriett's condition.

"Mr. Kepler?" questioned the approaching doctor. "Is there a Mr. Kepler here?"

"Yes, I am Eddy Kepler. Is my wife okay?"

"She is stable and resting. She currently does not want visitors. You should probably go home and get some rest yourself."

"I'm not going anywhere until I know what is going on with Harriett," Eddy insisted.

"She experienced an episode of extreme high blood pressure. We want to keep her in the hospital a couple of days to be sure this is an isolated event. I understand she received very troubling information immediately before the episode?" he looked at Eddy accusingly.

Oh God, thought Eddy. *This guy knows the whole story.*

"If you are sure, then I'll leave her in your capable hands. Please tell her that I love her."

"I'm sorry, sir. That is your job. Mine is to keep her from having a stroke after hearing most unwanted news!"

Wally raised an eyebrow and beckoned his friend to leave.

"Let's go collect your daughter," suggested Wally. "She'll feel safer staying with Daddy tonight."

Eddy and Wally solemnly rode to Alice's house to share Harriet's condition and retrieve Shelby. He omitted the cause of the episode. Shelby ran to her father, hugging him tightly.

"Where's Mama?" she said shyly, noticing Wally.

"Mama's not feeling very well tonight. The doctor wants to keep her at his house so that he can make sure she is okay."

"You mean she's in the hospital?"

"Like mother, like daughter," Eddy said, looking at Wally. "Yes, she is staying in the hospital for a couple of days. Honey, this is Uncle Wally. He is Daddy's new business partner." Wally, again, raised an eyebrow. "He will be staying at our house for a couple of days. Daddy and Uncle Wally have some things to discuss. You're okay with having him stay, aren't you?"

"Sure, Daddy. When may I visit Mama?" Shelby turned to Wally, thrust out her tiny hand, and said, "Pleasure to meet you, Uncle Wally."

The men grinned in delight. Shelby: as smart as her mother, as confident as her father.

***

The pound at the door came around midnight. Shelby, sound asleep in her bed, did not stir. Wally and Eddy were in the office enjoying their third nightcap. Slightly wobbly, Eddy opened the door to find Earl.

Without saying a word, Earl grabbed Eddy by the collar and pounded his face repeatedly.

"Stop!" shouted Wally, trying to separate the men. "You'll break his nose."

"He needs more than his nose broken," said Earl as he managed to land another punch. Finally, Earl let go of Eddy, who dropped to the floor.

"Christ, man. What the hell?" managed Eddy as he spit blood from his mouth.

"You don't deserve that woman! You selfish slime. Alice called Abigail to let her know of Harriett's hospitalization. I went over to get the scoop."

"She saw you?" questioned Eddy. "She refused to see me."

"Of course she didn't want to see her cheating, adulterous, insensitive prick of a husband. You have no right to that woman!"

Eddy sat looking at his older brother. It was suddenly clear.

"You're in love with her. Son of a bitch! You're in love with my wife. Did you ever make advances toward her?"

"No chance. I respect her too much!"

"How about when she was the grieving abandoned wife? How about then, big brother?"

Earl picked Eddy up and punched him again. "Fact is, I love her so much that I can't stand how you treat her. If I stay here, I swear I'll kill you. I'm moving to California."

"What? Don't be ridiculous." Eddy sputtered more blood.

"Tomorrow, I'll be on a train. But I promise you, that if you ever hurt her again, I'll be back, and you better hide. That is a threat you can count on."

Earl slammed the door and walked away from his once beloved little brother and the remarkable woman he loved—his little brother's wife.

Chapter 39

ALICE TOOK SHELBY TO THE hospital at Eddy's request. He was afraid that his appearance would upset Harriett enough to cause another blood pressure incident; however, Harriett was asking to see Shelby. Despite a puffy face from the altercation with Earl, Eddy continued to visit Harriett every day, although, he never entered her room. The nurses delivered flowers, candy, and cookies brought daily by Eddy.

Harriett's blood pressure and mood remained stable, although she was prescribed Valium. She requested to see her daughter, not her husband.

"Mama, mama, I am so glad to see you. I missed you terribly!" squealed Shelby as she ran to her mother.

"Hi, Bug. Are you okay?" asked Harriett. "Mama misses you."

"I miss you too. When can you come home?" asked Shelby. "Daddy, Uncle Wally, and I are having lots of fun. Wish you could play with us."

"What are you playing?" asked Harriett with speculation. She feared unthinkable thoughts with a strange man in the house.

"Every night, Uncle Wally reads a book to me while Daddy cooks dinner. Then we eat dinner, Daddy gives me my bath, and we play a game."

"Is Uncle Wally around while Daddy bathes you?"

"Oh no. Daddy and I go upstairs for my bath, and Uncle Wally stays in the kitchen and washes the dishes.

"That's good. Then what kind of games do you play?"

"They are so much fun, Mama. Some nights we play 'spelling' or 'name the country' or 'on the globe.' I have never played these games before, and I'm really good at them," Shelby ended proudly. "Can we play them when you come home?"

"Shelby Bug, it sounds like fun. I am glad Daddy is taking good care of you. Now, you need to go home with Aunt Alice, Mama's getting tired."

"Mama, I almost forgot, Uncle Earl moved to California. I can pick it out on the globe," informed Shelby, pleased with herself. "Can we visit him sometime?"

"Someday, Bug," replied a despondent Harriett.

"Night-night, Mama," wished Shelby as she gave her mother a huge hug and kiss. "Get better soon and come home."

Eluding sleep, Harriett thought all night about Earl and Eddy. Puzzled and trouble with Earl's leaving, she knew she must bear yet another void.

So unlike his older brother, Harriett was at least gratified by the care Eddy gave Shelby. She wished Eddy was a different man, more like Earl. She needed a man who loved her alone, dedicated his soul to her as she dedicated hers to him. Eddy was not that man. His list of weaknesses and faults was long; disloyalty, adultery, selfishness, immaturity, and a cad.

His redeeming qualities were few. Although he completely loved, protected, and cared for Shelby. Harriet knew from her own experience the specialness of a daughter-father relationship.

That night, Harriett subconsciously suppressed the blemished personality of Eddy, replacing it with the memory and attributes of a fantasy man to whom she wanted to be married. Eddy's shortcomings were filed away in her mind, never to be recalled again.

Two days after Shelby's visit, Harriett surprised everyone by asking for Eddy.

"Hello, Harriett." Eddy cautiously entered the room.

"Oh, my sweet darling Eddy! You're finally here," she exclaimed, motioning for him to approach the bed. Eddy walked over to his wife.

"Darling, give me a kiss!" she requested. "I missed you. I'm so glad to see you. The doctor said that I am well enough to go home tomorrow. Won't that be wonderful!"

Eddy sat looking at his wife, totally confused.

"Oh sweet Eddy. You are such a dear. How did I ever attract a man like you? I am just the luckiest woman alive!" Harriett continued fussing over her husband.

Eddy had no way of knowing about the internal mechanism and the secret place in which Harriett hid unpleasantries. Olive, Tobias's death, and now Eddy's betrayal lived in that mental file, hidden from the world and from herself. Harriett, in denial, decided she would rather live with a mental perfect image of a husband, than the real living man.

Chapter 40

Summer, 1976

As the years passed, Shelby demonstrated both intelligence and athleticism. Eddy and Harriett enrolled her in golf, swimming, and tennis lessons at the club. By her seventeenth birthday, she could beat both her mother and father in golf. Harriett, the better golfer of her parents, won several club championships. Eddy learned to tolerate being bested by his women.

"Daddy," yelled Shelby as she drove into the expanded garage. She owned her own car, a bright blue 1975 Camaro. An early high school graduation gift from both parents.

"Daddy, are you down here? I need help with the groceries."

"Coming, Bug," answered Eddy as he limped down the stairs. Arthritis set in his wounded leg, causing a more pronounced limp.

"I can't believe she is retiring from Dugan & Co.," exclaimed Shelby as she handed her father some bags.

"She's been there twenty-five years. Twenty as their CFO. She's worked hard and deserves to slow down."

"But Daddy, she's only forty-six years old! I hope I can retire at that age."

"You know she won't be inactive, she's taking on three more classes at Madison College, being promoted to associate professor and given tenure," explained Eddy. "For some people, that's their only successful career. For your mother, it's a successful second career."

"How am I ever to live up to her standards?" Shelby asked her father.

"You'll have no problem whatsoever. Now, stop worrying, Bug. Good grief, you're headed to Penn this fall!"

The two carried the groceries to the kitchen and unpacked the bags. Harriett expanded the back of the house and remodeled the kitchen mid-1960s. She used part of the rear flagstone terrace to add on a family room. The garage was expanded at the same time.

The Songer house was now referred to as Dr. Kepler's house. Again, Eddy learned to tolerate second billing. Perhaps that was his price for his previous indiscretion, perhaps not?

Eddy and Wally built their own achievement with a successful S/K Acq. The import business flourished to sustain both Wally and Eddy on a full-time basis. Eddy quit his job as supply manager to become a prosperous business partner.

Tomorrow, Eddy, Shelby, Wally, and Tom Roland were hosting an elaborate retirement party at Madison Country Club for their beloved Dr. Harriett B. Kepler.

"What kind of gift did you buy Mom?" Shelby asked her father.

Eddy laughed. "She has everything. But I bought her a new diamond ring—two full carats."

"Oh boy, she loves that tiny little thing you bought her when you proposed. Do you think she'll wear a new one?"

"I hope so. That ring is so pitifully small, but it was all I could afford at the time," explained Eddy.

"I know. Neither of you came by your wealth without working hard for it. Why do you think I never objected when you made me get a summer or after-school job? I was being taught the value of money."

Eddy smiled and hugged his daughter. "You always were wise beyond your years, Bug." Then he kissed her cheek. "Fair play—what did you get your mother?"

Shelby groaned. "That was a hard one. I saved my allowance and money from last summer to have enough. I hired a local artist to paint a picture of Mom as a little girl with Grandpa Tabs. I used an old photograph as the template."

Eddy looked at his daughter in wonder. How did an eighteen-year-old girl possess such maturity and wisdom? It was certainly not from his gene pool.

"Bug, she'll love it."

"I sure hope so," confessed Shelby.

***

Friends, relatives, colleagues, professionals, and clients joined Harriett at the club in celebrating her retirement. Harriett wore a darling pink St. Johns knit suit, matching pink pumps, the small pearl necklace, and her fox stole. She looked adorable, except for the stole.

"Mom, it's ninety degrees outside. Can you ditch the fox tonight?" asked Shelby as they piled into Eddy's Cadillac. "I know the story about Grandpa Tabs, but really!"

Harriett smiled at and blew a kiss to her criticizing daughter and then sat down in the passenger seat, complete with stole. The Club ballroom was packed. A side table for gifts and cards overflowed.

Half way through the evening, a man approached Harriett from behind. He laid his hand on her shoulder and said softly, "Congratulations, Harriett. They are well deserved."

Harriett whirled around to see Earl. "Earl, my goodness, what a delightful surprise. I am so happy to see you. You never said 'good-bye' when you left for California!" exclaimed Harriett as she hugged and kissed her brother-in-law.

Seeing Earl with Harriett, Eddy bounded across the room, not sure how either man would react. Harriett diffused any tension before it began.

"Eddy, darling, look who is here! It's brother Earl. This truly is a special night." Harriett leaned up and kissed Eddy. "Thank you, dear, for this perfect party."

The men looked at each other defensively for a moment and then with forgiveness. They clasped each other's hands and hugged.

"You are quite the specimen of manhood," Earl said to Eddy.

Not taking offense, Eddy retorted, "Better late than never."

***

After the party, the immediate family retired to the Kepler's cozy home office. Eddy and Wally carried two large baskets full of gifts and cards. Earl joined them and was pouring drinks as Harriett and Shelby entered the room.

"Me first," said Wally.

"Oh, I hate this part," admitted Harriett. "I already have everything I need. I hate for you to spend your money needlessly on me."

"Yeah, yeah…handle it," was Wally's retort. Harriett kissed her husband's lifelong business partner. Wally handed Harriett a large eight-by-eleven size envelope. She opened it to find one-thousand shares of Intel.

"Wally, this is too generous. I cannot accept this."

"Like hell you can't. You are the glue that keeps everything together. Without you, S/K flops," Wally expanded and then kissed Harriett. Eddy looked approvingly.

"Now me," said Earl. Eddy looked at his brother with suspicion. He too handed Harriett a large envelope. Three park passes to Disneyland fell out, along with three first-class plane tickets. "I want you to visit next month, as a family, before Shelby leaves the nest. Can you manage that?"

"Perfect!" exclaimed Harriett, agreeing. "We have missed you, Earl. It will be wonderful to spend some time visiting before Shelby's off to college."

"I'm glad you feel that way. How about you, Eddy?"

"Please, sweetie, we haven't scheduled any travel for this summer. May we?" asked Harriett.

Shelby interjected, "Wait, there are only three tickets, Uncle Earl, will you be joining us? I need a riding partner!"

"Of course, Bug," answered Earl. "I want this to be a family trip. Eddy, you okay with this?"

"Why not. Let's go," said Eddy while grinning at the women. He then looked at Shelby.

Shelby spoke first, saying, "I'm last."

"Then I guess I'm up," said Eddy as he handed Harriett a small square box. Harriett lifted the hinged lid to flaunt a beautiful marquis-cut two-carat diamond surrounded by small baguettes set in platinum, with a matching diamond-studded wedding band.

"My god, Eddy! It's beautiful. Why so extravagant?" she questioned, adding, "But I love my original ring. You gave that to me from the heart."

"I did," confessed Eddy. "It was one of the few decent things I did back then."

"Eddy, darling, whatever do you mean?" Harriett was genuinely baffled. "You have always been my sweetie."

The men exchanged glances. Shelby caught the innuendo.

"Of course, I'll wear this beautiful ring, but I think I'll wear the originals as a necklace from time to time." Harriett declared.

"Mom, wear your original rings on your right hand," suggested Shelby.

She is destined to solve problems, thought Eddy.

"Okay, now it's my turn," continued Shelby. She left the room, returning with a sheet-covered canvas.

"What in the world—" began Harriett. Shelby removed the sheet to display an oil painting of Janie sitting on her papa's lap, under the grape arbor. It was beautifully done and the likeness, true to life.

Harriett collapsed into a chair, sobbing. Shelby rushed to her mother's side.

"Mom, I'm so sorry. I didn't mean to upset you!" blurted Shelby. She was terrified that she would send her mother into another breakdown.

"Bug, I'm not upset. Darling Bug." Harriett embraced her daughter so tightly that Shelby winced. "Bug, my Shelby Bug. It is the best present I was ever given."

"Second to the fox stole." Shelby laughed. Harriett's intense emotions dissipated, to Shelby's delight. "Whew. No breakdown tonight! Just a loving family."

Chapter 41

"WHY DO YOU INSIST THAT I attend this woman's wake?" asked Harriett of Alice.

"Honey, it's the wake of Olive Bailey. Olive was our mother," answered Alice in frustration.

"I have no idea who and what you are talking about. I have no mother. I have no recollection of a mother! My only recollection of a parent was my beloved papa. He's the one who raised and loved me!"

"Well, Olive was your mother, even if you don't believe it."

"Stop! Do not continue with this nonsense. I shall neither attend her wake nor her funeral. That is all I have to say about that!" Harriett stomped out of the room.

Alice looked at Eddy. "What should we do about this?"

"Leave her be. If she doesn't remember her mother, then so be it." Eddy usually opted for the easy solution.

"What about Shelby? Will you bring her?"

"Aunt Alice, I'll come on my own. Daddy can stay home to watch over Mom," offered Shelby. "She is obviously distraught over the whole affair. Let's keep her at home to avoid another 'incident.'"

It was later that evening, after the group returned home from the club, when Alice phoned to say Olive was dead. None of the family tolerated living with the cantankerous woman; therefore, according to predictions, Olive lived alone in a county nursing home. None of her children willing to care for or even visit their callous mother, Olive died deserted.

Shelby met her grandmother twice; both times at Alice's, before Olive was moved to the nursing home. The first visit at age ten, she thought it odd that her grandmother made three cups of tea out of one tea bag. For Christmas that year, Shelby spent her allowance to buy her grandmother a box of one hundred tea bags. Upon presentation, Olive ill mannerly retorted with, "Harrumph. This will last a whole year! They'll be stale before I can drink them."

Without losing a beat, Shelby promptly responded, "If you use them correctly, they will only last three months and not go stale."

Shelby wasn't particularly fond of her grandmother Olive, especially compared with Abigail. However, she respected the title. It was this respect that motivated Shelby to attend Olive's funeral in her mother's stead.

It was also her concern of her mother. Shelby did not understand how Harriett was able to completely erase her memory. She also picked up on strange exchanges between her mother and father. Actions and reactions did not always match.

That night, the night her mother retired from Dugan and the night Olive died, Shelby decided to major in medicine, particularly psychiatry.

Part Four

Chapter 42

"I'll get it," yelled Shelby as she raced to get the ringing phone. The old man sat staring without any attempt to answer.

"Uncle Wally. How did you hear so quickly? I've only made a handful of calls," she said to the voice on the phone. "You're in town already? Do you need a place to stay? Thank you so much for coming. Daddy will be so happy to see you."

"I'm in a hotel. You have enough to worry about. How's he doing?" asked Wally. "How are you?"

"I'm fine, tired. She's been a handful the past couple of years. We never knew from day to day which personality we'd meet. Daddy did a fabulous job taking care of her. I gave him an out, more than once, suggesting hospitalization, especially after Uncle Earl died. His death didn't go over very well. For a woman feigning no memory, her reaction was rather violent to that news."

"Mother qualified for nursing home care, and they certainly could afford a luxury facility. He refused always, saying they had to stay together. She suffered from suppression with substitution and, finally, a dissociative disorder. I'm not sure how Daddy managed it every day. Sometimes, I was ready to throw in the towel, and I'm a geriatric psychiatrist," Shelby laughed.

"Smart as a whip, just like your mother. Loved school just like her too," commented Wally. "So what is Eddy's condition?"

"I'm not really sure. He is just staring into space. Not crying, just looking at nothing. I think I need to have an unofficial session tonight. I know he is toting tons of baggage. I have never pried, but I can read the signs. I may be a doctor, but I'm not his therapist, although I have suggested many times that he see one of my colleagues. He needs to unload. I'm his daughter and I love him. Tonight, I think I have to change role from little girl to psychiatrist."

"Good luck, honey. He does not share easily. God, I am a life-long witness to that behavior. Even after we went into business, I had trouble getting him to open up at times. What time is the funeral service and which church?"

"Service is at their home church, St. Martin. We have a break tomorrow, I managed to get everything done today after she was pronounced. Viewing is Wednesday at Sinclair Memorial. Only two to four in the afternoon, then six to nine Wednesday evening. Funeral is Thursday morning at ten. Be there early to get a seat, we're expecting a full congregation, considering everyone's social circles. Counting my colleagues, Richard's partners, her students, past associates at Dugan, S/K contacts and clients, and lastly, family, we shall have several hundred in attendance."

"Do you need me to stop over this evening?"

"No, but thank you. We'll be fine. I need to work with him tonight. If I'm not successful, he'll be a zombie. Love you. Come tomorrow night. I expect we'll still be talking, but he may need a break from me. Goodnight and thanks, Uncle Wally."

"Goodnight, Shelby Bug, if I may still call you that?" asked her father's long-time business partner.

"Of course. I'd be hurt if you didn't. You've called me that since I was six years old. Night." Shelby hung up the phone and went into the office.

She sat on the ottoman in front of her father and put her hand over his hands. Not recognizing her touch, Eddy continued to stare ahead.

Shelby squeezed his hands. Eddy finally looked toward his daughter. His eyes showed signs of welling tears, but no liquid fell.

"Daddy, we need to talk. You need to talk." She lovingly squeezed his hands again, hoping to evoke another response. "Do you want a sedative first?"

Eddy looked at his daughter and sighed. "It's no one's business but mine. Earl and Wally know too much."

"You are wrong. You need to talk about this, and unfortunately, it needs to be done tonight and tomorrow. I know we are both tired, so the sooner you start, the sooner we sleep," commanded Shelby.

Eddy looked at his daughter. He knew the look all too well. She was not going to budge until she got what she wanted. He capitulated. "I suppose I should tell you now that she is gone. I don't know where to start."

"Just start anywhere. We can weave the story together if we need. The important thing is for you to talk about it. You need to purge your skeletons. Otherwise, you shall never find peace."

"Can I have a drink?"

"Your choice, drink or sedative," prescribed his daughter.

"Drink! Make it a double. This is a long story."

"Start talking," said Shelby as she poured two whiskies; doubles, on the rocks.

Eddy complied.

Chapter 43

FIGHTING WAS HEAVY THE PAST several weeks. Private Kepler was in country for only three months. Arriving in April, the frosts of a bitter winter lingered, tormenting the men with thoughts of a spring thaw yet to come. When the thaw finally came, it thawed. July hot temperatures and high humidity created sopping-wet, uncomfortable men.

Mail caught up with Eddy, although several weeks later than if the senders had his correct address. His mother and Harriett corresponded faithfully. Wally wrote every couple of weeks.

Eddy hated Korea, especially after such a cake assignment in Italy. He hated the heat, he hated being soaked to his skivvies. He hated the trenches. He hated himself. He hated not finding Rosa, although he continued his search. He hated receiving daily loving letters from Harriett. He hated ignoring Harriett. He hated the total mess of his life. Eddy didn't care if he lived or died.

With nothing to do but dig, fight, eat, sleep, and then repeat, Eddy found it easy to stay out of trouble. They seemed to be on an endless quest for this hill. Gaining then losing real estate and then regaining again.

Morning began with heavy shelling from both sides in the distance. They were dug into the side of a rocky hill. Minimal vegetation provided little shade or cover. The trenches and foxholes were the only protection for the fighting men. Although early, the sun beat down scorching the ground. Water hung dense in the air. The smell of artillery smoke seemed to attach itself to the humidity. Command had predicted slow fighting today. The men took advantage of this prediction and exited their trenches to eat their breakfast of K rations outside in hopes of catching a breeze.

Eddy just finished a four-hour watch. He was happy to feed his hungry belly with undesirable beans and then catch some shut-eye between bomb blasts. Yelling up and down the line prompted the soldiers sitting beside Eddy to suddenly scramble back into the trench. In need of sleep, senses dull, he reacted too late to the yells and the sound of gunfire. The sniper's bullet entered Eddy's shin in the front of his leg. Splintering a piece of the tibia, it exited the back of the calf.

Eddy winced and then fainted.

"Medic!" yelled a corporal. "Kepler's hit."

The private awoke on a stretcher. Dozens of men lay on the ground in stretchers around him. Most were moaning, some screamed out in pain. There were trees and helicopters in the air above him. His brain rang with the *whop-whop* of the floating aircraft. A triage nurse loosened and then tightened the tourniquet on his leg.

"This one can wait. The bleeding is under control. There is bone damage. Don't put him too far down the list. He is still in danger of losing the leg."

Eddy fainted again as the nurse tagged him yellow.

The next time Eddy regained consciousness, he was in a hospital bed, with his leg in traction. He looked around him and found bleeding men on beds tightly wedged into a small pre-op tent. Eddy gagged at the blood and stench of the small, crammed space.

Glad to see both limbs intact but terrified one was in jeopardy, he wet his lips and then tried to speak. "Nurse. Nurse. Can someone help me?"

A busy orderly answered him with, "What need, Mac? If it isn't important, don't be interrupting."

Eddy attempted to sleep in avoidance of his imagined precarious situation. His fitful dreams were of Harriett and Rosa meeting each other. They were fighting over both Eddy and Joey. Eddy was the loser of the battle. Finally, a nurse shook him out of slumber. He was in yet a third area with bright overhead spotlights focused on surgeons, bleeding men, and attending staff.

"Private, we are going to try to set your leg. This will be painful. We've had lots of casualties today. You are one of the lucky ones," she said, comforting the scared soldier. Then she continued, "However, we are low on morphine. It's saved for the severest cases. I need you to bite down on this strap when the doctor tells you. Understand?"

Eddy's eyes were wide with horror. He nodded his head in understanding.

"Okay, son," said the doctor. "Bite hard."

The pain radiated up and down his leg as the surgeon manipulated the leg to forcefully slip the bone back in place. Eddy bit harder. He understood the phrase "seeing stars.'" Head spinning and ears ringing, Eddy collapsed into unconsciousness, the third time in one day.

"Private, private. Try to sit up and eat," said the orderly. He handed Eddy some warm broth. He was now in post-op, and a whole day had passed.

Eddy opened his eyes. He tried sitting up to take the broth. It was only chicken bouillon, but it tasted delightful compared to what he ate in field. Then he remembered. "Where am I?" he asked, fearing the answer.

"You're in the 8076 MASH unit. You were hit in the leg."

"My leg, is it still in one piece? Did I lose my leg?" asked Eddy frantically. His blood pressure increasing immediately, he began to sweat. He felt his head swoon.

"Nurse, this guy may be going into shock. Settle down, buddy. Take a big breath. Your leg is still attached," calmed the orderly.

Eddy slowed his breathing on command. Then he felt the searing pain in his leg. "Good god, can you give me something for this pain? My leg feels like it's on fire."

"We only have aspirin, but I'll get you two. It will help. We need you to stay awake while we cast your leg," concluded the orderly as he handed Eddy two white tablets and a glass of water. Eddy swallowed gladly.

Eddy watched the nurse clean and dry his leg. She wrapped it in gauze, beginning with his foot, toes exposed. She continued wrapping gauze until it reached above his knee. Then she applied a second layer of gauze.

"Holy hell! How big is this thing?" questioned Eddy when she finished.

"Sorry, son. Your whole leg will need to remain immobile. To do that, we need to also immobilize the ankle and knee. I don't envy you. This will be hot and itchy in this blasted weather. I assure you, it is necessary," answered the surgeon as he began applying a coat of plaster of Paris.

After several coats of plaster, the surgeon ordered the orderly to finish. The orderly smoothed the top coat, ensured that there were no sharp edges around the foot or upper leg opening, and then added a rubber heel pad. The walking cast was complete.

"Keep still, buddy. This will take an hour or so for the top coat to dry completely. You won't be out of bed for at least two more days. If you need to move your bowels, call for a bedpan." Handing Eddy a urinal, the orderly changed gloves and then hurriedly went to work on his next patient.

The doctor was correct. Eddy's leg was hot, itchy, and heavy to drag around. His surgeon decided that he should stay with the MASH unit rather than be transferred to an Evac hospital because of his blood type. Eddy was O-, a universal donor. For the MASH doctors, he was a walking blood bank, too valuable to transfer out.

The summer was hellish hot and humid. He cursed every day when he was required to walk for therapy. On one such walk, Eddy overheard the head surgeon and camp commander discussing the need for penicillin and bandages. Command neglected to send them in the last shipment, and they were dangerously low due to the continued fighting and many casualties. Eddy visited the company clerk's office, introduced himself, and then made two phone calls to Wally and Sgt. Williams. Three days later, bandages, penicillin, and a bonus of morphine (remembering his terrible pain), were delivered to the 8076th.

"Corporal Zarnecky, congratulations! How did you manage this?" asked Colonel Bowers.

"Well, sir. It wasn't me. It was Private Kepler," admitted the clerk.

"I don't remember a Private Kepler on my roster."

"He's a recovering patient. Leg wound, full leg cast. Walks daily through the camp for therapy. He's the vampire," explained Zarnecky.

"Corporal, bring Kepler to my office. *Stat.*"

Zarnecky found Eddy walking, as usual and ushered him to the camp commander's tent. It was sparsely furnished, with a desk, two chairs, one on either side of the desk, a file cabinet, and a picture of a woman, presumably his wife.

"Colonel, this is Private Kepler," said Zarnecky, "May I be dismissed?"

"Private Kepler. Pleased to meet you. Please have a seat."

"Yes, sir. Thank you, sir," Eddy was learning respect for army rank.

"How the hell did you manage to get penicillin, bandages, and morphine, son? I tried myself, only to be denied!" questioned the camp commander as he waved Zarnecky out.

"Well, sir, I have a few contacts back in Italy, sir," answered Eddy as the door closed behind the corporal.

"I see. I read your file. You were a good supply man until some silly business about going AWOL. Care to share what that was all about?" ordered the Colonel. "You were stripped rank! From the looks of it, you should be in Leavenworth, not Korea."

"Sir, what we did, what we do, is not illegal, not really. We just cut a few corners. Avoid purchase orders and such. Without all the red tape, things move faster. Then we have contacts outside of the army too, sir," Eddy hope he was not being insubordinate. The last thing he wanted was more trouble.

Colonel Bowers sat for a minute, rubbing his chin. "So this is an ongoing enterprise? And you have access to more than army surplus? Civilian items too?"

Eddy nodded his head affirmably. "Yes, sir, almost anything you want I can get, sir."

"Tell me about the girl."

Eddy shuddered. "Begging your pardon, sir, I would rather not, sir."

"Is that so? Well, if you want any hope of remaining here, then I suggest you change your mind."

Eddy shrank back and then relayed the story of Rosa, Joey, and Harriett.

Camp commander Colonel Bowers, a good judge of ability and character, immediately recognized Private Kepler, although possessing flaws, as a positive addition to the MASH Unit. Not only was Kepler a resourceful fount to expedite supplies, he was a walking blood bank. It was a no-brainer to keep Kepler and promote his abilities.

He understood that Kepler was just another stupid kid in love. Before releasing Eddy back to his unit, Bowers took advantage of the six weeks' time needed for recuperation. He made all the arrangements to permanently transfer Eddy to the 8076 MASH. Kepler's talents were needed, and Bowers, a surgeon himself, was not afraid to bend regulations if it meant better care for his wounded.

"Zarnecky, please bring Private Kepler to my office," ordered the Colonel.

Standing in the company command tent twice in two weeks unsettled Eddy. He feared S/K Acq. being in jeopardy just because he was showing off. Since his transfer to Korea, he toed the line. He even remained celibate; not that women were available on the side of that godforsaken mountain.

"Kepler, have a seat."

Eddy reluctantly sat across from Bowers. The colonel continued, "I contacted your unit commander. You have been in country only a short time. He confirmed your reformation attempt while in Korea. I intend to transfer you to my unit, provided you continue the good behavior," said Bowers. "Do you understand what I am asking of you?"

"Yes, sir. Ah, am I expected to be a monk, sir?"

Bowers laughed. "No, soldier. But you are expected to use birth control, preventing additional children. If you need information on this subject, our doctors shall happily provide. And you are certainly expected to remain active on base. *No* thoughts of AWOL ever again. Understood?"

How could Eddy refuse?

Although still a patient, Bowers moved Eddy in with Zarnecky to begin learning his way around the unit. Next week, Eddy hobbled over to Colonel Bower's tent with a bottle of aged Scotch in hand.

"Thank you, sir, for the transfer, sir," said Eddy as he gave Bowers the gift. Bowers smiled, affirming good decisions on the part of both men.

Zarnecky took Eddy "out" to celebrate the removal of his cast and his complete transfer from patient to member of the MASH. Eddy was happy to find a local bar with local girls. Korean girls were equally attracted to the tall blonde GI, although they were less receptive to his advances. When asked why, Zarnecky explained it had to do with fear of size. Eddy laughed and then successfully compensated by bringing trinkets to diminish their hesitation.

The girls were not the only recipients of Eddy's gifts. He frequented the officer's tent, bringing alcohol, perfume, and silk stockings used to entice the nurses. The officers, in turn, took good care of Eddy.

Eddy remained with the 8076th until April of 1953. Because of his relationship with Bowers and the other officers, he received a special "parting gift." When his orders finally arrived to rotate home, Bowers made all the travel arrangements; some of which were atypical non-army. Eddy's surgical staff benefactors paid for any out of the ordinary travel.

"Kepler, it's April. I have you exiting via Trieste. You will be sent back to Italy as a civilian. Once there, you have exactly one month to look for Rosa and Joey. If you don't find them by the end of June, you need to muster out in July as an army private. That's *your* last ride home," ventured the Colonel.

The men shook hands.

"Colonel, I don't deserve such kindness. I thank you from the bottom of my heart," thanked Eddy. "It's been a pleasure serving under you."

"It was my pleasure," said Bowers. "With your help, we were able to treat and help many more men successfully than we would have without you. You have done your country a great service."

With a last salute, Eddy exited the command tent, jumped onto the waiting helicopter, and began his journey back to Italy.

Chapter 44

SHELBY TOUCHED HER FATHER'S LEG. Eddy flinched, as if drawn out of a trance. "I'm sorry, Daddy, it is getting late. Do you want to take a break or continue?" she said. Eddy went on.

***

Arriving in Trieste mid-May, Eddy had a bonus two extra weeks to look for Rosa.

Wally, still at the base, once again provided transportation. Eddy continued to wear his uniform around the base without ever reporting for duty.

All of his mail caught up to him in Korea. Eddy kept it all bundled together. Considering Harriett wrote weekly, his mail made a comfortable pillow. Realizing that a letter possessed Isabella's last name, "Cortina," he and Wally headed out to Santa Croce to look for Rosa.

"This shouldn't be a problem," said a hopeful Eddy. "How many Isabella and Joseph Cortinas live in Santa Croce?"

"It's a pretty big place," retorted Wally. "I found that out when I went searching the first time."

"You didn't have a last name. I'm positive we shall find them. When we do, I'll finally write Harriett to tell her I am staying in Italy. She'll be hurt, but she'll move on."

"Dunce. She can't move on without a divorce. You are legally married in the United States. It's Italy where you only think you are married."

"Wally, don't be such a downer. I'll figure all of that out after I find Rosa!"

The search for the Cortinas was not as easy as anticipated. Cortina, a popular name in Santa Croce, resulted in five-hundred identified families. Of those Cortina, one hundred seventy-five were named Joseph.

"Holy shit! Is there a way we can check for spouse name?" asked Eddy.

"Nope. We need to make one hundred seventy-five house visits," replied a dejected Wally. "We need to visit six or seven houses each day if we want to have time to search places other than Santa Croce."

"Fuck!"

The men spent the next day mapping the addresses. To their delight, about thirty of the names shared the same address, taking them down to one hundred forty-five Joseph Cortinas. Remarkably, many Cortinas lived in the same sections of Santa Croce. Demographics saved a week of searching, allowing them time to concentrate on searching other names and areas.

After ten days of combing, the men hit a break. They found the house of Joseph and Isabella Cortina, but not Joseph or Isabella.

"*Si, Si*. I purchased this house from Joseph and Isabella Cortina. I believe it was fifteen months ago," offered the new owner. "I remember Isabella talking about her son-in-law, magistrate Romano."

"Did they leave a forwarding address?" asked Wally.

"Was a young girl and baby boy with them?" begged Eddy.

"*Si*. That's why I remember Isabella talking about the *magistrato*. She did not want him to know where she was moving. I think Joseph was deceased."

"So she told you where she was going but asked you to keep it a secret," hoped Eddy.

"No. She never said."

"Not even a city?" By now, Eddy was totally dejected. Wally was anxious.

"So sorry. Perhaps the postman can help?" suggested the helpful new owner.

Unfortunately for Eddy, the Italian post office was not efficient. They only kept a forwarding address for six months and then it was discarded. If any mail were delivered after that time, it was thrown into the "dead end" pile and sent back to the main post office of the region.

There was no way to search old mail.

Back to square one, the men spent the night thinking and drinking—mostly drinking. They decided to look for the name Kepler.

"Back to the phone books," said Wally.

The search resulted in zero Kepler's. Deciding to expand the search area, Wally rounded up phone books for a three-hundred-mile radius. It took both men three trips to carry them all into Eddy's apartment. Two days later, one Kepler was found in Venice. Hopping the train, they were in Venice before nightfall.

"Wally, you knock first. Please," pleaded Eddy. "I'm not sure my heart can handle seeing them."

"What kind of nonsense is that? We have spent three weeks, not to mention the past three years, looking for them. Of course you want to see them. Asshole!"

"Okay, you're right," Eddy conceded. He walked up the front steps and knocked on the door. Anxiously, he waited for an answer. The door opened. An old woman stood in front of Eddy.

"*Signora* Kepler?" asked Eddy. "*Parli* English?"

"*Si.* How may I help you?"

"Do you know Rosa and Joseph Kepler?"

"No. Who are they?"

"My wife and son. How about an Isabella Cortina? Do you know her?"

"Sorry, sir. I do not know these people."

"May I ask how you are named Kepler?"

The old woman looked at Eddy strangely, thinking that was a weird question.

"I met my husband during World War I," said the woman. "He is dead."

"*Molti Grazie, Signora* Kepler," thanked Eddy with a smile. "We are probably related."

***

"Well, that was worthless." Tired and exasperated, the guys spent the evening drinking at their favorite bar.

"What next?" asked Wally. "Should we head into Yugoslavia?"

"I think we should head north to Plave. She may have gone looking for me."

"Well, I have duty tomorrow, so you are on your own," said Wally. "I'll catch up with you Friday."

Eddy boarded the train. Memories washed over him, leaving him weak in the knees. This was the route taken twice a week while he and Rosa were together. He often talked of Luigi Rizzo; perhaps Rosa found the butcher.

His reunion with *Signore* Rizzo was emotional. The butcher feared that Eddy was either shot or court martialed when arrested. Luigi was so happy to see Eddy again.

"*Ciao,* Edwardo. *Bello rivederti!* So good to see you again, my friend. How is your wife and little Joey?"

"I was hoping you'd tell me," wished Eddy. "After I was arrested, did she come looking for me?"

"No. I watched for her. I had my brothers and cousins watching for a strange young woman and little boy in town. They were to bring her to me, but she never came."

"I had no way of telling her what happened." Eddy sat down and dropped his head into his hands. "They were all alone. No food. No heat. Oh God. How did I let this happen?"

Luigi tried to comfort the young man that he considered family. "If I had known, I would have sent my brother out to help her," offered Luigi. "I should have done that without your request. I let you down, my son."

"No. It's not your fault. It's mine," accepted Eddy. "It's all my fault."

***

On the way home, Eddy exited the train at Villa Opicina and walked forty-five minutes to the old cottage. The door was open. Dust, leaves, dirt, and a few dead mice inhabited the small hut, but there was no sign of humans. Even the flour sack curtains were missing.

Sobbing, Eddy sat on a chair, lay his head on the table to eventually fall asleep. Morning was a glorious Alpine dawn. Eddy remembered how much Rosa loved morning at this cottage. He made the doleful walk back to the train to return to Trieste.

Crestfallen, Eddy refused to leave his apartment. Wally called several times, wanting to discuss their next move. Eddy spent a gloomy night alone, pitying himself.

"Knock it off. You are such a baby!" Wally was yelling over the phone.

"It's not your wife and baby," argued Eddy.

"Well, it may as well be because I have traveled this journey with you from the very beginning. So cut the crap. Let's look in another direction!"

Eddy finally snapped out of his funk. His resolve restored, they began searching in Yugoslavia. Spending the remaining two weeks, the men looked for Cortina and Kepler in every small town between Trieste and Ljubljana without luck. Once in the metropolis of Ljubljana, they enlisted the local police, claiming they were missing persons.

"Eddy, we have to go back, or you'll miss your transport home. You'll be stuck here," disputed Wally.

"So what? I intend to stay if I find her. I'll stay and spend the rest of my life looking for them."

"Think Eddy. You can't do that. If she wanted to be found she would have made it easier for you. You have a loving wife at home. Return to Harriett. Don't screw up your life any more than it is already. If Harriett loves you, she'll forgive you. But you need to go home. You need to tell her about Rosa and Joey."

Eddy, ready to contest, thought a minute and then surrendered. "Let's go. I'll have Luigi and some of my other contacts keep up the search. God, I love her and Joey so much. I can't imagine leaving them forever."

"Well, that's what you are going to do. Now, write Harriett, tell her you are coming home. And when you have an address, write me and Sgt. Hill too."

***

Eddy looked at his daughter. Shelby sat patiently listening, holding her father's hand.

"That was it, Bug. I abandoned Rosa and Joey, came home, and treated your mother like shit."

Eddy hung his head in shame. "I never wanted you to know what a schmuck I am. Wally knew, Earl knew. I never told your mother the entire story. She knew just enough to go into labor early and to have a breakdown."

Shelby squeezed her father's arm and offered him some water. "You better drink some water. You've been talking for a long time. I can't have you dehydrated." She smiled lovingly at him.

"I'm such a coward. Can you ever forgive me, Bug? Oh God! I can't lose you too." Eddy sobbed.

"Shh. It's okay. This was a good session. We both need to get some rest. Tomorrow is open. I must sign the contract at the club and take Mom's clothes to the funeral home. You sleep in. When I return home, we'll have breakfast and continue this talk," said Shelby tenderly.

"How can I sleep wondering if you'll ever forgive me?" Eddy was agitated.

"Daddy, dear Daddy. I have known about Rosa and Joey for five years. Now, go to bed." Shelby kissed his cheek.

"What?" Eddy was astounded. "How could you know? And you don't hate me?"

"No, silly. I love you very much. Unlike Mom, I know how to forgive. She wanted to forgive but couldn't. We'll talk about that tomorrow too. Go to bed. All is right with the world."

Chapter 45

"Daddy, are you awake?" asked Shelby as she entered the kitchen.

"Yes, Bug, I got up about thirty minutes ago. Want a cup of coffee?"

"Sure. I picked up our lunch. Are you ready to eat?"

Shelby unpacked the boxed salads. The refrigerator was already full of dishes donated by neighbors; however, most were delicious-looking high calorie selections. Shelby, naturally thin like her mother, held her weight easily. She was tall like her father and cut a fashion model silhouette. However, at fifty-two, she chose her food carefully.

"How did you sleep?" she asked her father.

"Not good at first. I'm still bothered that you know about Rosa and never said anything."

"That bothers you? Why do you expect me to broach the subject when it's your secret? If you choose not to talk about it, then I respect your privacy," answered the doctor, not the daughter.

"But it didn't bother you?"

"It's none of my business. I'm your daughter. My job is to accept and love you, including faults. That's what I've done. But let's talk about this later. I picked up a couple papers. I have Mom's obituary."

The father and daughter ate their salad and drank a tall glass of ice water while Shelby flipped to the obits.

> Our distinguished Dr. Harriett Bailey Kepler, PhD., went to her Savior, yesterday Monday, October 12, 2010. Dr. Kepler, who died suddenly from a stroke, suffered severe memory loss the last years of her life. She had an illus-

trious twenty-five-year career as the first woman Vice President and CFO at Dugan & Co. She followed her business career with an eminent teaching career. Dr. Kepler was a tenured associate professor at Madison College. She taught business and finance classes for over thirty years. The diminutive Grand Lady of Campbellsville was well-known for her endless energy, infinite enthusiasm, superior intelligence, athletic prowess, and delicious baking skills. Dr. Kepler was admired by all. She was a long-time member of St. Martin Lutheran Church, Chamber of Commerce, Daughter of American Revolution, Madison Country Club, and Rotary Club.

She is survived by her beloved husband Edgar Gregor Kepler, Jr. and daughter Dr. Shelby Abigail Kepler-Patrick, son-in-law Richard Anthony Patrick, grandson Stephen (Patrick), granddaughter Jennifer (Patrick Avery), sister Alice (Bailey Jenson), brother Albert (Bailey), brothers-in law Theodore (Jenson), Roy (Kepler), George (Kepler), many nieces and nephews, and Walter Stuart, her husband's life long business partner.

Dr. Kepler was preceded in death by her loving father Tobias Bailey, mother Olive (Westchester) Bailey, mother-in-law Abigail (Kepler), father-in-law Edgar Sr. (Kepler), sisters Ester (Bailey Cline), June (Bailey Ralston), brothers-in-law Earl (Kepler), William (Kepler). She was the granddaughter of Henderson and Polly Westchester. Renowned maternal ancestors include Colin Westchester and husband's ancestors Gregor Campbell, original founders of Campbellsville.

Family shall receive visitors at Sinclair Memorial on Wednesday, October 13 from 2:00 to 4:00 p.m. and again at 6:00 to 9:00 p.m. Funeral services, including a DAR Celebration of Life is on Thursday, October 14, at St. Martin Lutheran Church, ten o'clock in the morning. Husband and daughter invite friends and family to join them at Madison Country Club immediately following burial, for a luncheon celebration of Dr. Kepler's remarkable life. Dr. Harriett Bailey Kepler was eighty-years old.

Shelby read the obituary to her father as he finished eating his lunch.

"What do you think, Daddy? Did I miss anything?"

"Nicely done, Bug. You are your mother's daughter."

"Thanks, but not quite. I want to talk about her for our afternoon session."

"I'd rather talk about how you know about Rosa!" demanded Eddy.

"All in time, we'll do that tonight. Would you like Uncle Wally to join us?"

"Wally's here?"

"He heard yesterday, shortly after her death. Arrived last night and stayed at the hotel. Shall I invite him to join us for dinner and to stay with us? Jenny and Steve are both coming in later today. They are staying at the hotel in Richard's suite."

"Damn. Friend to the end! Yes, Bug. I would like Wally to be here tonight."

Chapter 46

THE IMPRESSIVE MIND OF HARRIETT Bailey Kepler permitted her the ability to compartmentalize a multitude of data. It also allotted her to conceal damaging information.

As a child, Olive never taught Harriet how to either love or forgive. Lacking this ability, she was not capable of dealing with hostile life events.

Eliminating the memory of her mother enabled Harriett to accept the cause of her father's fall and subsequent death.

This tactic aided her capability to ignore Eddy's betrayal and deceit. Deeply in love with a fantasy, she desperately tried to fit Eddy into the mold of her perfect man. Unfortunately, Eddy continuously fell short of Harriett's measure.

To compensate for Eddy's faults, Harriett bundled and suppressed his adverse attributes. She filed them in the deep recesses of her mind. Then she substituted Eddy's negative traits with her own mental image of a perfect husband. She truly believed Eddy to be a dedicated, sweet, attentive, faithful husband; just as she believed Olive was not her mother. God gave her the ability of self-induced amnesia as a tool of pain alleviation.

Her memory of favorable events remained active throughout her professional life. Unfortunately, after retirement, her voluntary mental activity diminished. Too much empty thought time allowed her brain to take over on its own. Her brain continued to collect and erase memory data; a self-inflicted amnesia, until the once vibrant woman shriveled into a shadow of herself. Eventually agitated and frustrated, she became difficult to manage.

Eddy adamantly insisted that Harriett remain in her home. She was responsible for the purchase and elegance of the home; she would stay until the end. Eddy moved into a guest bedroom, leaving the master for Harriett.

As her capacity depleted, Eddy hired a nurse to help with her care. At the end, a live-in nurse, Judith, occupied a spare room— once a pantry—off the kitchen. It was Judith who found her in her bedroom early yesterday morning.

Although Shelby lived six hours away from Campbellsville, as a geriatric psychiatrist, she tried to help and advise her father on Harriett's care.

***

"So you see Daddy, she wanted to forgive you, but she didn't know how to do so," concluded Shelby.

"Bug, I was a real prick. I treated her poorly. I am guilty of mental abuse. Her condition was my fault," admitted Eddy.

"Actually, it is Grandma Bailey's fault. She failed her in her childhood. Yes, I agree you were a terrible husband in the beginning. But you compensated for your failure in the end. She forgave you in her own way. By God's grace, she found peace and lived a very full life. It's time to forgive yourself."

Offended by his daughter's indictment, Eddy protested.

"Daddy, stop. If you want harmony, you must acknowledge your mistakes. Did I accuse you unjustly?" asked Shelby.

"No," admitted Eddy.

"Then let's start with this explanation of her mental health. Believe that you were deservedly loved."

Skeptically, Eddy capitulated.

"Thank you. Now time for a nap. Despite sleeping late, this activity is emotionally draining. I'll call Wally and arrange for your reunion."

"Don't forget, I love you despite yourself." Shelby giggled and then kissed her father. It reminded Eddy of her mother.

Eddy hobbled up the stairs. Shelby, watching, made a mental note to have a chair lift installed in the kitchen staircase. It was harder and harder for her father to traverse steps.

Judith, the nurse, agreed to stay on to care for Eddy. He would be easier duty than Harriett. With the addition of the chair lift, Eddy would increase mobility. Judith could resume working an eight-hour day.

Despite it being afternoon, Eddy fell asleep much more quickly than anticipated. Shelby continued completing chores.

"Uncle Wally. Any chance you are willing to checkout of the hotel and stay with us tonight?" Shelby asked.

"That depends, Bug. Do you need me there?"

"Actually, we made great progress last night and this morning. However, we are at the part of the story where you need to be there to hear the ending," explained Dr. Kepler-Patrick.

"Bug, I already know the ending. No Rosa. No Joey. Only Harriett. Eddy treated her like a jerk most of his life," clarified Wally.

Shelby laughed. "*Au Contraire!* I have a surprise for both of you. Did you know that I knew about Rosa and Joey?" she asked.

"Hell no. When did you find out? I thought only Earl, Eddy, and I knew. Your mother knew but chose to deny," expounded Wally.

"Come over tonight, around five. We'll eat some of the tasty treats donated by the neighbors, then I'll fill in some information that just may surprise both of you," requested a self-assured Shelby.

"How can I pass on such intrigue?" asked Wally. "See you around five, and I'll stay the night."

Chapter 47

"We have tuna casserole, lasagna, cold cuts, mac and cheese, spiral cut ham, potato salad, apple pie, chocolate cake, raisin cookies, three bottles of wine, a case of beer, bagels and cream cheese, and a broccoli quiche. Anything sound good?" Shelby shouted to the men who were already making themselves comfortable with whiskies in the office.

"Whatever you decide, I'll make up trays so that we can be more comfortable eating in the office," she offered.

"Ham and potato salad," chose Eddy.

"Sounds good," matched Wally.

Shelby pulled wooden TV trays out of the office closet and placed one in front of each of them. "Get comfortable. Daddy, be sure you have plenty of whiskey ready. I guarantee this is going to be a long night. Get your food orders in now because you will not want me stopping to replenish your plates," ordered Shelby.

The men looked at each other. "What is she going to tell us?" asked Eddy as Shelby left to get the food.

"How the hell do I know? I thought you and I were the only ones left with knowledge of this fiasco. She sure makes it sound otherwise," conceded Wally. "I'm almost afraid!"

"I am terrified," professed Eddy.

Shelby return with three plates of food. Sitting a plate in front of each participant and a tray of cookies on the desk, she sat. "Shall we begin?"

"You know, Bug, I am afraid to hear what you have to say," declared Eddy.

"I want you both to remember one thing. I am both a daughter and a doctor. As a doctor, I collect information, analyze, and process.

211

As a daughter, I listen, accept, forgive (if necessary), and move on. I make no judgement. I love you both."

"Good God, Bug, you sound like I am on trial for my life," stated an anxious Eddy. "Or my eternal life."

"Not your life, just your soul." She smiled lovingly at her father. "You may finally find self-forgiveness and peace of mind. God willing."

"Let's get on with it. I can't stand this waiting. I'll not be able to eat if you don't start talking," concluded a fearful Eddy. "Begin already! How do you know about Rosa?"

***

"Do you remember several years ago? I was trying to prove ancestry to an obscure patriot for DAR? I thought it might be helpful if I took a DNA test, so I did. I was able to justify the ancestor to earn another patriot pin, but the test had another outcome."

"I got a call from a man living in Switzerland. He said that our DNA matched as sibling DNA, having at least one common parent. We discussed age, shared pictures via the internet, and basic history. Daddy, we look like twins. His name is Joey Novak."

Eddy gasped. Wally reached to stabilize him. "Joey?' he asked.

"Yes, Daddy. Joey," confirmed Shelby. "Joseph Earl Novak."

Eddy stopped breathing. Fearing this reaction, Shelby was quick with the smelling salts. Reviving her father, she reclined him slightly, propped him with pillows, and raised his legs on the ottoman.

"Feel well enough to go on?" Shelby questioned.

"Yes," Eddy agreed weakly.

"I'm not sure I'm ready," braved Wally.

"Okay, I'll give you a few minutes to let this sink in. I have had contact with Joey. But ready yourselves, there is more, and some of it may be disturbing."

The men drained their glasses. Wally poured more.

"Okay. Let's go," yielded Eddy.

Well, do you remember when Richard and I traveled to Italy four years ago? It was to meet Joey. We could be twins, Daddy. We both look so much like you. Here, I have a picture."

Shelby showed Eddy a picture of Joey and she standing together in front of the Trevi fountain. Both inkblots of Eddy. A very handsome pair. Eddy fondly fondled the picture.

"My tiny little Joey," he said softly. "I'm so sorry I left you. I love you very much."

Looking at Shelby, Eddy braved the question. "Is Rosa still alive?"

"Why don't I tell you the entire story?" granted Shelby. "It will all come together. This is the story told by Joey."

Chapter 48

"Joey," Rosa smiled at her baby boy. "Daddy is coming home today." The excited tone of her voice made the baby bounce on the bed.

"You sweet little man! You look just like him." The baby grunted and reached for his mother. Picking him up, Rosa took stock of supplies.

"Good thing he's coming too. We are low on just about everything. Why don't we make a stew from this salted beef bone and some wild onions?" She nibbled the baby's neck. She was rewarded with a hug from tiny but strong hands.

Rosa had no conversation other than with the baby, except for weekends with Eddy. "If I'm going to cook, I need to stoke this fire," she said, tickling Joey. Walking over to the fireplace, she chose two appropriate cooking logs. Alarmed to realize she had little wood, she staved off panic.

"Eddy will be home tonight. It will be okay."

Rosa sat the baby back on the bed. He immediately began to play with a ragged cloth toy. His attention captured until it was his turn to eat. Letting his mother know he was hungry, Rosa picked him up and bared her breast to let him feed. She hummed softly to the child; both mother and son content.

Rosa's milk production was low due to malnutrition. At the same time, Joey was growing rapidly and required much more than she provided. Sadly, Mama and baby both went to bed hungry on most nights.

"Here, little man, try to eat some of Mama's noodles." She offered mashed pasta on a spoon. Joey gladly accepted extra food for his belly. Full belly, the baby compliantly fell asleep. Rosa continued her meal preparation for Eddy.

He usually arrived around eleven in the evening on Friday night, having to finish work, close the shop, take the train, and then walk forty-five minutes to the cabin. Although meager, the aroma of the beef and onion stew was inviting; as inviting as the thoughts of having Eddy's strong arms around her waist.

Rosa set the table and then lay down on the bed with Joey to wait for Eddy's arrival. She awoke with a start to find she was alone. Without a timepiece, it was hard to know the exact time; however, Rosa knew that it was close to midnight.

"Maybe Papa missed his train," she whispered to Joey. "We'll see him in the morning."

Eating only a spoonful of their dinner, she tightly covered the pot, placed it under some rocks, and packed it in snow. Having so little, the stew would be reheated for tomorrow's supper.

Rosa crawled under the quilt, snuggled Joey, and dreamt all night of her soldier.

Early morning light shone through the flour sacks on the window. Rosa donned her threadbare coat, wrapped herself with her shawl, and went searching for firewood. Joey would sleep for another hour before demanding his breakfast.

Incapable of chopping trees—Eddy's job—Rosa gathered shrubs and twigs. Forced to go farther from the cabin to scour, she filled a basket and headed back, trying to beat Joey's awakening. Opening the cabin door, Rosa was met with the howl of a hungry, frightened baby.

"There, there, Joey dear. Mama is here," Rosa said, lifting the child into her arms to hug him tightly. Somewhat satisfied that he was no longer alone, Joey changed his demand to one of food.

Exposing her breast, Joey suckled earnestly. "Better little guy? Feeling better?"

He ignored his mother. Feeding was the only thing on his mind this morning.

It's amazing how quickly a baby will return to sleep if their belly is full. That's exactly the response given by Joey. As he slept, Rosa went about cleaning the cottage and taking stock.

She had enough wood for probably four days. She was low on flour, sugar, bacon fat, and rice. Four jars of jelly remained in the pantry, along with an additional salted bone. Two potatoes, one apple, two carrots, three tea bags, one cup of ground coffee, and one bottle of cow's milk completed her food inventory.

Checking her coin purse, she possessed a total of four U.S. pennies, one U.S. dime, and one Italian ten lira coin. Eddy desperately needed to resupply her stocks.

As the day lapsed, Rosa carried Joey, anxiously prancing around the cottage.

"Let's sing songs," she suggested. The boy was open to suggestion as long as Mama was involved. Rosa tried singing every song she knew. Soon, Joey was once again fast asleep.

Putting him down, Rosa tried knitting to take her mind off Eddy. She needed a new pair of socks; this was a good time to make them.

Without a phone, it was impossible to relay a message. The nearest telegraph line was a forty-five-minute walk to the train station in Villa Opicina. That was also the nearest place to secure transport. The walk was difficult in the spring and summer. During the cold winter, toting a baby, it was near impossible.

That night, she prayed. "Dear Jesus in heaven. Please keep Eddy safe. Please bring him back to me. Watch over us, keeping Joey and me in your tender care. Protect *Nonna* and Papa. I pray in the name of God the Father, God the Son, and God the Holy Spirit, Amen."

Knowing she needed to keep her strength up for Joey's sake, Rosa heated some of the beef stew for her supper. There was enough left for tomorrow. After that, she would be down to the last of her provisions.

Holding the baby tightly to her chest, she wept, eluding rest. Shortly before dawn, exhausted, she surrendered to sleep.

Sunday morning, Rosa lit a candle and said all the prayers she could remember from mass. She knew Eddy would not venture home today. Sunday journey to Plave required he start out around one in the afternoon. Arriving at 10:00 a.m. and leaving at 1:00 p.m. is senseless.

Wrapping Joey tightly in the bed blanket, Rosa tied him in the sled and went out in search of kindling. She took along the axe just in case she found a sapling small enough for her to cut.

"Come on, big boy," she encouraged Joey. He was not yet walking, but he was old enough to thoroughly enjoy a sled ride. Rosa sang as they trekked through the woods. Her choice of a different direction yielded a sled full of kindling and a few small branches.

"We can stay warm this week," she divulged to Joey. He appraised their situation by clapping his hands with a giggle.

Weekend and disappointment over, Rosa and Joey's routine went back to their normal weekly routine. She rationed her food stuffs, saving enough to make dinner for Eddy on Friday night. He would bring items to restock.

A downhearted Rosa and happy Joey occupied the cabin most of the week. Trying to disguise her hunger, Rosa used physical activity to suppress belly grumbles. Joey ate enough between mother's milk and the bottle of cow's milk. Rosa cooked a potato and the apple to supplement Joey's nutritional intake.

After a long hungry week, Friday finally arrived. Elated, Rosa danced around the cottage all day.

Rosa sang as she danced, "Papa's on his way. Yeah, Yeah. Papa's on his way."

Midday, Joey looked at his mother and said, "Papa."

"Joey, you said your first word!" She kissed the baby all over. Giggling, loving the added attention, he again said, "Papa."

"Wait until your papa arrives tonight to hear you call him by name. He's going to be so excited. What a smart little boy you are." Joey continued to giggle.

Using the last of her limited supplies, Rosa made a pot of broth. When Eddy arrived, he would have bits and pieces of meat and vegetable to make a proper soup. She would add them later. She spent the afternoon knitting her new socks. Holes in the heel and toes, the old socks were no more than rags. She looked at her shoes. Soles and sides separated, Rosa made a mental note for Eddy to have them repaired in Plave.

"When we save enough money, your daddy and I will buy a little house, and the three of us can live happily ever after with real shoes." Rosa smiled. "Where would you like to live? Italy, Yugoslavia,

Switzerland, Germany, France? We can live anywhere we want, as long as we are a family!" The baby cooed.

Evening approached with no sign of Eddy. The pit of Rosa's stomach churned as she washed and dressed Joey for bed.

"Little man, something terrible may have happened to Papa," she admitted, talking aloud to the boy.

"Papa," said Joey giggling.

"Oh yes, my sweet darling. Papa." Rosa burst into tears with the realization that she and Joey were on their own. Joey, safely in bed and sleeping, Rosa began the task of inventory and packing.

With little to pack, she filled a rucksack with all her worldly possessions.

"Where are my pearls?" she asked the sleeping child. "I need to trade them for our train tickets." Remembering wearing them on Eddy's last weekend home, she also remembered putting them in Eddy's pants pocket to prevent Joey from reaching for them.

"Oh no," she whimpered. "We have no money, and I have nothing to use as barter."

She cuddled close to her son. "Baby boy, I will find a way. I will find a way." She closed her eyes and fell asleep.

Morning was cold and windy but without snow. It snowed the week past. The walk, normally difficult, would hinder a young girl with a baby.

She layered most of her clothing on her body. Most of her dresses were threadbare, but in mass, they offered some protection. She did the same with Joey, who fussed. He was used to having his limbs free. Then she wrapped him in the bed blanket, tied him to the sled in front of the rucksack, and covered him with the checked tablecloth.

Glad her new socks were complete, she layered her old socks, new socks, split shoes, and then wrapped each foot tightly in one of the flour bag curtains from the kitchen window.

Taking down the curtains, she looked at the snowy scenery. The hillside was beautiful, even in snow. It was the special home that she and Eddy shared. Knowing she would die if she stayed, she still hated to leave it. One last look at the blue sky dotted with white clouds, mountains beyond, throwing her shawl over her head and shoulders, she lifted the strap to the sled and began pulling.

Out in the cold, Joey no longer fussed. He was quite happy to be bundled and warm. Rosa checked on him every ten minutes. Plowing on, stopping once in a grove of trees to feed Joey, Rosa finally arrived at Villa Opicina three hours after their journey started.

Now cold, hungry, and fussy, Joey demanded the attention of his mother. Rosa was exhausted and near frozen. Her feet were numb. She hobbled up the wooden step and across the platform. Pushing open the door, she entered the station.

Consisting of two long benches placed back to back, the train station was small and dark. The tile floor was surprisingly warm due to the large stove in the corner. The walls were dirty gray plaster in need of a fresh coat of paint. It smelled of wet leather and fur.

One lightbulb hung overhead. The station master's wooden desk with a locked drawer was the only space in which to do business. A time schedule hung on the wall behind the desk.

Three trains per day, she thought. *This is certainly a secondary stop.*

She shuffled over to the *Kachelofen*—masonry stove—sat down, and tried to thaw her hands and feet; unwrapping each layer to allow them to dry.

"How much for a ticket to Santa Croce for me and my baby?" She finally had enough energy to ask the station master."

"The train to Santa Croce already left for the day," said the station master. "One ticket costs seventy-five lire."

Gasping, Rosa opened her coin purse. "Is this enough?"

"I'm afraid not," he replied.

"Sir, I have no money. Is there a way for me to earn transport?" she asked, fearing he may request sexual favors.

"You are welcome to sit in that far corner and beg until you have enough for fare," he answered. "You may remain inside as long as the station is open for business. However, each night, you must leave the building. I am sorry. There is a small shack behind the station that will provide some shelter during the night."

"Oh, thank you, sir," Rosa said, kissing his hand. "You are most generous." At that, Joey let both adults know that he was hungry.

"Forgive me, my son is hungry, I need to nurse," she said as she turned away, encouraging Joey to suckle. Her breasts produced little milk. The station master noticed that the nursing finished sooner than the baby's need for milk.

Rosa took out a jar of jelly, ate a spoonful, and then fed some to Joey. The sugar satisfied his need for energy. Rosa hoped he would sleep soon.

"Are there any trains coming through today?" asked Rosa, wondering how long she would be destined to beg?

"Two more trains today, *signore*, then I close to go home."

All pride aside, Rosa Romano, the spoiled, prima donna daughter of a wealthy Trieste magistrate, Miss Untouchable, with her 6 mm matching strand of pearls, sat in the station corner and begged for money. She would do whatever was needed to keep her son safe.

***

"Stop. Oh God, Stop!" Eddy shouted. "I can't bear to hear this. My God, what did I do to them?"

"Daddy, I'm afraid you have to hear this. Then you must accept that you are the cause of this pain if you are to move forward."

"I can't. I can't listen to this."

"Yes, you can, buddy," said Wally, embracing his old comrade. "You wanted to know your entire life. Now you will know. Think what a blessing that is. You don't want to die never knowing their fate, do you?"

"No! I don't want that, but I never wanted them to suffer."

"I'm afraid you are notorious for causing suffering to those who love you." It was Wally again. "Look what you did to Harriet. Why is Rosa less immune to the curse of Eddy Kepler?"

Eddy clenched his fist as if to punch Wally, Shelby on the ready to intercede. Before he could follow through, Eddy released his own fist.

Looking at Wally, he said, "I should thump you, but at eighty, my whacking days are over."

"Lucky for you, I'm only seventy-nine. I can still whack." The men relaxed. Eddy calmed himself and then agreed for Shelby to go on.

Chapter 49

THE SHED BEHIND THE STATION was more of a three-sided lean-to. Rosa and Joey crouched behind a one-wheeled garden cart as a wind break. It provided some protection; it was still very cold for an improperly dressed mother and child. The next morning, the station master appeared earlier than usual. He knew the two would be freezing outside. He let Rosa and Joey back into the station and lit the stove fire. Then he gave Rosa some milk for Joey and some stale bread for herself.

"*Grazie!*" Rosa gratefully accepted and hungrily ate.

Mortified that someone would pass through that knew her; she secretly prayed for the embarrassment. "Please end this journey quickly."

It took four days of passenger petitioning and three nights of wakeful intolerable cold, until finally, Rosa had enough five lire coins for a ticket to Santa Croce; the ticket master contributing that last bit himself. The sled, donated as firewood, was to remain in Villa Opicina. Boarding the train, she blessed the gentle ticket master for his kindness, found a seat, and fell asleep.

The train stopped six blocks from Isabella and Joseph Cortina's house. Tired, cold, and hungry, Rosa carried Joey the last length of their excursion in search of safety, warmth, and food.

Knocking on the door, she could barely hold herself up. Isabella opened the door, gasped, called for Joseph, and then reached for Joey.

"*Nonna,*" mouthed Rosa through parched lips. Isabella grabbed Joey and helped Rosa prop herself against the doorframe. Rosa was ready to collapse.

"Shh, little one," she said to her fussing great-grandson. "Let me help your mama."

"Joseph. Come quickly. Rosa needs help!"

Her grandfather, although old, hoisted the failing teen into his arms and brought her inside. Meanwhile, Isabella comforted Joey. Heating some milk for the baby and some broth for Rosa, she sought to nourish both. She unwrapped Joey and rewrapped him in soft cashmere blankets. Joseph carried Rosa to a plump down-filled bed, unwrapped her feet, then tucked her in completely clothed.

"Let her sleep," said Isabella. "She can have a warm bath and change of clothes in the morning. Now let's find something to use to feed this hungry boy!"

Isabella and Joseph again welcomed their granddaughter and great-grandson. Next day, Isabella undressed Rosa. "Darling, what happened? Where is your young soldier?"

"*Nonna*, I don't know. He must be in some sort of trouble. He would never abandon us," she declared as her grandmother helped her into a warm bath.

"Ahh. This feels wonderful. I had forgotten how wonderful it is to have a bath and be warm." Then she coughed.

Isabella helped her into a warm flannel nightgown, felt her forehead, and lifted the tiny girl into bed.

"Joseph, please fetch the doctor. I'm afraid the journey has made Rosa sick," she called with concern to her husband. "We better check Joey too."

Both Rosa and Joey were sick due to overexposure.

"Keep them warm and hydrated with plenty of broth and tea. The boy should be weaned and bottle fed, adding cereal. His mother can no longer produce enough milk to nourish this brute," instructed the doctor.

Rosa remained in bed for a month. Isabella brought Joey to her daily for playtime, not for feeding.

In five weeks, Joey was rattling off lots of words. Along with *Papa*, he added *Mama*, *Bella*, *Non*, and *Lat*. *Nonno* and *Latte* to follow.

"*Nonna*, I have to find Eddy," insisted a weakened Rosa. "This is not like him. We have pledged our love. Please contact Mama and Papa. Surely they will tell me if he's contacted them."

Agreeing with Rosa and concerned over the whereabouts of Eddy, Isabella contacted her son-in-law.

"Giovanni, for god's sake, if you know the whereabouts of this young soldier, or if he has contacted you, you must tell her! They are in love. How can you be so cruel?" grilled Isabella.

Romano made no response, just as he made no response to Eddy's letters, with the exception of, "Stay out of my business old woman!"

It was spring before Rosa fully recovered, but her lungs were left weak and susceptible to infection. Joey grew into a handsome toddler; Rosa regained the beauty of her youth.

By summertime, she was once again the envy of all her peers. Rosa shied away from soldiers. In May, finally feeling well enough to venture out, Rosa visited the base, looking for Eddy.

"Sir," she asked the sentry at the base gate, "Do you know a soldier named Eddy Kepler? What about a Walter? I don't know the last name."

"Kepler, he was in prison, maybe he was transferred to Leavenworth?" offered an unknowing sentry. "Anyway, he's not here now. Don't know any Walter," he added, never realizing that Wally is short for Walter.

Rosa, dejected, was sure Eddy would come for her, but if he was back in the USA in jail, that was an impossibility.

Hoping beyond hope for Eddy to rescue her, Rosa rejected all offers of men. By fall, a handsome Yugoslavian business man by the name of Anton Novak noticed and fell in love with Rosa. Anton was fifteen years older than Rosa.

"Rosa, I understand you wait for your son's father. But you must accept that he is not coming for you."

"Anton, I do have feelings for you, but yes, I love Joey's father."

"I know not why he would abandon a beautiful woman—he must have a very good reason. I promise to love you and little Joey. I can offer security, safety, stability, and love. Will you not consider marriage?" asked Anton Novak.

"Anton, please allow me to try one last time to find Eddy," pleaded Rosa.

"If that is what you please, then of course," capitulated Anton.

Shocked that her mother took her call, Rosa questioned, "Mother, I am desperate! Has Eddy contacted you in search of me?"

Sofia Romano lied, "He has never tried to find you," she said, denying any contact from Eddy, even though Sofia had a large stack of letters and money from him tied into a bundle with one of Rosa's silk hair ribbons.

***

"Why that no good lying bitch!" blurted Eddy. "I wrote hundreds of letters and sent money!"

"Daddy, do you want another drink? Uncle Wally!" Wally obediently mixed three more drinks. "Just settle in and listen. I promise you must bear the pain to reap the reward," analyzed Dr. Kepler-Patrick.

***

"Anton, my grandfather's health is failing. I cannot leave him alone. I shall marry you on one condition—all four of us come as a package."

"My darling Rosa—that is no condition. It is the duty of the man. Of course, your grandparents are welcome in my home. As for Joey, if you permit, I shall take him as my own son and give him my own name."

Rosa leaned up to kiss Anton. As she did, he slipped a beautiful emerald ring on her finger.

"To match your eyes," he whispered. "Trust that I love you. And I have room for you loving Eddy, if you love me too."

"I do not deserve such a kind man," confessed Rosa.

"My darling, you deserve much, much more."

Rosa moved Eddy's faux wedding band to her right hand. She never moved it again.

Anton and Rosa married late summer of 1952. The Novak family moved to Yugoslavia, Anton's native country, outside of Split. The same fall, Joseph Cortina died and was buried in Anton's family plot in Split; Isabella, Rosa, and Joey left on their own with Anton.

***

"Sheer madness! I searched for her, she searched for me, but we could not find each other," whispered Eddy.

"It does sound a bit like a Russian tragedy," chuckled Shelby, trying to lessen the tension in the room.

"Can't say I've ever read one, but I have to agree," replied Wally.

"Is that it?" asked Eddy.

"No. But I think you need a break. Let's take a minute, go to the bathroom, mix another drink, take a short nap, whatever you need," offered Shelby. "We can start again in twenty minutes."

"Wally, Daddy, do you want to hear more of this story, or have you heard enough?"

"Holy shit, Bug! If there is more to hear, we need to hear it," Wally answered for both men.

Laughing, Shelby agreed to finish the story.

***

Anton, Rosa, Isabella, and Joey lived happily in Split for several years until Anton became suspicious of the direction of the communist government. The government threatened nationalization of all industry. Anton, a businessman manufacturing steel wire, decided it better to relocate his business and family.

In the summer of 1956, Anton, Rosa, and Joey Novak, taking Isabella Cortina and the wire mill with them, moved to Kilchberg, Switzerland, on the west banks of Lake Zurich.

Anton, Rosa, and Joey lived a charmed life in the beautiful setting of an Alpine lake. His factory, located just outside the idyllic town, prospered. Anton provided his family a beautiful home with a wonderful water view. Neither Joey nor Rosa wanted for anything. Anton was a generous, kind, and gentle man.

"Rosa, now that we are settled in Switzerland, my business is running successfully, and your health is improved, I would like to ask a favor of you."

"Why, Anton, anything. Whatever can I give you that you don't already possess?" replied Rosa.

"I want my own child. It is no matter whether girl or boy, but I want us to have a baby."

Rosa smiled tenderly at her husband, "I'm surprised it hasn't happened already." She giggled. "I got pregnant with Joey my first time! Can you believe it?"

"We shall try harder to make you a baby," she agreed flirtingly. "It shall be a fun quest."

Rosa found herself pregnant by November.

"Another summer to carry a baby through all the heat," she gently complained to Anton, who smothered his wife with kisses.

"My darling, I have a gift for you," Anton said as he handed Rosa an elongated jewelry case.

"You have given me so much already, this is not necessary."

"I understand, from *Nonna*, that, as a teen, your father gave you a beautiful strand of matching 6mm pearls but absconded with them when he discovered you pregnant with Joey. I know these will never replace the originals, however…"

Rosa opened the box and found a perfectly matching set of 8 mm rare black pearls.

"Oh." She gasped. "Wherever did you find such a beautiful rarity? This is too extravagant."

"Nothing is too extravagant for the mother of my child."

A seven-pound, twelve-ounce, twenty-inch baby boy was born to Rosa and Anton Novak on August twenty-eight, 1957.

Rosa's hospital room was filled with flowers from Anton, his workers, their Swiss friends, family from Split, and Isabella; the only relative of Rosa.

"My dearest darling," said Anton, kissing his wife. "What shall we name my perfect son?" Anton was holding six-year old Joey in his arms.

"Mama, Mama, I want kisses too," required Joey.

"Come here, my sweetie, and meet your brother," urged Rosa. Anton placed Joey on the bed.

"Do not bounce. It will make your brother sick," he warned.

Joey snuggled into his mother's arms as they held the new baby together.

"Shall we call him Anton, after his father?" Rosa smiled at her husband, hoping she pleased him with such an honor.

"Darling, you are so generous, but I can't. Look at our boys together. If I name him Anton, will Joey feel less mine? That I cannot risk," stipulated Anton. "We shall name him Danis, after my father."

"Danis Anton Novak," sighed Rosa.

"No, Danis Edgar Novak," explained Anton. "We mix all parts of the family together to make it ours. This way, Joey and Danis shall be blood brothers for all times."

The family enjoyed the beauty of a lakeside home. Anton amply provided for his family. The boys grew under Rosa's and Isabella's supervision.

In 1960, Isabella succumbed to a bout of influenza and died. Anton ensured that Isabella be transported back to Split, to be buried beside Joseph.

Joey was encouraged to excel at both academics and athletics. Having Eddy's gene pool and Anton's support, Eddy played team sports of rugby, soccer, lacrosse, and polo. His father kept a boat on the lake; Joey learned to sail and water ski. However, his best sport was downhill skiing. Switzerland was a wonderful place for a sportsman to grow up.

It was a wonderful, endowed childhood. Danis, six years behind his brother, attempted to keep stride. The parents deeply loved both boys; Anton's pride and joy. The boys loved each other.

Rosa, although very fond and grateful of her husband's kindness and love, reserved a small place in her heart for Eddy. Anton understood and accepted Rosa's sense of hurt and abandonment.

In 1962, Rosa received word that her father died. She neither grieved nor attended the funeral. She felt nothing toward the man who disowned her for getting pregnant. She correctly blamed her father for Eddy's trouble and absence. If her father had accepted Eddy, he would not have gone AWOL, she would not have been destitute, and she and Eddy would remain together in love.

Shortly after her husband's death, Sofia Romano sent a package addressed to Isabella in Switzerland. Sofia, unaware of her mother's death, had kept the return address from one of Isabella's letters, pleading forgiveness for Rosa. To Rosa's surprise, she opened *Nonna*'s mail to find a large bundle of letters wrapped in a silk ribbon.

"Anton, My God, come here quickly," she called as she fell into a chair.

"What is it darling?" he questioned, worried by Rosa's pale face.

"From mother to *Nonna*. All letters from Eddy." She opened the oldest, on the top of the pile. "This was written three weeks after his disappearance."

Twenty American dollars fell out of the envelope. Rosa read aloud, shaking. Anton held her hand.

Dearest Rosa,

I have been arrested. I foolishly went skiing with Luigi and his family, was recognized and now I am in the stockade at the base. I love you so much. I pray you and Joey are surviving.

I sent Wally to the cottage with food, firewood and money, but you were gone? Where did you go? How did you get there? What did you use for money? Please dear God. Please don't let her sell her body!

I am still in jail. Next week I can receive visitors. If you get this will you visit? We will make this right. When I get out of the army, I intend to stay in Italy with you and Joey.

Dear, dear, Rosa. You and Joey are my life. Please forgive my stupidity. I shall continue to search for you.

Please visit at the brig next week.

With my everlasting love,
Eddy

Rosa burst into tears. "He didn't abandon me. He tried. She threw the collection of at least one hundred letters in the air. Look, Anton, he tried!" Rosa fell into her husband's arms. He held her tightly, afraid that if he loosened his grip, he may lose her forever.

"Rosa," Anton asked gently, "Do you want to resume your search for Eddy? I have resources."

Secretly hoping she would say no, Anton was too much of a gentleman not to offer his wife her lifelong dream.

Rosa realized the essence of her husband's love to make such an offer. "No, my dearest Anton. No. I wish to live my life with you, Joey, and Danis, here in Switzerland, for however long that may be."

Anton scooped his wife into his arms and twirled her around. Hearing the commotion, the boys questioned the reason for an afternoon dance.

Rosa answered them by grabbing their hands. "We shall all dance together forever. Mama and Daddy are so happy today. Let's have a decadent dinner, ending with cake tonight."

The next day, Rosa and Anton sat arm in arm and read Eddy's letters. At times, Rosa would cry, sometimes she would laugh. Stacking and counting the money, Anton figured they had enough to start a generous college fund for Joey.

"Although higher education in Switzerland is free," reminded Rosa with a smile.

"Then enough to set him up in business." Anton altered its use. "A legacy from his father."

Rosa was beyond forgiveness. She neither responded to her mother nor told her of Joseph's and Isabella's death; their gravesite hidden from Sofia Cortina Romano.

Chapter 50

"DADDY. THESE ARE FOR YOU," said Shelby, handing Eddy a large envelope. "Open it. I think you will enjoy the contents."

Eddy shook the objects in the package onto his lap. He inspected several photographs questioningly.

"That's Joey, his wife Claudia, son Anton, son Peter, and daughter Bella. It was taken five years ago," Shelby explained. "Here is Joey, Richard, and me. Don't we look alike? I think the similarity is astounding. This is Anton, he's in his ninety's. Oh look, Rosa and Anton's wedding. Nonna Cortina is holding Joey—do you remember her?"

Eddy lovingly viewed each photo. "Shelby, why did you keep these from me?"

"Joey asked that I wait until you told me yourself about your army 'adventures.' So I waited. Here is Joey and his brother Danis, thirty years ago. Here is the three of us together."

"Rosa had other children?"

"Yes, another son—Danis Edgar Novak."

"Edgar?"

"Yes, Rosa's husband Anton picked the name. He said the name would integrate both families into one."

"Do you have any other pictures of Rosa?"

"Yes, just one. Here. This was from 1976. Anton Novak, her husband, Joey, Danis, and Rosa. Aren't they a beautiful family?"

"Shelby. I need to know. Is Rosa still alive," demanded Eddy. "I can wait no longer, tell me now!"

"Daddy, here's a letter to you from Rosa."

"So she is still alive?" asked Eddy anxiously.

"Read it first. Then I'll tell you about our trip," agreed Shelby. Eddy read aloud.

July 1975

My Dearest Eddy,

I have procrastinated for the past thirteen years about writing you. I have remarried. He is a loving, caring, decent man. We have two children, Joey, who Anton adopted as his own, and Danis, six years younger. Please do not be upset over Anton adopting Joey. He is a wonderful father and role model. You would approve. On Anton's request, our second son is named Danis Edgar, to unite the two families.

My despicable mother kept your letters from me. I know that you did not abandon us and that you tried very hard to find us for several years. Anton and I have read and reread your letters many times. He held me as I cried and mourned the loss of our union. We saved all the money for Joey to open his own business.

Joey is finishing the last phase of his education. He will graduate with the highest degree. His intention is teaching at university level. He is a very smart lad. He looks just like you, tall, blonde, strapping example of manhood. The girls swoon around him. Just like I swooned around you.

Please know that my love for you was—is very deep and true. Anton understands the fire of a first love. With your package of letters, mother also sent mail from the USA. I have your home address.

Don't be angry, my love, for not writing sooner. I have Anton and you have Harriett. I truly hope that you are happy and have children. I only write now because I have little time left in this life. I suffer from consumption, I think you call it tuberculosis? My case is advanced and not curable.

Eddy dear, thank you for the beautiful gift of Joey, and for the wonderful gift of first love. You will always be in my heart.

With unending devotion,
Rosa

Eddy handed the letter to Wally. "Hand me a cigarette."

"You silly old man, you quit forty years ago!" declared Shelby.

Eddy sat speechless for several minutes. Trying to comprehend his loss, he said, "She's gone. Harriett's gone!"

Shelby was the first to speak. She put her arm around her father. "They are both gone. They both deeply loved you. In their own way, they both forgave you."

"Daddy, do you want to meet Joey? We can set it up for you if you like."

"He wants to meet me?" asked a surprised Eddy. "In person?"

"Yes, he does. Knowing your age, he is willing to fly his family to the USA for the occasion. Danis wants to come also."

"Yes. I would like that," murmured Eddy. "I'll send money if he needs it to buy tickets."

Shelby laughed. "Not necessary. He is quite wealthy on his own account. In fact, he was wondering if he may sponsor a Rosa Kepler Novak scholarship in your name at his university."

Eddy sat thinking. "No. I don't want that. Joey may do whatever Joey wishes as far as scholarships are concerned. I would rather sponsor a scholarship in the name of Dr. Harriett Bailey Kepler at Madison College."

"I'll contribute to that!" Wally finally joined the conversation. "In fact, I'll write a check tonight and spread the word tomorrow."

Shelby teared. "Mother would love that. Of course, Richard and I shall contribute too. I'm sure Richard's firm will be generous. This is a great idea—loving tribute to a woman who loved knowledge."

Eddy broke into the conversation. "Will you two pray with me?"

Shocked at the request, Shelby nodded in consent. "Let's hold hands."

Eddy began. "Dear Heavenly Father. I know I do not deserve your love. I continue my daily prayer for absolution. Please have mercy on my eighty years of sin and transgression. I have lied to, abandoned, and betrayed those who love me. Thank you for the love of two amazing women—Amen."

At the end of his prayer, Eddy looked at Wally and asked, "Will you make a stop with me tomorrow morning before we head over to Sinclair Memorial?"

"Sure, buddy, what do you have in mind?"

"I want to stop at the jewelry store to buy a string of pearls. Harriett deserves her own strand of pearls. I want her to wear these pearls throughout all of eternity. She has done nothing but love me unconditionally. I shall desperately miss her."

With that, Eddy broke down and cried. The tears of loss, and the tears of burdens lifted. The weight of guilt completely gone. He forgave himself. Through the grace of God, Eddy was finally at peace.

Author's Notes

ALL CHARACTERS AND EVENTS IN this book are fictional, including the Revolutionary War patriots. Any similarity or resemblance to actual events or people, real or past, is strictly coincidental.

The National Society of the Daughters of the American Revolution is a real organization, with headquarters in Washington DC. Membership qualification requires applicant to trace and verify a direct bloodline to a participating or contributing patriot of the American Revolution. Membership is subject to approval by NSDAR.

DAR chapters referenced (Jacob Ferree, Massey Harbison, Fort McIntosh, General Richard Butler) are actual Pennsylvania DAR chapters from the Pittsburgh metro area.

The author is a DAR member in good standing, having full membership in Pennsylvania Jacob Ferree chapter and associate membership in Florida Myakka chapter.

The town of Campbellsville is fictional. Many towns in west central Pennsylvania exhibit similar attributes to that of the fictional town.

About the Author

THIS IS THE FIRST NOVEL by S. Lee Fisher. Author, clothing designer, artist, and traveler, S. Lee Fisher splits the year living in both Pennsylvania and Florida with her husband Ralph Progar.

Her website containing information about current and upcoming projects is: sleefisher.com

CPSIA information can be obtained
at www.ICGtesting.com
Printed in the USA
FSHW020637140619
58994FS

9 781640 969070